Killer Secrets Buried Truth

CJ Tuttle

Published by CJ Tuttle, 2024.

This is a work of fiction. Similarities to real people, places, or events are entirely coincidental.

KILLER SECRETS BURIED TRUTH

First edition. October 22, 2024.

Copyright © 2024 CJ Tuttle.

ISBN: 979-8227533173

Written by CJ Tuttle.

Dedication

Writing a book is never a solitary journey, and I am deeply grateful to the many people who have supported me along the way.

First and foremost, my heartfelt thanks go to my daughters—Skylar, Rylan, and Piper. You are my everything, and this book is a testament to the boundless inspiration you provide. I hope it shows you that you can achieve anything you set your mind to. I love you all more than words can express.

Sue, thank you for your unwavering belief in me, even when my dreams seemed far-fetched. You allowed me the space to fail and the support to rise again, for which I am eternally grateful.

To Abbey, there aren't enough pages to list the ways you've transformed my life for the better. Beyond this book, the very person I am is because of you. Thank you for believing in me even when I couldn't believe in myself. I owe everything to you, and I love you deeply.

This book began as a personal challenge, a project I returned to time and again over the years. Completing it fills me with immense pride, and I sincerely hope you enjoy it. Thank you for accompanying me on this journey.

Chapter 1

"Another cloudy day out there with plenty of rain and possible thunderstorms...there's a friggen' shocker. On a lighter note, here's some new metal from the Lunatic Fringe with their hit..."

"God damnit," Jay groaned as he fumbled to silence the radio alarm clock that blared from his nightstand. The old clock had been his companion since middle school, its chipped paint and worn-out buttons a testament to years of use. He stretched in front of the full-sized mirror that hung on the back of his bedroom door, his jet-black hair slightly tousled from sleep, framing his sharp features. His blue eyes, striking against his pale skin, stared back at him.

Jay's room was a small sanctuary, cluttered with posters of his favorite bands, a worn-out guitar in the corner, and bookshelves crammed with novels he had devoured over the years. Despite the clutter, it was his retreat—a place where he could escape the pressures of his world. The walls, adorned with concert tickets and snapshots of memories with friends, told the story of his teenage years.

He threw on the clothes he had laid out on his chair the night before—a pair of jeans and his favorite button-down shirt. It was his go-to shirt, the one everyone said made his blue eyes pop even more. Though he wasn't one to dwell on compliments, he couldn't deny that it gave him a small boost of confidence.

Descending the narrow staircase, Jay could hear the familiar clatter of dishes in the kitchen. The smell of chocolate chip pancakes and bacon wafted through the air, triggering a growl in his stomach. His mother had breakfast ready for him, as always. The kitchen, with its warm yellow walls and mismatched furniture, was a place of comfort and routine. It was the kind of place Jay knew he would miss, even as he yearned for the independence that lay just beyond graduation.

"I can't believe my baby is almost done with high school!" his mother exclaimed, her voice a little too cheerful for Jay's taste this early in the morning. She bustled around the kitchen, her apron tied snugly around her waist, flipping pancakes with practiced ease. Jay and his mother had always been close. As an only child, he had spent his life striving to make her proud.

"Ma, will you cut that shit out, I'm 18, I'm not your freakin' baby anymore."

"Oh Jason, you'll always be my baby, you know that," his mother laughed, dishing out a plate of pancakes and bacon. Her laughter was light and melodic—a sound Jay knew he would miss more than he wanted to admit. She placed the plate on the table, the rich aroma filling the room.

"Yeah, whatever," Jay muttered, walking through the kitchen without a glance at the meal she'd prepared.

"You're not even going to eat? I made your favorite," she said, gesturing to the plate.

The food smelled irresistible, but Jay wasn't in the mood for a lengthy morning conversation. "Nah, I gotta pick up Darren and Georgey. I'll just grab something on the way. Love ya!" he called as he grabbed his bag and headed out the side door into the pouring rain.

The rain was relentless, a steady downpour that matched Jay's stormy thoughts. Each drop hit the ground with a force that felt almost personal. "Where the fuck is my car?" he muttered, scanning the driveway. "Ma, where is my car?" he yelled back toward the house.

Mrs. Galentino poked her head out the side door, just enough to avoid getting wet. "Your father took your car this morning. He said you can take the Jeep. And Jason, I really wish you'd wear a jacket in this rain; you're going to catch pneumonia."

Jay ignored the comment, trudging through the rain to the Jeep. "I'll see you later," he called back as he climbed into the vehicle, hoping his parents would give it to him after graduation. Even after everything that had happened in the past few months, he wished his parents would stop babying him. He was about to graduate high school; it was time for him to live his own life.

The windshield wipers struggled to keep up with the deluge as Jay drove the short distance to Darren's house. The rain pounded against the Jeep's roof, a constant reminder of the storm both outside and within. The streets were slick, and Jay navigated them cautiously, aware of the responsibility of driving his father's cherished Jeep. Seeing Darren in the morning was always a relief. No matter what mood Jay was in, Darren could always lift his spirits. With his perfect blend of smartass and wise guy, Darren had a way of commanding attention. You either loved him or hated him—there was no in-between.

Jen stood in front of her bedroom mirror, carefully braiding her long, chestnut-brown hair. The rain pattered against the window, creating a soothing rhythm that contrasted with her racing thoughts. The lamp on her nightstand cast a gentle, golden light across the room, wrapping her in a familiar sense of warmth and security. At 5'8", Jen was taller than most girls in her school, a height she used to her advantage as the captain of both the volleyball and basketball teams. She reached down to her desk and squeezed out a dollop of lotion, smiling as she caught a glimpse of a picture of her boyfriend, framed and smiling back at her. Jay and Jen had been together since the 7th grade, officially, but they had actually grown up together, their parents being very close friends. Their childhood friendship had blossomed into something more when they each reached puberty.

As she rubbed the lotion into her sun-kissed skin, she glanced at the clock on her nightstand. It was almost time to leave for school.

"Jenny, breakfast is ready!" her father's voice echoed from downstairs. He was the only person in the world she allowed to call her "Jenny." He often used a funny voice, calling her "Jenn-ay" and quoting a movie from before she was born, talking about how they were "like peas and

carrots."

"Coming, Dad!" she replied in a teasing tone as she secured the end of her braid with a small elastic band. She took one last look in the mirror, adjusting her favorite silver necklace that her father had given her for her sixteenth birthday. The emerald pendant matched her striking green eyes perfectly.

Jen crept down the stairs, her backpack slung over one shoulder. Ever since she was little, she and her father had played pranks on each other. Whether it was hiding to scare each other, rigging the kitchen sink to spray the other when turned on, or replacing the sugar with salt, there was always some kind of prank going on between the two of them. It was one of the things Jen was going to miss most about home—her relationship with her father. Jen had a great relationship with both of her parents, but she had always been a bit of a daddy's girl. Her older brother, Mark, had moved out years ago, leaving her as the focus of her father's protective instincts.

"Morning!" Jen's father jumped out from his hiding spot beside the wall at the bottom of the stairs. Jen jumped back, giving him the familiar grumpy look of defeat.

"Breakfast is ready!" he said through his wry smile. Jen's father, Michael Morgan, was known as Big Mike since middle school due to his 6'6" height. He had always been in good shape and played multiple sports growing up. He was thrilled when his only daughter ended up being a chip off the old block, excelling in sports just like him. He had secretly hoped to watch her dance and do gymnastics without the pressure to perform the athletics he did when he was younger. Little did he know that Jen would become every bit the athlete he had been.

"The old man's still got it!" he turned towards the dining room table, already set up for their usual morning breakfast date.

"You're just lucky I don't want to scare an old fart!" Jen retorted playfully as she followed her father to the table. A nice spread of French toast, scrambled eggs, and sausage links awaited them. A cup of coffee and a glass of orange juice accompanied each plate. Despite Jen's petite look, she wasn't shy about enjoying a hearty meal, and she sat down eagerly. Morning breakfasts with her father were a ritual Jen cherished. No matter how she was feeling, her morning dates with her dad always lifted her spirits.

"You going to be home for dinner tonight?" her father asked.

"I think we're going to go over the plan for the weekend. Jay wants to make sure everything is perfect," Jen replied, rolling her eyes affectionately at her boyfriend's meticulous nature.

"Of course he does," chuckled Jen's father. Jay was one of his favorite people. Jen's parents had grown up with Jay's parents, going to the same school their kids now attended, and had been best friends since grade school. Their kids growing up together was expected. Jay had been like a godson to Jen's parents since he was born. When the friendship turned to romance, it took Jen's dad a little time to adjust, but in the end, he knew that if anyone was going to take his daughter's heart, it was in good hands with Jay. He just hoped he wouldn't have to hunt him down one day for breaking his baby girl's heart.

"Is it supposed to stay like this all week?" Jen nodded towards the window and the steady rain outside.

"I think so, Jenny," replied her father, matching her gaze. "You guys might wanna pack your waders."

"Very funny!" Jen rolled her eyes mockingly.

"You know, I'm really proud of you, Jenny," he said, using his silly voice from that movie again.

"I know, Daddy," she smiled, reaching her hand out on top of his.

He picked up his cup of coffee and squinted, "I just wish you could have beaten out that little shit for valedictorian!"

"Oh, stop it!" she slapped the hand that she was just covering, making him laugh even harder at his joke. Jen was the salutatorian of their class, second only to Jay. They had always been the top two in their class, but no matter what Jen did, she could never beat him academically.

"No, I couldn't be more proud of you, baby girl," he said, his tone softening. When her father spoke like this, Jen knew to listen.

"Thanks, Dad. That means a lot," she replied, feeling a lump form in her throat. She was going to miss her father more than anything.

After finishing breakfast, Jen helped her father clear the table and wash the dishes. She then grabbed her backpack and headed for the door, her father following behind.

"Drive safe and have a great day," Michael said, giving her a quick kiss on the forehead.

"I will, Daddy. See you later," Jen replied, stepping out into the crisp morning rain. She bounded to her car, trying to avoid the inevitable drops that relentlessly dove from the sky.

As she drove to school, Jen's mind wandered to the upcoming week. Their last week of senior year. She couldn't believe it was finally here. The camping trip they had planned forever. She was excited but also a little anxious. These last few months had been tough on everyone. Jay, in particular, had been acting a little off lately—not that she could blame him. They all had. Ever since what happened six months ago, things had never quite been the same. She shook the thought away, forcing herself to focus on the fun ahead.

MMMAAAMMMPH!!!!
MMMAAAMMMPH!!!!
MMMAAAMMMPH!!!!

A swinging hand came down with the force of a felled redwood tree on top of the alarm clock, silencing its relentless blare. Groggy and disoriented, Darren Walters wiped his tired eyes, squinting to make sense of the room through the morning blur.

"Ugh, what the fuck," he muttered to the empty room, his voice rough with sleep. He sat up, stretching his arms wide, his joints popping in protest. Darren was one of the most popular kids in school, a status cemented by his athletic prowess. He was the best athlete in the school, an All-State award winner in both football and lacrosse. He had reluctantly run indoor track during the winter season until his senior year, a decision forced upon him by the football coaches. Despite being one of the fastest kids in the region, Darren despised the long waits and monotonous nature of track meets.

Being such a good athlete his whole life, Darren took great pride in his physical appearance. He didn't care for expensive clothes or flashy accessories, but his physique was important to him. He worked out like a maniac, driven by a desire to excel that was rooted deep in his childhood. Darren was an only child, and his father had left when he was just two years old. His mother had remarried twice, and each time, Darren had been adopted by the new husband. Yet, he never truly felt wanted by these father figures. Sports became his refuge, the one area where he could shine and prove to himself that he was worthy.

Darren's dark brown hair was usually kept in a buzz-cut, a practical choice for someone who spent so much time wearing a helmet. His ice-blue eyes, which often drew compliments, had earned him a reputation as a charmer since childhood. Even his first-grade teacher had noted his charisma, dubbing him the Don Juan of the class. His six-pack was almost visible through his t-shirts, a testament to his dedication in the gym.

He groggily made his way to the bathroom, grateful for the small luxury of having his own. Unlike many of his friends, who had to share a bathroom with siblings or other family members, Darren enjoyed this bit of personal space.

His bedroom walls were adorned with posters of his idols. One wall featured Aaron Judge in various action poses, while another showcased a framed image of Tom Brady and Rob Gronkowski celebrating their Super Bowl win in Tampa. Around these central pieces were

numerous plaques and awards, the most prized being his second-team All-American award from his senior year of football. He had led his school to a state title and broken the state record, only to be overshadowed by a phenomenal running back from Florida who had set a new national record.

As Darren brushed his teeth vigorously, he peeked at the clock through the bathroom doorway. Jay was supposed to arrive in fifteen minutes. His stomach grumbled, reminding him that he hadn't eaten yet. He contemplated grabbing a quick bowl of cereal but knew he would have to hurry.

After getting dressed, he grabbed his bag from the computer chair in the corner of his room and gave himself a final once-over in the mirror on the back of the door. Satisfied with his appearance, he headed downstairs.

He could hear his mother's voice drifting from the kitchen, engaged in a conversation about politics with her husband, Gary, Darren's adoptive father.

"Hey!" his mother greeted him with a warm smile as he entered the kitchen. The scent of freshly brewed coffee and frying bacon filled the air, mingling with the soft sounds of the radio playing in the background.

"Hey, Mom," Darren replied, returning her smile. He nodded at Gary, who was seated across the table. Gary was a portly man with a yellow mustache that matched the thinning hair on his head. He and Darren had a strained relationship. Despite being his adoptive father for eight years—longer than any of his mother's previous husbands—Darren never felt fully accepted. Gary seemed to only notice him when he excelled in sports.

"Yeah, Ma. Big week." Darren rolled his eyes. Lately, even the smallest things got under his skin. He couldn't pinpoint why, but ever since what happened six months ago, everything felt... different.

"You idiots still camping in this?" Gary asked between bites of his breakfast. The kitchen was cozy, with wooden cabinets and a round table that had seen years of family meals and debates.

"Yeah. We've been planning this forever. A little rain won't hurt anyone," Darren replied, glancing out the window at the relentless downpour. He spotted Gary's wallet sitting at the end of the counter, a twenty-dollar bill sticking out.

Darren hesitated. He couldn't take money from his own father. But then he remembered Gary had never paid up on their bet on last weekend's Subway Series.

As Jay's parents' Jeep pulled into the driveway, Darren made his move.

"Hey, Gary," Darren smirked, creeping along the counter towards the wallet.

"What?" Gary grunted, not bothering to look up.

Darren took one last glance at him. "Pay up, bitch!" he laughed, grabbing the twenty-dollar bill and bolting out the door before Gary could react.

Jay's fingers fumbled towards the radio dial. "The Yankees win their tenth in a row and move 6 ½ games ahead of idle Bost..." static "...better be careful out on the roads today, the weather shows no sign of letting up and..." static "...enjoying their seventeenth week at the number one spot on the pop charts...here is ADD 47 with their latest 'we sold out.'"

Jay wiped his tired eyes as he waited for Darren to get out of the house. "Jesus Christ, what the hell is takin' so long?" He glanced up at Darren's window, searching for any sign of movement. Even though Darren was usually adamant about being picked up on time, Jay wouldn't put it past him to skip school. After all, it was Darren's senior year too, and while Jay took school seriously, Darren was just riding the wave to graduation.

Suddenly, Darren burst out of the house like a bat out of hell. "Let's get the fuck outta here!!!" he yelled, his eyes wide with a mix of adrenaline and mischief. "I'm not fuckin' around, get the fuck outta here!!!"

"What the hell did you do now?" Jay asked as his tires squealed on the wet pavement.

"My stepdad is accusing me of takin' money again."

"You mean your broke ass stole money from your dad again," laughed Jay as they sped away from Darren's house. "You'll never change."

"Fock you. You know I wouldn't steal from my own father. What kind of person do you think I am? What a terrible thing to say," Darren mocked himself, shaking his head. "And what the hell is this garbage doing on your radio? You really are a female. If I ever saw these guys in concert, I think I'd have to kick my own ass!" Darren was in rare form this morning.

"Anyway, hurry up and pick up Georgey so we can hit up some Arches. Breakfast is on me. I
found an extra 20 bucks under my pillow this morning," Darren said, grinning like a kid who had just pulled off the perfect prank.

"You're such an asshole," Jay muttered, trying to suppress his own smile. Darren continued to fiddle with the radio, while Jay focused on navigating through the relentless rain. The downpour
made it nearly impossible to see, even with the wipers on full blast. George only lived a few blocks away, but Jay was being extra cautious with his father's cherished Jeep. The last thing he needed was to damage it.

"GEORGY, YOU FAT BASTARD!!! GET THE FUCK OUT HERE!!!" Darren yelled, half of his body hanging out the passenger seat window, completely ignoring the rain that was now pouring inside the Jeep. "I'M CRAVIN' A NUMBER 3, AND I KNOW YOU GOT AT LEAST A FEW DOZEN HOT CAKES IN YA THIS MORNING!!!"

"Get in the car, you moron," Jay scolded as he pulled into George's driveway. "Are you ever gonna grow up?"

"Oh, what's the fun in that, Jay-Jay?"

George finally emerged from the house, wiping crumbs from his mouth. Even though he knew they were planning on grabbing breakfast, he couldn't turn down his mother's home cooking. The warm glow of the kitchen light behind him contrasted sharply with the gloomy weather outside, painting a picture of cozy domesticity.

"What's up, Slim?" Darren called out. "You down for some Arches or what?" George shot him a look as he climbed into the backseat. "You're right, dumb question."

George was a lineman on the football team, and he and Darren had been playing together since they were old enough to walk. When they were younger, George had struggled with his weight, and there were a few seasons where he wasn't going to be allowed to play because he was too heavy for their age group. Darren had run with him every day to help him drop the pounds before weigh-in.

Like Darren, George kept his hair cut short. His baby face barely managed to sprout a few whiskers, despite his efforts. Since he'd started dating Amy, who was very into fashion, George had taken more care with his appearance, trying to look his best at all times. He was an imposing figure at 6'3" and around 320 lbs—intimidating on the football field, but off of it, he was a gentle giant.

Jay backed out of George's driveway and started the trip out of the neighborhood.

"Oh, it's my jam!" Darren yelled as a new song started on the radio. He reached toward the console and turned it up. The bass made a thundering boom, louder than any storm the quiet neighborhood had experienced in the last few days. The vibrations from the speakers made the car's windows rattle, and the boys could feel the beat in their chests.

"Turn that shit down!" George exclaimed from the back seat, covering his ears in mock agony.

"Come on, Darren," Jay began to reach for the dial to turn the music back down, the corners of his mouth twitching in amusement.

"Don't you dare!" Darren slapped his hand away, drawing an annoyed glance from Jay. Darren smirked back as he performed a ridiculous dance, lip-syncing the words to the song with exaggerated enthusiasm. Jay couldn't help but laugh at his friend's performance. He was so entertained that he completely neglected to notice the light in front of him turn red as he glided right on through.

The music was so loud that the boys couldn't hear the overwhelming horn from one of the drivers in the lane whose light had just turned green. Harold Grimes, on his way to work, instantly recognized the boy in the passenger seat as Darren Walters.

Darren Walters. Just hearing the name sent a shiver down the old man's spine. Harold was past the age of retirement, but aside from his daughter, his job was all he had. He couldn't imagine leaving the school. He'd been there for 47 years this coming fall. Starting as a custodial assistant, he had worked his way up through sheer determination and grit to become Head of Grounds. It was a title he took very seriously, and any student who stepped out of line heard about it.

Which is what made Harold so familiar with Darren Walters. It wasn't that Darren was a troublemaker. Sure, he mouthed off just like the rest of the punks at the school, but Darren reminded Harold too much of his own time in school, when he was picked on by the most popular kid. It haunted him all these years later, fueling a grudge so large that smiling or acting kind was out of the question for the old man.

"Fuckin' punk kids!" He yelled over his own horn to the empty car. His face twisted into a scowl, deep lines etching into his weathered skin. His knuckles turned white as he gripped the steering wheel, trying to suppress the anger bubbling within him.

He was still glaring at the vehicle speeding down the road and didn't notice he was holding up his own lane until a chorus of small beeps behind him startled him back to reality. He glanced in the rearview mirror, seeing the line of cars forming and the irritated faces of other drivers.

It didn't take much to put Harold in a bad mood, and this was just the ticket to get his day started off extra shitty.

He muttered to himself the whole way to work about how "these damn kids have no respect these days" and "if I was 20 years younger, I'd teach them respect." His voice was a low growl, barely audible over the hum of his car's engine. Each word was like a release valve for his frustration, though it did little to calm him down.

Harold pulled into the employee parking lot at 6:50 on the dot. He parked in the back row, where he had parked since he started his job. He figured he deserved at least a spot up front,

considering he was the longest-tenured employee at the school, but he got barely any more respect from the other staff members than he did from the students. Probably because most of the staff were former students who had known Harold since their school days and didn't like him then, either. His reputation as a stern and unyielding presence had followed him throughout the years.

He stepped out of his car, the rain pattering relentlessly on his coat, and took a deep breath of the damp morning air. The school loomed in front of him, a place of both pride and resentment. He walked toward the entrance, each step heavy with the weight of decades of memories, most of them bitter. As he approached the doors, he could already hear the faint sounds of students inside, laughing and talking, oblivious to the storm cloud that was Harold Grimes.

"I can't believe we're eating here instead of taking it to go. We're gonna miss Ms. Davenport's class," Jay complained, glancing at his watch.

"Do you have the tightest asshole in the world, or is it just my imagination?" Darren exclaimed, his face a picture of disbelief. "We're about to graduate in less than two weeks, and you're worried about missing Ms. 'I wanna fuck Darren-port's' first block class? Come on, man! Although, she is the hottest teacher in school," Darren added, shooting a look at George, who was completely uninterested in his antics. "I wouldn't mind her keeping me after school for a little extra discipline, if you know what I mean." He started grinding provocatively against the table, drawing disgusted looks from other patrons.

"So, what's the plan for the trip this weekend? Is everyone still in?" George asked, trying to ignore Darren's inappropriate thrusting. "I need to know so I can get the beer and everything in time. Plus, Amy's been asking."

"I WIN!!!" Darren suddenly exclaimed, shoving Jay almost off his chair. "Fork it over." "What?" George asked, confused and a little embarrassed.

Darren pointed at a stranger waiting in line to order. "I told him, but he didn't want to believe me.

'No way,' he said, 'he'll hold out 'til lunch at least...'"

"You had to ask, didn't you? Couldn't wait 'til after lunch?" Jay shook his head at George while Darren reveled in his victory.

"Don't blame him. You know Chunky's been waiting for this for over three years," Darren said with a grin as he started dancing on his chair in the middle of the restaurant. "Jay was wrong, and I was right," he sang, basking in his moment.

"You just lost me 20 bucks. I hope you realize that," Jay grumbled, ignoring Darren's over-the-top celebration. Darren announced to the entire restaurant, "Mr. Galentino is simply not as clever as he thought. Yet another win for Thee Darren Walters!"

"Yes, we're still on, and yes, the girls are still coming. The four of us planned this thing forever, and now that it's here, you think we're going to back out? You, me, this idiot," Jay gestured to Darren, "and Will. The girls too. Nothing changes. And speaking of the girls coming, I really don't know why you're so excited," Jay turned to Darren, interrupting his annoying friend. "It's not like you're gonna get any, dickhead!"

"Fuck you, it's PROM WEEKEND. Em's gonna have to take off the locks and chains; it's a given," Darren shot back, jumping down from the chair. "Look at me. Not even you could resist this!" He rubbed his nipples through his t-shirt, flicking his tongue in and out of his mouth with exaggerated enthusiasm.

"Huh? What the hell are you talking about?" George asked, his mouth full of sausage, clearly paying no attention to Darren. "I just figured since..."

"Oh, you didn't know? King Ding-A-Ling over here hasn't been so lucky lately," Jay said with a sly smile, interrupting George, who was left with a look of bewilderment.

"What?" George nearly spat out his food, his eyes bulging as he focused on Darren for clarity.

"Yeah, Em's been stingy with it, but whatever, it's all good. She's worth the wait," Darren replied, flashing a wink.

"Yeah, right. You've probably got ex-girlfriends coming over every night to satisfy your horny ass," George laughed, glancing at Jay for approval of his joke.

"Fuck that. I'm not cheating on her."

George and Jay's laughter grew louder. "Yeah, right!" They knew their friend too well and were aware that his reputation was well-deserved.

"I'm not! What the hell do you two know? You've both been married all of high school," Darren retorted defensively.

"You've been with Emily for almost a year now, and you haven't gotten laid yet? That's a long time for you to hold out. Maybe the Great Darren Walters is finally in love," Jay teased, holding up his fingers to mock Darren's dramatic quotes.

"Whatever, bitch. At least I'm not whipped. You can't even walk down the street without a permission slip signed by Jen. And you, fat chops, you're so far up Amy's ass I can't tell where she ends and you begin, which is a pretty fuckin' scary thought."

The teasing continued as the boys finished their meal. "I really don't know why we're in such a hurry," Darren grumbled. "We're already late. We might as well just skip today!"

The boys lumbered towards the school, over an hour late and drenched from the walk from the parking lot. "Oh shit, here comes Harold," Jay muttered, trying not to make eye contact.

"Who gives a shit about this old man? I say we walk right by him like the guy ain't even there," Darren suggested.

"You know you boys are over an hour late?" the old security guard grumbled, his face set in its usual frown.

"Yes, sir, well..." Jay began, but Darren quickly cut him off.

"The thing about that one is, you see, my boys had to come pick me up for school this morning, but the damndest thing happened."

"Oh yeah, Walters, what might that be?" the old man prompted, barely containing his snarl.

"I told her I didn't want to come over because I had school in the morning. And I know how forgetful she is with the alarm clock in her old age," Darren continued as George and Jay exchanged knowing glances, sensing what was coming.

"What the hell are you talking about, Walters?"

"And on top of all that, she kept me up all night long. Look at my back; that old lady has got some nails," Darren said, turning his back towards the old man and starting to lift up his shirt.

"Walters, I have had it up to here with your shit!" Harold's scowl deepened, his tired eyes narrowing into slits as he glared at Darren. There was something unsettling about the way his jaw clenched, the way his fists tightened at his sides. For a moment, Jay swore he saw a flicker of something darker beneath the surface, but just as quickly, it was gone. Harold's voice dripped with venom as he growled, "Someday, your mouth is going to write a check your ass can't cash, and I just hope I'm there to see it when it happens."

"Oh Harry, come on now, you didn't really just say that. Ha ha," Darren mocked. "Besides, old man, you only have two weeks left of us. And you know you're gonna miss me more than anyone in this entire school."

"Just get the hell out of here, Walters, before I write your ass up!"

"Yes, sir," Darren responded with a mock military salute as the boys passed through the old man's barricade. "Wouldn't want that now, would we?"

"Why you gotta mess with Harold every single day?" Jay scolded as they left Harold fuming.

"One of these days, he's gonna have enough of your shit and go postal on you or something."

"Oh shut up, bro. Harry's harmless. I'm just havin' some fun with him," Darren defended himself as they walked through the door, dripping wet. Their feet made sloshing noises as they made their way down the hall past the gymnasiums. While Jay and George tried to move quietly, Darren exaggerated every step, making his entrance as dramatic as possible.

"Well, I'll see you guys later. I gotta go see Amy before second block," George announced as he shook himself off one last time.

"Exactly my point," Darren mocked. "I hope she'll let you sit with us at lunch today."

"Fuck off," George retorted, slapping up his best friends before heading down the hall.

"Such a shame! That kid couldn't take a shit if Amy didn't approve," Darren cracked as he and Jay walked the opposite way. "So what's up with this weekend, anyway? Are you absolutely sure EVERYONE is still going?"

"Yeah, EVERYONE is still going. How many times have I told you that?" Jay responded defensively, wondering why Darren was suddenly so focused on people backing out.

"Well, you know I got nothing but love for everyone involved, but ever since that shit happened...I dunno. Shit's different. I don't want to be like Georgy...but things have changed, ya know," Darren actually sounded serious for the first time all day. The boys walked on past the second gymnasium, their shoes squeaking on the tiles as Darren snuck a peek into the girls' class.

"You're so sensitive, you know that?" Jay ignored his friend's antics, concentrating on Darren's previous statement. He hoped the comment would steer Darren away from the topic.

Darren waved into the cracked door, giving a whistle and a wry smile. "Oh shut up. You know I feel bad, but it's kinda hard when the kid couldn't even acknowledge me anymore. I mean, we all practically grew up with him. It feels like when he needs us the most, he's nowhere to be found. It's just weird, I guess. I never understood it. Probably never will."

"Well, I think this weekend will be good for us. We need to get away from all this shit, ya know?" Jay replied, sounding as though he was trying to convince himself as much as Darren.

"I guess. I just hope we can get things back to normal. I miss havin' the whole crew, ya know what I'm sayin'? Maybe this trip will bring things back to...I dunno."

"Well, you better keep your eye on the prize Mandingo," Jay cracked, trying to lighten the mood, hoping Darren would take the bait.

"Yeah, I definitely do," Darren joked shamelessly as they sauntered into their math class. Without missing a beat, he exclaimed, "Ms. Davenport, my love, how are you? You know, Jay here wanted to skip your class, but I told him that I just couldn't go on with my day unless I saw your beautiful smile!"

Jay rolled his eyes at his math teacher. Although the entire class snickered at the joke, Ms. Davenport seemed a little more annoyed with Darren's escapades today than usual. Jay felt even guiltier as he could see that something was obviously bothering her this morning.

"Sit down, boys," she ordered, then turned to the rest of the class. "Look at this class; Mr. Walters and Mr. Galentino decided to grace us with their presence this morning. Please, let's make sure we give them the attention they so desperately crave..." she mocked, hoping to embarrass the tardy boys.

Darren stood up and waved to his classmates as if he were the main float in a parade. "You know, Ms. Davenport, to tell you the truth, I was only thinking of you when I made it here today." "Well, that's very kind of you, Mr. Walters. Do you mind if we get back to the lesson?"

"Oh, by all means. I wouldn't want to impede on the knowledge you bring to us on a daily basis," Darren grinned, egged on by the muffled laughter of his fellow classmates.

Jay rummaged through his bag for his notebook. Even though he was the only student who took notes in math, and class was almost over, he still felt obligated to try since they were late, and his friend was making such a spectacle. After all, even though it was his senior year, and most of his classmates, especially Darren, were goofing off and not doing any work, Jay had a reputation to uphold.

The bell rang a minute after Ms. Davenport finally got back to the lesson, and the rest of the students quickly got up to leave.

"Well, thank you for wasting our time," said Ms. Davenport as the class started to file out. "Do you mind staying here for a few minutes while I have a word with you?"

"I told you she wanted me," whispered Darren as Jay walked out the door. "I'll see you at lunch, bro."

"I was talking to Jason, Mr. Walters," Ms. Davenport said in a harsher tone.

"Oh, well, um... okay," Darren shrugged, a playful smirk on his face. He was used to being the center of attention, but Jay getting singled out by Ms. Davenport was a rarity. He playfully sulked away from the room, diving into the usual chaos of the hallway. Conversations seemed to magnetically pull Darren in, and he had already high-fived a few classmates when he spotted Emily walking toward him. The crowd seemed to part for her naturally, as if she was walking down a red carpet.

"Hey, baby!" Emily greeted, playfully pinching his jeans and catching a bit of flesh.

"Jesus!" Darren yelped, jumping slightly. "You scared the shit outta me, babe!"

Emily giggled, her laugh as light and melodic as a summer breeze. She was widely recognized as the most beautiful girl in school, a reputation she wore with effortless grace. Her perfectly straight, light brown hair always fell just right, never a strand out of place. Her eyes, a mesmerizing shade of blue, were the kind that people couldn't help but get lost in—they were almost hypnotic, a color all their own. Though Darren would never admit it to anyone, Emily had been his secret crush for years. He'd been too shy to approach her, content to admire from afar, until Will dared him to ask her to the Junior Prom last year. That dare changed everything.

Emily wasn't just beautiful; she was also smart, compassionate, and fiercely loyal. She had a warmth about her that drew people in, and while she could have easily fallen in with the more superficial crowd, she chose to surround herself with people who valued her for more than just her looks. Her kindness was genuine, and she always made time for others, even when it wasn't convenient. Yet, despite her outward confidence, Emily often felt the pressure to live up to the expectations placed on her, both by others and by herself. Being with Darren had helped her find a balance, teaching her to let go and embrace spontaneity.

"I can't wait to spend the whole weekend with you," Emily said, her perfect smile lighting up the dimly lit hallway. There was something almost regal about the way they walked hand in hand, the other students naturally moving aside to give them space. It was as if the couple commanded the center of the crowded hall without even trying.

"I know, it's gonna be a blast!" Darren grinned, his mind already wandering to thoughts of having Emily all to himself in a tent. She carried on about her morning, filling him in on the little details he usually tuned out, but today, he found himself listening more closely, appreciating the sound of her voice.

As they reached her class, Darren pulled Emily in for a kiss. Neither of them noticed her entire class watching through the window, but it wouldn't have mattered if they had. When they were together, the world around them often faded into the background. "I'll see you at lunch, baby... love you."

"I love you too," Emily blushed, her heart swelling with affection. She turned and started toward her seat as the bell rang. She set her books down on her desk, the laughter of her classmates finally pulling her out of her daze. She looked up and saw Darren in the window at the top of the classroom, pressing his lips to the glass.

"I LOVE YOU MORE!!!" he exclaimed, his voice muffled but full of enthusiasm.

Emily shook her head, a wide smile spreading across her face. She loved Darren's unpredictability, his ability to turn even the most mundane moments into something special. To the rest of the school, he might have been the jock or the sarcastic showoff, but she knew there was so much more to him than that. She loved him for all the layers that only she got to see.

"Thank you, Mr. Walters," Mr. Bradley responded sarcastically, closing the shade that covered the top of the door. "I am very fond of you as well," he added with a wry smile. Turning his attention to

Emily, who was still blushing from Darren's antics, he asked, "Now, Mrs. Waterson, do you mind if we begin class?"

"Yes, Mr. Bradley. By all means," Emily replied, her smile still lingering. While she was a good student, disciplined and diligent, being with Darren had opened her up in ways she never thought possible. Before Darren, Emily had been the girl who always followed the rules, never spoke out of turn, and kept her head down. But Darren had shown her how to embrace her inner confidence, how to speak her mind, and how to let loose when the moment called for it. She was no longer afraid to challenge someone or give a little attitude if it was deserved. In many ways, Darren had brought out the best in her, and she was grateful for it every day.

The bathroom was dimly lit, with flickering fluorescent lights buzzing overhead, casting uneven shadows across the grimy tiles, as if the very room was unsettled. The faint smell of disinfectant mixed with something old and musty, lingering in the air. The constant hum of conversation from the hallway felt miles away, subdued by the solid, echoing walls. Jay approached the sink, letting the cold water flow over his hands, relishing its cleansing promise.

He looked up at the mirror next to him. He smiled to himself for a moment as he saw Will standing by him, clad in the all-too-familiar gray sweatshirt and faded jeans—a comforting constant amid six months of chaos. Their eyes met in the mirror.

"I can't believe this weekend is almost here," Jay said, his voice bouncing lightly off the ceramic walls, desperately looking for a match.

"Yup," Will replied, tone flat but present, as if the weight of the universe rested on his shoulders.

Jay's eyes darted around the bathroom, trying to hide the inquisition behind their gaze. "Darren and George don't think you're still in. Well...I mean, they just..." He hesitated, the sentence unfinished, left to live on without closure.

Will stood there, his gaze fixed somewhere distant, like he was half-listening or maybe not listening at all. His hands remained in his sweatshirt pockets, unmoving, as if he hadn't noticed the tension in Jay's voice.

Before the silence thickened again, Jay shifted. "How about Oswald today, huh?" he ventured, his voice brimming with an attempted lightness. "Can you believe he said that—"

The creak of the bathroom door punctured the moment, and Connor Smith, a frail sophomore with oversized glasses, hesitantly shuffled in. It was an unwritten rule that the third floor bathroom was meant for seniors—initially dismissed by Jay and Will, until senior year lent it meaning. Now this bathroom had become their haven after first period since the school year started.

Connor's eyes flickered from Jay's mirror, then to Will's, and back, stopping on Jay with a questioning look that seemed to ask more than it answered.

"What are you staring at, Connor?" Jay asked, his tone protective and firm. Connor stammered a quick apology, retreating swiftly, the door swinging closed with a final thud. Jay turned back to find the mirror next to his vacant.

The atmosphere was heavy with the pressure of unsaid words.

He looked at the now-closed bathroom stall and wondered what Will must be going through. Had Will noticed the way Connor had looked at him and retreated to the stall to be alone? Was he under this constant microscope with people not knowing how to talk or even act around him? His heart hurt.

"I've got your back...always," he affirmed over the stall, nodding as if to implant those words in stone.

The silent response was deafening, as Will left Jay to his own thoughts, staring at his own reflection and wondering if things could ever be the same again.

Darren burst into the lunchroom, his eyes watering from laughing so hard. "Yo, you guys missed it!" he gasped, barely able to catch his breath.

"What did we miss?" George asked, looking up from his already half-empty plate.

"You... know Abby Hanson, right..." Darren managed between fits of laughter. "Well... she just bit it sooo hard walking up the stairs. Her books went flying everywhere, man! She had to go to the nurse's office. Dude, I was rolling! I can't believe you guys missed that shit. Then again," Darren added, not missing a beat, "I bet George would miss it if a meteor hit the school during lunch, huh tubby!"

"You are such a dick," Jay responded, though he couldn't hide his smile. "The biggest geek in the whole school, and you just laughed at her during probably the most embarrassing moment
of her life."

"Oh, that ain't her most embarrassing," George grinned between bites. "Remember in ninth grade when we were all in the same earth science class, and Abby had that... you know...
situation?"

He got interrupted by Amy, who appeared at the table like she always did, effortlessly. "Hey baby, how's your day going?"

Amy, dressed in her usual preppy style, smiled warmly at everyone except Darren. She was a genuinely nice girl, and both Jay and Darren often wondered aloud how George managed to land her. While not as popular or striking as Emily or Jen, Amy had a quiet beauty about her. Her dirty blonde hair, cut just to her shoulders, framed her face perfectly, and her dark brown eyes—so dark they sometimes seemed black—held an intelligence that made her all the more attractive. She was always impeccably dressed, often dragging George to the mall to shop for the latest trends.

"Hey Amy! George was just in the middle of telling us about Abby Hanson's little incident back in ninth grade. You should really pull up a chair," Darren said with his usual smirk. Although Amy tolerated Darren for George's sake, she wasn't his biggest fan. She often told George that Darren didn't treat him like a true friend, what with all the jokes and ridicule. George always brushed it off, saying that's just how Darren was.

"No thanks, Darren," Amy replied with a mocking smile. "I'm going to sit with the girls. I'll see you in a few minutes, babe."

"Ok," George mumbled after Amy bent down to kiss him and walked away.

"You are such a pussy-whipped bitch!" Darren exclaimed, shaking his head at George.

"What's up?" Jay asked Will, noticing their quiet friend had slipped into the seat next to him without the others noticing. It was hit or miss whether Will showed up to school nowadays, and even when he did, it was rare that he lasted until lunch. Still, Jay insisted on keeping his seat open just in case.

"Sup," Will mumbled, his face as expressionless as always.

"Looking forward to this weekend, boys?" Darren asked the table, ignoring Jay's subtle warning glance. "Should be an awesome time, fellas," he grinned.

"What if the rain doesn't stop?" George stammered. "It'll all be for nothing."

"We're gonna be in the middle of the woods, a hundred miles from here, ass-clown," Darren retorted. "Your fat ass won't get a drop on you. Anyway... what did Ms. Davenport want with you after class, Jay?"

Jay shot Darren a look, trying to stop him before he finished the sentence, but it was too late. "I thought she wanted to give me an extra tutoring session," Darren teased, mimicking the ridiculous thrusting motion he'd demonstrated earlier.

Jay couldn't help but notice Will's glare but he didn't respond. Will and Jay had known each other the longest. They lived across the park from each other ever since they were born and had been best friends for nearly as long. There wasn't much about Will that Jay didn't know, but since that day six months ago, Jay could feel the distance between them growing wider and wider.

"Oh well, boys, I'll catch you after school. There's my baby," Darren announced, loud enough for the entire lunchroom to hear. "Hey, hun!" he called out as Emily walked by, slipping his arm around her waist. As they walked off, he looked over her shoulder at her short skirt, then back at his friends, flicking his tongue in and out with a mischievous grin.

"I know she's the hottest girl in school, but if you ask me, he's the one that's whipped," George said, drawing a laugh from Jay, who was relieved to see a faint smirk from Will. George and Jay chatted about Darren's facade—the tough-guy act he put on for everyone else. Jay didn't push Will into the conversation; he was just glad that Will still sat with them on the days he decided to come to school.

But even with Will sitting right there, something felt off. The way he stayed silent, how his presence almost... faded. Jay couldn't shake the feeling that things were slipping away, like a memory you couldn't quite hold onto.

Chapter 2

George and Jay huddled under the meager shelter provided by the Jeep's overhang, the relentless rain drumming a steady rhythm on the roof. The school day had ended, but the storm showed no signs of letting up as the boys waited for Darren. "Where the hell is he?" Jay muttered, his eyes scanning the damp and emptying parking lot.

"Huh?" George responded, his mind clearly elsewhere, not catching Jay's question. He had complained enough about them hacing to wait in the rain, he didn't want to make Jay any madder than he already seemed to be.

"BYE HARRY," Darren's voice echoed across the lot, filled with mock cheerfulness as he waved off the old man.

"So, are we gonna chill tonight and go over everything or what?" George asked, trying to stay focused on the weekend plans.

"Yeah, I'm down," Jay replied, only half-listening as his eyes searched for Darren, who had already been swallowed up by the mass of students leaving the building, "but we gotta make sure everyone else will be there."

"Be where?" Darren finally arrived, shaking off the rain as he reached the Jeep.

"I dunno, but we gotta talk about this weekend somewhere," George said, sounding eager to get out of the downpour.

"Of course we do," Darren shot back sarcastically, tapping Jay on the chest. "Well, let's wait for Liz. She's still included in this too."

"Of course she is!" Jay shot a look of disgust at Darren. "They both are!"

"Right..of course," Darren nodded in agreement and looked over at George, who was too busy squinting through the rain.

"Well where is she?" George asked impatiently, visibly annoyed by the rain now.

"This rain ain't gonna fuckin' kill ya," Darren joked, giving George a playful shove. "Besides, I bet you're starting to turn some of these ladies on with that wet t-shirt."

"There she is," Jay pointed out as Liz appeared in the distance. "Hey Liz!" he waved to draw her attention through the crowd filling out of the school.

It was a rare occurrence for Jay to see Will by the end of the school day, but Liz was still trying to make it through the last days of the school year as best she could. Darren and Liz were actually the closest out of the group. Darren's mother had been best friends with Liz's mother since college. The rumor was that they actually got pregnant at the same party during college so they would have kids at the same time. But that was just a nasty little rumor the small town had made up. But naturally, Darren and Liz grew up together as kids. Much like Jay and Jen. But their bond did not turn to romance. In fact, it was much closer to a sibling rivalry than anything else. Deep down, they loved each other like brother and sister, but they bickered with each other as if they hated the sight of one another.

Oddly enough, when Will and Liz started dating a few years ago, Darren found himself acting very protective of her. Very much like a big brother. The horror that they had gone through was something that the group couldn't imagine. But they wanted to be there in any way they could.

Liz trudged over to join the group, her head down, hoodie pulled tight against the elements. There was a heaviness about her, a weight that seemed to drag her down, even more than the rain-soaked fabric clinging to her frame. Jay couldn't shake the feeling that something was off with her, but he was in no position to question how she should handle things.

"We're gonna meet tonight to get shit straight for this weekend," George hurriedly said, eager to get the conversation over with.

"Where?" Liz asked, her eyes fixed on his shoes.

"How 'bout the Warehouse? There's a special on meatballs every Monday," George suggested, a hopeful smile tugging at his lips. "I could really go for some Italian."

"Yeah, me too. You think your mom will mind a late-night visit, Jay-Jay?" Darren quipped, unable to resist poking fun at Jay.

"Fock you," Jay shoved Darren lightly. "Yeah, the Warehouse is cool with me. I think Jen and Amy are coming, so you guys might want to bring Emily and -"

"Alright, so it's set!" George cut him off, eager to wrap up the conversation. "We'll meet there around 5:30,"

"Ok," Liz said flatly before turning toward the parking lot, walking away without a backward glance or a word of goodbye.

Jay's eyes scanned the parking lot, searching for Will's car. But it seemed no one else cared. George was already halfway inside the Jeep, and Darren hadn't even mentioned Will's name once. It was as if... they had moved on. But Jay couldn't.

He felt so far away from a friend he had considered a brother. Will wasn't the same. And neither was Liz. No one else in the group could sense it. But Jay could. Things were different.

Things had to be different.

Jay's mind raced as Darren carried on in the seat next to him, "...and you would know the daily specials at every restaurant in town, you fat fuck!" Darren teased, turning to George, who was busy texting on his phone. "Are you fuckin' serious? Please tell me you're not texting Amy... you just saw her! Holy hell! Are you that excited about the Warehouse that you can't wait to tell her?"

Jay barely registered the banter as he drove, his mind stuck on Will and the burden he seemed to carry alone. Jay felt increasingly like the glue holding their group together, but the strain was starting to show.

"Well, I'll meet you guys at the Warehouse at 5:30," George said as they reached his house. He quickly jumped out of the Jeep and dashed through the rain.

"What is up with that?" Darren asked, watching George disappear.

"He's just excited about the trip, that's all," Jay replied, but he knew Darren wasn't talking about George.

"Well, what the hell, man? She's like a sister to me but I feel like she doesn't even have an opinion on life anymore," Darren continued, ignoring Jay's weak attempt at changing the subject. "I don't mean to harp on it, but damn, bro. Sometimes I wonder about all of it. I mean, I don't understand any of it. How could something like that go unsolved? And who the hell would ever be fucked up enough to do something like that?"

Jay gripped the steering wheel tighter, wanting nothing more than to get Darren home and out of his head. "I dunno, man," he muttered, trying to sound nonchalant.

"Well, anyway, what did Ms. D want you to stay after for?" Darren asked as they approached a stoplight.

"Uh, she just wanted to tell me, um, that I have to make up the quiz from last week 'cuz I failed."

"Bullshit, you haven't failed a fucking quiz your whole life," Darren retorted, but then his tone shifted, a glint of mischief in his eyes. "You taggin' Ms. D, bro? I mean, I ain't gonna say shit to Jen, but if you are, congrata-fuckin'-lations!"

"Are you fucking kidding me!" Jay snapped, his frustration boiling over. "I fucked up on a quiz,
  that's it!"

"Whoa... alright, bro. God damn... didn't mean to get your panties in a bunch."

The rest of the ride was tense and silent, but Jay couldn't shake the feeling that Darren had been too close to the truth. He had kept this secret buried for so long, and with high school nearly over, the last thing he needed was for Darren to find out. Because if he did, all hell would break loose.

"Why are we meeting at the Warehouse?" Jen asked as soon as she climbed into the Jeep, shaking off the dampness from the relentless rain.

"It's nice to see you too, dear," Jay quipped, leaning over the center console to give her a quick kiss. He smiled as he started the Jeep and pulled out of the driveway. "I don't know, George probably wants to stuff his face."

"When is this rain gonna stop? I feel like we're living in Seattle or something," Jen sighed, watching the raindrops race down the window. "I hope it's not like this all weekend." She had always been cute, but her senior year had seen her blossom into a true beauty.

"Don't let Darren hear you saying that," Jay chuckled, squinting through the windshield. "He'll flip his shit."

"What else is new?" Jen rolled her eyes. She liked Darren, unlike many girls at their school who had probably been on the receiving end of his short-lived affections. But she had admitted to Jay that she was nervous about spending a whole weekend in the same place as his obnoxious friend.

They pulled into the parking lot at 5:40, and Jay parked as close to the building as possible to spare Jen from getting drenched. He dashed through the downpour, joining Darren and George just inside the entrance.

"Liz isn't here yet, but Tubby over here wanted to sit down and go to town on the breadsticks," Darren reported, nodding toward George, who was already eyeing the menu.

"It's almost quarter to six. Where the hell are they?" Jay asked himself, concern creeping into his voice.

"I figured you'd be bringing the ladies," Darren joked, shrugging.

"Well, I ain't waiting all day," George grumbled, impatient as always.

"Oh, calm down, it's not like you're wasting away," Darren teased, earning a half-hearted glare from George.

"We need to make sure everyone's here," Jay insisted.

"Well, I'm just sayin'—" George started, but was cut off as Liz walked in, her hoodie pulled tight against the elements, head down to avoid the rain. She didn't look up until she was right in front of them, and even then, her usual light-hearted smile was missing.

Jay greeted her. "Hey, Liz. You doing alright?"

Liz gave a small nod, her eyes not quite meeting his. "Yeah, I'm okay," she said softly, her voice barely audible over the sounds of the bustling restaurant.

Jay hesitated for a moment, glancing at a typically silent Will standing there, his hands stuffed in his sweatshirt pockets as usual. "So, you're still in for the trip, right?" he asked, trying to include his best friend in the conversation.

A tense silence followed.

Liz's eyes flickered, her hand tightening on her cup. "Yeah," she whispered, her voice cracking slightly. She cleared her throat, forcing a small smile, but the weight behind her words was impossible to miss. "Of course."

Jen shot Jay a gentle, concerned look, reaching out to give his hand a quick squeeze under the table. The rest of the group remained awkwardly quiet for a beat too long. Darren shifted uncomfortably in his seat, and George stared at his plate, clearly avoiding eye contact.

Darren was the first to break the tension. "Well, good," he said, trying to shake off the awkwardness. "Now George won't have a heart attack waiting for his food."

The group chuckled half-heartedly, but the mood remained heavy. Liz's smile faded again as she dropped her gaze to her lap, her fingers tracing the edge of the table absentmindedly.

The girls quickly dove into a lighter conversation, and Liz managed to join in after a few minutes, but Jay couldn't shake the feeling that something was off—more than usual.

"So," Darren announced, clapping his hands to change the subject. "Let's get this weekend's plan hammered out."

"Well, we know that Georgy and Amy are taking care of the beer and liquor, right?" Jay started, trying to get back on track.

"Make sure you go heavy on the booze, Georgy. This ain't no picnic," Darren interjected, earning a laugh from the group.

Liz remained quiet, occasionally nodding as the others divided up responsibilities, but her mind seemed far away.

"So, you guys still remember that spot you want to go to?" Jay asked, his eyes lingering towards the silent couple. He was certain Will's presence should have been more comforting, but lately, it felt like there was a gap between them—a growing silence Jay couldn't explain.

Liz looked down for a second, then nodded again. "Yeah, I think I still remember how to get there. It's a really isolated spot... no one around for miles." She forced a smile, but it didn't reach her eyes.

Jay's stomach knotted. He wanted to believe everything was fine, but something in the way Liz avoided his gaze told him otherwise. Still, no one else seemed to notice.

The group shifted to trivial subjects throughout the meal, a welcome relief for Jay, who had enough on his mind.

As they left the restaurant, the rain continued its relentless downpour. Jay lingered for a moment, his thoughts weighed down by the awkwardness of the conversation earlier. Liz and Jen walked ahead of him. Will was trudging beside him. Head down and hands in his hoodie.

Silent.

"Yo... me and Georgey are gonna drop off the girls then head up to the pool hall. You down?" Darren caught up to them.

"No thanks, bro, I gotta get some stuff done," Jay lied, desperate for some time to think.

Will just shook his head, his mood unchanged.

"Aright, see you in the morning," Darren shrugged, turning back to George.

For a moment, Jay was caught between the two groups, a metaphor that wasn't lost on him. He hurried to catch up.

"Hey Will, wait up." he pleaded, hoping for a response from his friend.

Liz gave Jay a sidelong glance, her lips pressing together as if holding something back. Before she could speak, Jen stepped in, her voice gentle. "Jay, why don't I ride with Liz? You know, keep her company?"

Liz glanced over at Jen, offering her a faint smile of gratitude. "Yeah, that'd be nice." Jay hesitated, looking between them, then nodded slowly. "Sure... yeah, that works." He looked over at Will who only nodded, his expression still distant.

The rain tapped lightly against the car windows as Liz drove in silence for the first few minutes. The windshield wipers swished rhythmically, creating a steady beat in the background. Jen glanced over at Liz, who was staring out the windshield, her hands gripping the steering wheel. She looked smaller than usual, like the weight of the past few months had physically diminished her.

"You okay, Liz?" Jen asked, her voice soft but filled with concern.

Liz didn't turn away from the immediately. She let the question hang in the air for a moment before answering, "Yeah... I'm fine." Her tone wasn't convincing, but Jen didn't push it—at least not right away.

"You sure? You've seemed... I don't know... kinda distant lately. Like you're not really here, even when you are." Jen kept her eyes on the road but shot Liz another glance, gauging her reaction.

Liz shifted in her seat, tucking a strand of hair behind her ear, her fingers fidgeting nervously. "It's just... everything, you know? It's hard to be around everyone sometimes. They all act like things are normal, but nothing feels normal to me anymore."

Jen nodded, understanding exactly what she meant. "I know it's been rough, but you don't have to keep all of that in, Liz. I mean, we're all here for you."

Liz sighed, her breath fogging up the glass for a moment. "It's not just what happened. It's the way people look at me now, you know? Like I'm some fragile thing that's gonna break at any moment. Like they don't know how to talk to me without tiptoeing around everything."

"I can't imagine how hard it is," Jen admitted, her voice laced with empathy. "But I don't think any of us are tiptoeing. We just care. Everyone's trying to figure out how to help, even if we don't always know how."

Liz let out a small, humorless laugh. "Yeah, I guess. I just don't want to feel like I'm being treated differently. I miss when things were... simple."

Jen looked back at her friend who was looking at the road through teary eyes. She could feel Liz's pain radiating, but there was something more beneath the surface. Something unspoken. "Things were never that simple, though, were they?" Jen ventured cautiously.

Liz's eyes flickered for a moment, allowing a tear to roll innocently down her cheek. She met Jen's eyes briefly, then turned back to the road. "No... I guess they weren't," she murmured, her voice barely above a whisper.

Jen didn't press further, sensing Liz wasn't ready to open up completely. But something about

Liz's expression struck her—there was more that Liz wasn't saying. It felt like everyone in their group was keeping some kind of secret, something just under the surface, waiting to break through. And Liz wasn't the only one.

"Do you ever wonder if things will ever feel normal again?" Jen asked, more to herself than to Liz, as the thought hung heavy between them.

"I don't know. I hope so." Liz's response was so quiet, it was almost drowned out by the rain.

The rest of the ride passed in near silence, the unspoken weight of their words lingering between them. Liz drove on, lost in her thoughts, while Jen couldn't shake the feeling that there was more to all of this—more to Liz, more to what happened six months ago, more to the strange tension in their group. But whatever it was, it remained just out of reach, buried beneath layers of grief and silence.

Jay turned to Wil in the passenger seatl. The night felt heavier now, the earlier light-heartedness with their friends a distant memory. "So, what's up, man?" Jay asked, his voice quieter than before, trying to ease into the conversation that he knew was coming.

"Nothing," Will replied flatly, his tone making it clear that he wasn't in the mood for small talk. Jay knew that wasn't entirely true, but Will's walls were up, and he wasn't budging. Not even for Jay.

Jay hesitated, choosing his words carefully. "You really seem like something's bothering you... I mean, more than usual... I mean..." He trailed off, realizing how clumsy he sounded, unsure of how to approach the subject without pushing Will further away.

"It's ok, Jay," Will interrupted, his voice softening as he finally lifted his head, meeting Jay's gaze for the first time. The look in his eyes was unsettling—something between gratitude and resignation. "You know, through all of this... all the bullshit and fake sympathy, people not knowing what to say... you've always been there. You've been a best friend to me through everything—the good and the bad. I just want to thank you for that."

Jay was taken aback, his mind scrambling to process the unexpected depth of Will's words. It took him a moment to respond, "Yeah, well... what are friends for, right?" Even as he said it, Jay cringed inwardly at how hollow it sounded. "If the roles were reversed, you'd do the same for me."

Will looked away, his expression unreadable as he stared at the floor of the Jeep. "But the roles aren't reversed, Jay."

"True." Jay's voice was barely above a whisper, the weight of Will's words pressing down on him. There was so much he wanted to say, so many questions he wanted to ask, but he couldn't find the right words. The silence between them grew heavier with each passing second, filled with everything they weren't saying.

They drove the rest of the way in silence, the tension thick in the confined space of the Jeep as the rain drummed steadily on the roof, a relentless reminder of the storm both outside and within. Jay's hands tightened on the steering wheel, knuckles tensing, as his mind raced with thoughts of what he wanted—needed—to say but couldn't bring himself to voice. The occasional streetlight cast fleeting, pale glows inside the Jeep, illuminating Will's blank stare before plunging the passenger seat into emptiness.

When they finally pulled up in front of Will's house, the weight of the silence seemed almost unbearable. Jay hesitated, his hand hovering over the gearshift, not quite ready to let Will go. "Well, you know if you ever need anything...anything at all," Jay began, his voice cracking slightly under the pressure of the unsaid.

"I know," Will replied, his tone distant as he opened the door and stepped out into the night. He didn't look back as he walked up the path to his front door, his movements slow, almost mechanical, as if each step took more effort than the last. The front light flickered on casting a harsh, artificial glow over the worn-out porch and peeling paint—a house that seemed to sag under the weight of its own secrets.

Jay watched Will disappear inside, his stomach knotting with a sense of dread he couldn't shake. The light in the living room flicked on, and through the thin curtains, Jay saw Will's silhouette moving through the house, a solitary figure swallowed by the darkness within. There was an eerie stillness to the house—almost as if it wasn't truly lived in, despite Will being there. *How does he do it?* Jay wondered, his heart heavy with the realization that no one should have to face what Will was enduring. *How can he go home to this, day after day? No wonder he acts the way he does...*

Jay sat there for a long moment, staring at the house, half-expecting—half-hoping—that Will would come back out, maybe say something more, or maybe just need someone to talk to. But the house remained silent, the only sound the relentless patter of rain on the Jeep's roof.

Finally, with a heavy sigh, Jay shifted into gear and pulled away, the tires splashing through puddles as he drove off into the night. His mind was a whirlwind of thoughts, Darren's earlier questions replaying in his head. The way Darren had pushed about Will, the seriousness in his tone, it all gnawed at Jay, adding to the unease that had settled deep in his gut.

Jay tossed and turned in bed, his mind a tangled mess of thoughts. No matter how hard he tried, he couldn't shake the feeling that something was off with Darren—and with Will too. His friends were drifting, and he felt powerless to stop it. He was the one trying to hold them all together, but at what cost?

Eventually, exhaustion pulled Jay into a fitful sleep.

Suddenly, Jay jolted awake, his heart pounding in his chest as he realized Darren was sitting at his desk in the corner of the room, staring at him. The room was dimly lit by the early morning light filtering through the rain-soaked windows, casting eerie shadows on the walls. The sound of rain tapping against the glass was soothing yet unnerving, given the strange circumstances.

"What the hell, dude? How long have you been there? How did you get in?" Jay's voice trembled, startled from being awoken so suddenly. His heart raced as he tried to shake off the remnants of his dream. He glanced at his alarm clock—7:30 AM. He should have been up by now.

Darren sat motionless, his eyes fixed on Jay, something unsettling simmering beneath his calm exterior. "Don't think I don't know about everything," Darren whispered, but it wasn't Darren's usual voice. There was a coldness to it, an edge that sent shivers down Jay's spine. His heart thudded in his chest.

"Darren?" Jay stammered, his mouth dry, a sense of unease settling in. Darren's face, usually filled with mischief or humor, was blank, devoid of any emotion. The rain outside seemed louder now, like a distant roar, amplifying the tension in the room.

"Don't think I don't know about everything," Darren repeated, his voice a monotone whisper.

Jay's pulse quickened—something wasn't right. This wasn't Darren. Not the Darren he knew.

"What the hell is wrong with your voice, bro? You sound like—" Jay tried to joke, but his voice faltered. He swung his legs over the side of the bed, feeling the cool hardwood floor under his feet, grounding himself. His mind raced. What was happening?

Darren's gaze remained locked on Jay, but now his eyes seemed darker, more menacing. "Don't think I don't know about everything!!!" Darren suddenly shouted, his voice booming as he stood up, walking toward Jay's bed. Jay's heart pounded, adrenaline surging through his veins.

"What the hell are you talking about?" Jay demanded, his throat tightening. Was Darren accusing him of something? Did he know? What did he know?

Darren now stood at the edge of Jay's bed, his presence looming. The two friends were just a few feet apart, the tension suffocating. Jay could feel the heat rising in his own chest, panic threatening to consume him. Was Darren talking about Ms. Davenport? No... he couldn't possibly know. Could he? Darren had asked all those questions earlier, but... it couldn't be.

"Don't think I don't know about everything!!!" Darren roared, lunging toward Jay with a force that knocked him backward. Jay gasped, shocked, as Darren's hands closed around his neck, his grip like iron.

"CHILL!!!" Jay choked, his hands flailing to pry Darren's fingers off his throat, but Darren's strength was overpowering, his eyes burning with a rage Jay had never seen before.

"Don't think I don't know about everything!" Darren growled through clenched teeth, his grip tightening, cutting off Jay's air. Jay's vision blurred as his lungs burned for oxygen, his thoughts racing. Why was this happening? What did Darren know?

"I...can't...breathe..." Jay gasped, feeling himself slipping away. His vision darkened, the room spinning as his body fought for air.

Then, just as suddenly as it had started, it stopped.

Jay sat up, gasping for breath, drenched in sweat. His chest heaved as he looked around the room, his heart still racing. The room was quiet, except for the soft patter of rain against the windows and the occasional rumble of distant thunder. He glanced at his desk—empty. No Darren. No one.

"What the hell?" Jay whispered, running a hand through his damp hair. It took him a moment to realize he had been dreaming. But it felt so real... He rubbed his sore throat, still feeling the ghost of Darren's hands gripping him, the fear lingering like a shadow.

"This is really starting to freak me out," he muttered to the empty room, his voice shaky. Why would he dream something like that? And it felt so real, too real.

Another crash of thunder shook the house, rattling the windows. Jay lay back down, his eyes fixed on the ceiling, wide open. He tried to will himself to sleep, but every time he closed his eyes, he saw Darren's face—angry, accusing, merciless.

The rain continued to fall, relentless, matching the unease that gnawed at Jay's insides. He turned onto his side, curling into himself, but sleep wouldn't come. What if the next dream is worse? The thought lingered, dark and unsettling, as Jay lay there, waiting for the dawn to break.

Chapter 3

"Another stormy day outside, making it two and a half weeks in a row, by far surpassing the old record. Highs in the mid-60s, and rain all day…" Jay's radio alarm blared, delivering a grim weather update that matched the dreariness in his mind.

Jay sat up in bed, his body heavy with the fatigue of a restless night. "What is going on," he muttered to himself as he stretched, his muscles stiff from tension. He caught a glimpse of his reflection in the mirror—dark circles shadowed his eyes, a stark reminder of the turmoil that had kept him awake. He scoffed at his own image, the night's events replaying in his mind like a half-remembered nightmare. Everything had felt so vivid, yet now, in the cold light of morning, it was slipping away, leaving behind only unease.

As he made his way downstairs, the house was eerily quiet. His mother was nowhere to be seen, which was unusual for a Tuesday morning. No comforting smell of breakfast, no chatter from the morning talk shows that she usually watched. It felt almost surreal, as if he hadn't fully escaped the dream yet.

"Mom?" Jay called out, his voice echoing slightly in the stillness. There was no response, just the distant sound of rain drumming against the windows. He sighed and sat down at the kitchen table, pouring himself a bowl of cereal. The flakes floated lazily in the milk, and he stirred them absentmindedly, his mind elsewhere. He wasn't hungry, but he left the bowl in front of him, untouched, knowing his mother would check to see if he had eaten.

As he sat in the silent kitchen, his thoughts drifted to Will. Will, who had been through so much and seemed to be holding on by a thread. Jay wondered how his friend was coping, if at all. And then there was Darren, who had been acting strange—stranger than usual. Jay knew that his own nightmare was coloring his perception, but still, something felt off. He decided that he had to find out what Darren knew, or thought he knew. Maybe it was just paranoia, but the nagging feeling wouldn't leave him alone.

Suddenly, a loud crash at the door jolted him from his thoughts. The sound was sharp and unexpected, causing Jay to freeze. His heart raced as he sat there, his mind still clouded with remnants of his daydream. It took him a moment to muster the courage to investigate. He pulled back the curtain on the side door, peering out into the rain-soaked morning. The sky was a dull gray, the kind that seemed to press down on everything beneath it. His father had left him the Jeep again, parked just outside. "Sweet," Jay muttered, more out of habit than genuine enthusiasm, trying to distract himself from the unsettling sound.

"Whattup, loser!" Darren suddenly jumped out from under the window, his laughter cutting through the tension like a knife. Jay's heart leaped into his throat as he stumbled back, nearly losing his balance. "Oh my god, somebody's a little jumpy today," Darren teased, his voice brimming with amusement as he opened the door and helped Jay to his feet.

"W-what are you doing here?" Jay stammered, his mind racing to catch up. Was this still part of the dream? The edges of reality felt blurred, like he was caught between the waking and sleeping worlds.

"You never came to pick me up this morning, bro. You have any idea what time it is? I could've driven myself to school, but I didn't feel like it. Georgey's on his way over."

"What are you talking about?" Jay asked, still disoriented. Everything felt off-kilter, like he was a step behind in a conversation he didn't remember starting.

"Dude, are you feeling all right?" Darren eyed him with a mix of concern and curiosity.

"What time is it?" Jay's confusion deepened. He couldn't shake the feeling that something was wrong.

"Wow, you really are out of it, aren't you? It's quarter to eleven. I could only watch SportsCenter so many times before I had to come over and see what the hell was up."

"Quarter to eleven?" Jay's brow furrowed as he tried to process what Darren was saying.

"Yeah, dude. So why didn't you come pick me up?" Darren asked, seemingly unfazed by Jay's bewilderment.

"I-I don't know. I guess I overslept," Jay shrugged, turning away to hide the unease creeping back into his chest. He walked toward the kitchen, his thoughts still tangled in the remnants of his nightmare. How could he have overslept so much?

"Yeah right...don't think I don't know!" Darren called out, his tone suddenly taking on a sharper edge.

Jay stopped dead in his tracks, his heart pounding in his ears. "W-what did you just say?"

"I said, don't think I don't know," Darren replied, his eyes narrowing as he studied Jay's reaction.

"Know what, Darren?" Jay demanded, his voice strained as he turned to face his friend.

"You know."

"No, I don't," Jay shot back, his irritation rising. His gaze locked onto Darren's, trying to read what was behind his friend's cryptic words. "Why don't you tell me?"

"About Ms. D," Darren smiled, a sly grin spreading across his face as he shrugged his shoulders.

"What...how could you know?" Jay's voice quivered slightly, his mind racing as he tried to piece together how Darren could possibly have found out.

"It's obvious, Jay. You don't have to hide it from me. We're supposed to be boys. This isn't just some minor detail; this is huge," Darren's tone was light, but there was an undercurrent of something more intense, something that made Jay's skin prickle.

Jay's confusion deepened, his thoughts spiraling. "Well, how did you find out? Does Will know that you know?" he asked, his voice tinged with desperation.

"Will? What are you talking about?" Darren's brow furrowed, his confusion mirroring Jay's, but for entirely different reasons.

"Huh?" Jay felt like the ground was slipping from under him, the conversation twisting in directions he hadn't anticipated.

"You don't have to hide it from me, man. I'm not gonna say anything. I just want the details," Darren laughed, the sound echoing unnervingly in the quiet room. "Is she good? I bet she's a closet freak. She's freaky, isn't she? Jay, you dog! You've finally topped me. Not even I have hooked up with one of my teachers...let alone Ms. Davenport. She's so damn hot. How the hell did you pull that off? I always see stories on the news about teachers getting caught with students, but I never thought any of that stuff was real. I'm proud of you! Is it because you're such a nerd and hand in all your homework on time? I bet she's into your uncanny intellect."

Jay's sense of relief was almost palpable, the tension in his shoulders easing slightly. "You are such an idiot. You really are."

"What?" Darren grinned wide, leaning back with a satisfied look. "Can't I be proud of my boy?"

"You really amaze me sometimes," Jay said, shaking his head. The earlier anxiety was still there, but it was starting to fade into the background. At least Darren wasn't harassing him about what Jay had initially feared.

"Don't deny it, bro. If I were you, I'd be advertising that all over the place," Darren boasted, his eyes glinting with mischief. "I'd go from table to table in the cafeteria like, 'So, I hooked up with Ms.

Davenport,' and then walk away, like that dumb commercial where the guy tells strangers he lowered his cholesterol. Only this time, people would definitely care. Do you realize what kind of play you could get now? You're an experienced man. I'm so proud!"

"I didn't hook up with Ms. Davenport, you moron!" Jay snapped, his voice edged with frustration. "Don't deny, glorify!" Darren declared, his voice booming through the room as he struck a triumphant pose, a mischievous grin plastered on his face.

Jay sighed, trying to tamp down his growing nervousness. He knew Darren well enough to anticipate where this conversation was heading, and he didn't like it. He cast a glance at the rain-soaked window, the storm outside feeling like a reflection of the turmoil brewing inside him. "Why would you walk all the way over here in a thunderstorm?"

"I didn't walk, I drove. What, are you kidding me?" Darren laughed, the sound loud and unrestrained, as if the thought of walking in the storm was absurd. He shrugged off his jacket, shaking the raindrops from it before hanging it on the back of a chair. "Anyway, I had to ask you about this, plus I was worried about you, baby," Darren teased, playfully throwing an arm around Jay's shoulder—a gesture that felt uncomfortably close to Jay.

Jay forced a laugh, trying to distance himself from Darren's probing. "Well, was it worth it?" he asked, his voice betraying the nervousness he felt. His heart pounded, the conversation treading dangerously close to things he didn't want to discuss.

Darren ignored the question, his expression shifting to one of genuine curiosity. "Well then...if you're not hooking up with Ms. Davenport, then why is she always talking to you alone in the halls, and having you stay after class and stuff?"

The question hung in the air, heavy and unavoidable. Jay's earlier relief vanished, replaced by a sinking feeling in his stomach. He knew Darren's earlier line of questioning was just a setup, a way to get to the real issue on his mind. Jay could feel the walls closing in, the tension in the room thickening as he struggled to find an answer. His mind raced, trying to come up with something, anything, that would deflect Darren's suspicions.

'Is he trying to see what I know again? Does he really know what's going on? Maybe he knows, but no one realizes that he knows, and he's going to use me as the scapegoat for telling him. Why the hell is he so persistent?' Jay's thoughts spiraled as he searched desperately for a response, feeling cornered.

"Yo," Darren waved his hand in front of Jay's face, snapping him out of his thoughts. "You gonna ignore me?"

Jay blinked, trying to gather himself. "I told you, I've been struggling in class lately, and—"

"Bullshit!" Darren interrupted, his voice sharp, cutting through Jay's excuse like a knife. "You haven't struggled since you were learning to tie your shoes! Don't mess with me!"

The tone in Darren's voice was unmistakable—he was frustrated, maybe even angry. Jay could sense that Darren was getting fed up with whatever secret Jay was keeping from him, if there even was a secret.

Just as Jay opened his mouth to try and explain, George burst through the door, the wind and rain following him in a gust of cold air. The door slammed shut behind him with a bang, the storm outside a fitting backdrop to the brewing tension inside.

"Holy crap, is this rain ever gonna stop?" George cried as he stumbled into the kitchen, water streaming from his soaked clothes. His hair clung to his forehead, and his coat dripped, leaving small puddles on the floor. He looked like a drowned rat, and Jay couldn't help but let out a small sigh of relief at the sight of his friend.

'Maybe the interrogation is over,' Jay thought, feeling his heart rate start to slow down. His mind raced, trying to make sense of everything. Why had he overslept like that?

"Will you quit your whining already? You're worse than Em," Darren joked, flashing a quick look at Jay, one that seemed to say, This isn't over. Darren's attempt at humor only partially lifted the tension that lingered between them.

"Yeah, so Jay was just telling me how he and Ms. Davenp—" Darren's sentence was cut off by the sharp sound of glass shattering on the kitchen floor. He snapped his head around just in time to see Jay's cereal bowl explode into pieces, milk and mush splattering across the tiles like a messy crime scene.

"What the hell, Jay? Got some butterfingers or what?" Darren asked, raising an eyebrow at his friend, who was now kneeling on the floor, hastily trying to gather the broken shards. Jay's hands shook slightly as he cleaned up the mess, his nerves clearly frayed.

"N-no...I just...dropped it," Jay stammered, his voice shaky as he fumbled to pick up the pieces.

'Darren can't know. There's no way. But what if he does?'

"Anyway, what were you saying, Darren?" George asked, seeming unfazed by Jay's clumsiness as he dismissed it with a wave of his hand. He was more focused on the conversation that had been interrupted.

"Huh," Darren muttered, still fixated on the mess Jay had made. His mind seemed to drift for a moment before he shook his head, snapping himself out of it. "Oh, nothing," he said, his voice trailing off. Then, as if trying to shake off the tension, he added with forced enthusiasm, "What do you guys say we grab a case and chill today? My treat."

Jay blinked in surprise at the sudden shift in Darren's mood. Was he trying to throw him off, or was Jay just being paranoid? The whole situation felt surreal.

"Sure, as long as you're buying," George replied, equally surprised but more than willing to go along with the plan.

"Jay?" Darren turned to him, eyebrows raised.

"What? Yeah, whatever," Jay mumbled, trying to sound indifferent, though his mind was still racing.

"Wow, don't be so damn enthusiastic about it. I buy once a semester, and you can't even crack a smile. Whatever's lodged up your ass better be out by the time I get back," Darren teased, half-joking as he headed for the door.

He stepped out into the relentless downpour, his jacket already soaked through. He noticed George's car blocking his way out of the driveway but didn't bother asking him to move it.

Instead, he decided to put his truck in four-wheel drive and cut through Jay's neighbor's lawn.

But as he reached his truck, a strange, eerie chill ran down his spine. It was the kind of feeling you get when you know someone's watching you. He scanned the house, but there was no one in the windows. He looked down the street and saw a dark SUV parked nearby, its windows so tinted they looked like they were painted black. The sight of it made him uneasy, though he couldn't put his finger on why. He shook his head and laughed it off.

'It's a good thing Jay and George aren't here to see what a wuss I'm being,' he thought to himself.

As he backed his truck through the neighbor's lawn, he glanced back at where the SUV had been, but it was gone. A shiver ran through him again, but he brushed it off, attributing it to the cold rain and his overactive imagination.

"So anyway..." George turned back to Jay, who was lost in his own world, his mind racing to piece everything together. He couldn't shake the feeling that Darren was getting too close.

'He's really starting to freak me out,' Jay thought, barely registering George's voice. 'What's going on with him? Why all the questions?'

"HELLO!!!" George waved his arms in the air, trying to snap Jay out of his thoughts. "I said, do you think the campsite will be flooded by the time the weekend hits?"

"I doubt it... Liz picked it out, I'm sure nothing can go wrong with it," Jay lied smoothly, trying to reassure George. And anyway, it was Will's idea too, right? Or was it?

"Yeah right, it would be just my luck to have the one thing I was looking forward to get totally screwed up," George grumbled, his face creasing with worry.

"Why does everything have to be so perfect, George?" Jay snapped, his frustration boiling over. It was the first time he'd let his emotions slip all day. He'd been trying to keep calm, but the pressure was getting to him.

"I don't know. It would just be nice if it was. For once, ya know? No reason..." George's voice trailed off, caught off guard by Jay's sudden outburst. "I just think we've been planning this for so long that I don't want it to get messed up. That's all."

Jay turned away and started walking out of the kitchen, the whole situation feeling more surreal by the minute. It was like being trapped in a bad dream, the kind where everything is just real enough to make you question what's actually happening. But as he reached the doorway, the storm outside seemed to echo the storm raging inside him, and he couldn't shake the feeling that something was about to go very, very wrong.

Jay's mind continued to spiral as he tried to make sense of Darren's behavior. Darren couldn't know anything. 'I haven't told him, and I know Will hasn't said a word.'

But why does it feel like he's pushing so hard? He's not just fishing—he's trying to catch something. But what?

"You want anything from Captain Tony's?" George's voice broke through Jay's thoughts as he reached for the phone, completely unaware of the turmoil brewing inside his friend.

"Nah. I'm not that hungry," Jay replied, his voice distant, eyes still clouded with doubt.

"You alright, Jay? You look like you've seen a ghost." George's tone shifted, finally picking up on Jay's unease.

"I'm fine," Jay muttered, though he knew it was a lie. He didn't feel like talking or even being around his friends right now, but there was no escaping it. They were here, and Darren wasn't going to let things slide easily. Jay resolved to play it cool, to act normal, even though his insides felt like they were twisting into knots. After all, these were his best friends. Nothing could come between them. Right?

The door swung open with a bang, and Darren burst in, grinning from ear to ear, two 18-packs of beer in hand. "You guys ready to drink or what?" he hollered, his voice filled with the reckless enthusiasm that always accompanied him when he started drinking. His face was already flushed, the telltale sign that he had begun indulging before arriving.

"What's all that for?" Jay asked, eyeing the beers with a mix of apprehension and resignation. He wasn't sure if he was more worried about what Darren might say next or the path the day might take.

"Em and Amy are on their way over," Darren announced, already halfway through his first beer. "They're skipping fourth block to come hit the sauce with us. I figured we could fire up some beer pong. No good?" Darren's voice held a slight edge, as if he was waiting for Jay to reject the idea, ready to pounce on any hesitation.

"I'm not really in the mood," Jay replied, trying to sound casual. "But you guys go ahead. I might have a few later." He forced a smile, hoping it would deflect any suspicion Darren might have about his state of mind. He couldn't let on that the dream—or whatever it was—was still gnawing at him.

Darren's expression flickered with something that looked like disappointment, but he shrugged it off quickly. "Alright, where's

Georgy?" he asked, scanning the room as if expecting George to materialize out of thin air.

"He went to Captain Tony's to pick up some food," Jay answered, leaning against the counter, trying to steady his nerves.

"That fat bastard better have gotten me something," Darren joked, his tone lightening. "Maybe I can call and add something to his order before he gets there." He darted to the kitchen, grabbed the phone, and began dialing, his fingers moving quickly across the keypad.

Jay felt a small wave of relief wash over him. Darren's intense questioning seemed to have passed, at least for the moment. Darren returned to the living room, still on the phone, but with a beer in hand for Jay. "Here you go, sweetheart. That should put a little hitch in your giddy-up."

Jay hesitated for a split second before taking the beer. Maybe this was what he needed—a chance to relax and shake off the unsettling feeling that had been clinging to him since he woke up. After all, Darren was his friend, and the dream was just that—a dream. Nothing more. He tipped his beer against Darren's, trying to convince himself that everything was fine.

The rest of the day unfolded more smoothly than Jay expected. Emily and Amy arrived, and soon enough, the five of them were deep into the beer, their laughter filling the house as they joked and played games. The rain outside was relentless, but inside, the atmosphere was warm and lively. Darren, as usual, was the life of the party, his earlier intensity forgotten as he chugged beer after beer, his jokes growing louder and more outrageous.

Jay found himself relaxing more as the hours passed. The beers dulled the edge of his anxiety, and he almost managed to forget about the morning's tension. Almost. But every now and then, Darren's eyes would flicker toward him, a brief flash of something that reminded Jay that the questions weren't entirely gone. They were just waiting, lurking beneath the surface, ready to reappear when he least expected it.

By the time the evening rolled around, Jay was leaning back on the couch, a half-empty beer in hand, watching Darren and George argue over the rules of beer pong. For a moment, everything felt normal.

But as Jay glanced over at Darren, who was cracking another joke at George's expense, that uneasy feeling returned. The day had gone well—better than he had expected—but something still didn't sit right with him. The dream, Darren's questions, the tension that had hung over them all day like a storm cloud—it all lingered in the back of his mind, refusing to let him fully relax.

And as the night wore on, Jay couldn't shake the feeling that this was just the calm before the storm. Something was coming, and whatever it was, it wasn't going to be as easy to shake off as today's lingering unease.

But for now, all he could do was tip back his beer, laugh with his friends, and hope that whatever was coming, they would face it together. Just like they always had.

"I dunno, Jen, he just seems different lately. You really haven't noticed?" Jay stared blankly at the wall, his mind racing as he waited for his girlfriend's response. The rain outside had softened to a gentle drizzle, the rhythmic tapping against the windowpane blending with the quiet hum of the house. It was a comforting sound, but tonight it felt more like a reminder of the unease that had settled over him.

"Well, not really. I mean, he's always kind of an ass, but you're used to that by now," Jen replied, her voice crackling slightly over the phone, a familiar sound that usually soothed Jay. But tonight, it only added to his growing discomfort.

"It's not that he's being an ass," Jay said, his tone more contemplative than defensive. "That part of Darren doesn't phase me anymore. It's just...he's been a little pushy, I guess. Like he's digging for something, but I don't know what. Maybe I'm just being paranoid again." Jay sighed, running a hand through his hair as if trying to massage the tension out of his skull. He had enjoyed the day with his friends, the beer, the laughs, even Darren's usual antics. But now, with the alcohol wearing off, the exhaustion was settling in, and with it, the nagging feeling that something was off.

"Well, what did you guys do today?" Jen asked, sensing the need to shift the conversation, to pull Jay out of his head and into something more tangible.

"I guess I overslept this morning, so Darren and George came over here. Darren wanted to drink, of course, and George couldn't resist grabbing food from Captain Tony's, so we just stayed here, hung out, nothing special." Jay tried to keep his voice light, but there was a weight to his words that he couldn't shake.

"Oh," Jen replied, her confusion evident. "I thought you were sick."

"Nope...just overslept." Jay frowned, pulling the phone away from his ear for a moment. Part of him wanted to tell Jen about everything. To confide in her about it all. About his dream the night before. Or about his talk with Will on the way home. Or...

He snapped out of his daydream

"Well I was just calling to check up on you, babe. Making sure you're not changing your mind on me about the dance!"

"Never!," Jay quickly responded. His mind was still wrestling with itself. Trying to make sense of all of the chaos. "My mind is just going in a million different directions. Everything's been so hectic lately. I just want things to go back to normal."

"Jay, things are never going to be the same. They can't. Not after…" Jen's voice trailed off, not wanting to finish the thought that they both knew was true.

"I know," Jay whispered, his heart heavy with the weight of unspoken words.

"Well…I'm gonna go wash my hair. Promise you'll call me before you go to bed?" Jen's voice was gentle again, a peace offering of sorts, signaling that she didn't want to dwell on the conversation any longer than necessary.

"Yeah, babe," Jay mumbled, feeling the fatigue pulling at him more now than before.

"I love you, honey."

"Love you too." Jay replied automatically, but even as he said the words, his mind was still racing, still trying to piece together the fragments of the day. He hung up the phone and sat in the quiet of his room, listening to the rain as it tapped persistently against the window, mirroring the unease that refused to leave him.

As he sat there, he couldn't shake the feeling that Jen was right. Things weren't the same. They couldn't be. Not after everything that had happened. And no matter how much he tried to push it aside, the truth was always there, lurking in the shadows of his thoughts, waiting to be acknowledged.

He sighed deeply, running a hand through his hair once more, before finally lying back on his bed, staring up at the ceiling. The rain continued its relentless pattern, a steady reminder that some storms couldn't be avoided—they could only be weathered. And Jay knew, deep down, that this was just the beginning.

Chapter 4

Jay was overtaken by the darkness of his room as he restlessly lay in bed that night, his mind a whirlpool of thoughts he couldn't escape. The storm outside raged on, lightning flashing in erratic intervals, casting eerie shadows on the walls. The house shook with each thunderclap, but Jay barely noticed.

The storm had become background noise, blending with the turmoil in his head. The dream from the night before still lingered, its intensity unsettling him more than he wanted to admit. Darren's odd behavior earlier that day only added to his unease, but as he lay there, it wasn't Darren that occupied his thoughts—it was Will.

Jay tried to push the thoughts away, but they kept coming back, relentless. He remembered the good times he and Will had shared before everything changed. Those memories seemed like a lifetime ago, yet they were as clear as if they'd happened yesterday.

He could still picture their first day of school. It was a day that felt almost predestined given how close their families were. Jay tossed to his left side, trying to get comfortable, but sleep was a distant hope.

The faint glow from his alarm clock illuminated the framed picture on his desk—a photo of him and Will on their first day of school. Jay's heart ached at the sight. It had been so long, but he could remember that day perfectly...

"Are you nervous?" young Jay asked, tugging at the collar of the preppy outfit his mother had picked out for his first day of school. The fabric felt stiff and unfamiliar, and his anxiety was palpable.

"No, why would I be?" Will's response was confident, almost dismissive, as if the idea of being nervous was foreign to him.

"I dunno, I just don't know about this, ya know?" Jay mumbled, his voice tinged with apprehension. "I heard the older kids just pick on the kindergartners on the bus something fierce. I'm not looking forward to that at all."

"Well, I wouldn't worry about it," Will replied, his tone unwavering. "I don't see anyone messing with us."

Jay had always admired Will's confidence. It wasn't overbearing like Darren's; it was quiet and assured. Will's self-assurance had a way of calming Jay's nerves, even when things seemed

bleak. Jay smiled to himself, recalling how Will had led the way that morning, his confidence infectious.

"Well, what about Lenny Thompson? I heard he punched a kid out on the first day last year...just for looking at him!" Jay's voice shook as he voiced his fear.

"Don't worry about it," Will said again, this time with a reassuring smile. "I don't think he'll try that with us."

Jay couldn't believe how composed Will was. As the bus approached, Jay's anxiety skyrocketed. The massive yellow vehicle seemed like a monster looming on the horizon. His heart pounded in his chest, his palms sweating as he tried to steady himself. Will, on the other hand, was calm, almost excited. He led the way onto the bus, heading straight for the back seat, completely unfazed by the stares from the other kids.

Jay trailed behind, clinging to Will's confidence like a lifeline.

The bus ride started uneventfully, with the boys engrossed in their lunchbox treasures, trading snacks and joking around. Jay had almost forgotten his fears until a loud voice boomed from the front of the bus, "Who is in my seat???"

Jay froze. It was Lenny Thompson, the kid he'd been dreading all morning. His worst fears were coming true. As Lenny stormed down the aisle, Jay shrank into his seat, sweating profusely. But Will didn't flinch. He didn't even acknowledge the looming threat.

"You two little punk kids think you can..." Lenny's words were cut off abruptly as Will's fist met his jaw with surprising force.

WHAM!!!

Lenny crumpled to the floor, out cold. The bus went silent, every eye fixed on Will, who sat back as if nothing had happened. Jay's heart raced, not from fear but from admiration.

"*So your banana for my fruit roll?*" *Will asked, his tone as casual as ever, as if knocking out Lenny was just another part of the morning routine.*

Jay chuckled to himself as the thunder crashed outside, pulling him back to the present. Even as a kid, Will had a way of handling things that left everyone else in awe. He had always been the one Jay looked up to, the one who could take on anything without breaking a sweat. But now...things were different. Will wasn't the same, and that change gnawed at Jay.

Suddenly, his cell phone rang, shattering the silence of the room. The bright screen lit up the darkness, the sound startling Jay out of his thoughts. "Who the hell would call me this late?" he muttered, glancing at the clock. The red digits glowed—2:24 AM.

"Hello?" Jay answered, his voice groggy as he rubbed his eyes, trying to shake off the haze of sleep.

"Jay...did I...uh...wake you up?"

It was Will. Of all the people in the world, Will was the last person Jay expected to call him—especially this late. Something must be wrong. Jay's mind instantly flashed back to the night six months prior, a chill creeping up his spine. He shot up in his bed, "No...why, what's up,

Will?"

"You think you could...uh...meet me in the...um...park in a little while? I...gotta talk to you about something."

"Now? It's 2:30 in the morning, and it's pouring out there, man."

"I wouldn't ask if it wasn't important."

Jay hesitated, but Will had a point. He wouldn't ask unless it was serious. "Yeah, OK. I'll be there in like five minutes."

"OK, hurry, bro."

As they hung up, Jay's mind raced. What could possibly be so urgent? The urgency in Will's voice unsettled him. It wasn't like Will to reach out, especially not recently. Jay pulled on the hoodie draped over his chair and quietly made his way down the stairs. The last thing he wanted was to explain this to his parents. He crept to the side door, carefully opening it before stepping outside into the cold, wet night.

The rain was relentless, drenching him instantly. Jay decided against starting the car—it would make too much noise, and he didn't want to risk waking anyone. He'd walk. The park wasn't far, and he could tough it out through a little rain. He zipped up his hoodie and pulled the hood tighter around his face, bracing against the biting wind.

The park had always been their meeting spot, the halfway point between their houses. Even though it was a little closer to Will's, Jay had never minded the extra few steps. Tonight, though, each step felt heavier, as if the weight of the rain was trying to pull him back. The streets were eerily silent, the usual hum of distant traffic muffled by the downpour. Jay's thoughts raced as he approached the park. "What could be wrong? Why did Will call me now? What does he need to tell me that couldn't wait until morning?" His voice cut through the stillness, the only sound besides the rain and his own hurried footsteps.

When Jay reached the park, the empty swings swayed slightly in the wind, the playground deserted and shadowy. He checked his watch—2:58 AM. "Where the hell is he?" Jay muttered, his breath visible in the cold air. The park was devoid of life, save for Jay standing in the middle, drenched and anxious. He waited for a few more minutes, scanning the dark pathways for any sign of movement, but Will was nowhere to be seen.

Growing more uneasy with each passing second, Jay decided to head toward Will's house. Maybe he'd meet him on the way. At least if he was moving, he wouldn't feel as exposed to the elements—or the rising dread in his gut. The rain continued to pour, soaking through his hoodie, making him shiver as he trudged down the empty street.

As he approached Will's street, Jay saw a dark SUV pulling out of Will's driveway. The vehicle's windows were tinted so dark that they appeared almost black, obscuring any view of the driver. Jay squinted, trying to make out who it was, but the rain made it impossible. The SUV sped off, leaving a spray of water in its wake. Jay stood there, frozen in place, watching the vehicle disappear into the night. "Who the hell was that?" he wondered aloud, his voice swallowed by the rain.

His heart raced as he approached Will's house, his mind spinning with questions. The door was slightly ajar, as if Will had been waiting for him. Jay hesitated for a moment, then steeled himself and walked up the driveway, his footsteps splashing in the puddles that had formed. He reached out and rang the doorbell, the sound sharp and intrusive in the quiet night. The door opened almost immediately, and Will stood there, looking disheveled and confused.

"Wh-what are you doing here?" stammered Will, his eyes wide with surprise. Jay could see the puffiness around Will's eyes, evidence that he had been crying.

"Me? What are you still doing here? I was freezing, man... anyway, what was so important that you couldn't tell me over the phone?"

"What are you talking about?" Will's confusion deepened, his brows knitting together.

"You called me like 45 minutes ago... You told me to meet you at the park. You said it was important and to hurry. I've been waiting in this downpour the whole time, bro."

"I...never called you, Jay," Will replied, shaking his head as if trying to clear it of some fog.

Jay's heart skipped a beat. He was sure it had been Will on the phone—wasn't he? Who else would know about the park? The familiar spot that had been their meeting place for years?

Will began to close the door, "Look, it's really not a good time. I'll see you tomorrow."

"Well, at least tell me what's wrong. I walked all the way over here in this rain...you owe me that at least." Jay pressed, hoping to get some answers. "You said it was important. Who was just here?"

"LOOK...I NEVER CALLED YOU, AND I DON'T WANNA TALK RIGHT NOW," Will exploded, taking a step back and slamming the door in Jay's face with a force that seemed to cause the house to shake.

Jay stood at the door, half-expecting his friend to open it back up, laughing at the joke. But it was no joke, and the days of Will doing something like that as a joke were long gone. He slowly turned and started back down the driveway.

"What the hell was that all about?" he muttered to himself. "I know it was him...it was his voice and everything. He knows I'm here for him if he needs me, why would he be embarrassed to talk to me?" He stepped back onto the cold street. He turned to take another look at Will's front door, with one last hope that his friend would open it.

Jay was concentrating so much, trying to sort through every thought that he was having, that he did not notice the SUV about 50 yards down the street. Suddenly, the bright lights of the truck flicked on, cutting through the rain and casting long, eerie shadows. The tires screeched on the wet pavement. Jay's heart leapt into his throat, his chest heaving as his eyes widened in shock. Without thinking, he took off running in the pouring rain, not wanting to find out if the truck was after him.

The SUV's engine roared as it barreled down the street, water spraying from the tires as it closed in on Jay. He sprinted toward the park, knowing the truck wouldn't be able to follow him in there. But as he reached the park entrance, he heard a loud skid and the unmistakable sound of a car door slamming. He glanced back, seeing the truck parked haphazardly on the side of the road, the driver's door wide open. The dome light flickered inside, revealing an empty interior.

"Where the hell did he go?" Jay's thoughts raced as he stood there, panting, the rain pouring down his face. He began walking backward, his eyes darting from side to side, scanning the darkness for any sign of movement.

CRASH.

A bolt of lightning split the sky, illuminating the park in a brief flash of white light. In that split second, Jay saw a dark figure bolt from behind the truck, heading straight toward him. Panic surged through him as he turned to run, but his foot slipped in the mud, sending him crashing to the ground. He scrambled to his feet, hearing the figure's footsteps pounding behind him, growing closer with each second.

Jay ran faster than he ever had, his lungs burning, his legs feeling like they were wading through quicksand. The figure was right on top of him now, close enough that Jay could feel the person's breath on the back of his neck. He could hear the fabric of his sweatshirt tearing as the figure grabbed at him, trying to pull him down.

Up ahead, Jay saw the headlights of a truck approaching on the road. Desperation gave him a burst of speed as he veered toward the road, hoping to intercept the vehicle and escape his pursuer. He dashed in front of the truck, throwing himself onto the hood, praying that the driver would stop.

The truck screeched to a halt, inches from Jay's face.

"What the hell are you doing, boy?" demanded an older man, jumping out of the truck, his voice filled with concern.

"S-s-someone's chasing me, sir," Jay gasped, pointing back toward the park, his voice trembling with fear.

The old man squinted into the darkness, then looked back at Jay, his expression softening.

"Ain't nobody there...you OK, son?"

Jay turned around, his heart still racing. The park was empty, the figure gone as if it had never been there. He tried to catch his breath, nodding slowly. "I don't know... I think I'm just losing it."

The man gave Jay a once-over, noticing the torn sweatshirt, the mud on his clothes. "You sure you're alright? Where do you live? I can give you a ride home."

"Sure, sir. Thank you," Jay mumbled, feeling the adrenaline start to fade, replaced by a cold, creeping exhaustion. He knew his house was only a block and a half away, but he didn't want to chance getting caught by whoever—or whatever—had been after him.

The ride home was short and silent, the old man glancing at Jay occasionally, but saying nothing. Jay stared out the window, his mind racing with questions, but too tired to find any answers. When they pulled up to his house, Jay thanked the man repeatedly, his voice barely above a whisper.

After the truck drove away, Jay stood in the driveway for a moment, trying to process what had just happened. Was he imagining things? Was there even anyone after him? He turned to go inside, but something caught his eye. The SUV was parked across the street, its lights off, but clearly there. It must have crept up while he was walking up the driveway, hiding in the shadows behind the old man's truck.

Jay's breath caught in his throat. He bolted for the door, slamming it shut behind him and locking it. "What the hell is going on?" he whispered to the empty house, his voice shaking.

He hurried up the stairs, shedding his muddy sweatshirt as he went. He flopped down onto his bed, his heart still pounding in his chest. The curiosity was unbearable, but he forced himself to get up and peer out the window, pulling the shade back just enough to see the street below.

The SUV was gone.

Jay sank back onto his bed, his mind spinning. He knew he wasn't going to sleep, but he had to try to rest. His thoughts kept returning to Will. Had it really been him on the phone? It had to be. It sounded just like him. But if it wasn't Will, then who? And why had they told him to meet at the park?

He checked his phone, hoping for some clue. No missed calls. The last call was from a blocked number—just like Will's house phone always showed up. But that was no help. The rest of the night, Jay tossed and turned, his mind replaying the events over and over, searching for answers that wouldn't come. He couldn't shake the feeling that he hadn't seen the last of the person in the SUV—and that whatever was happening, it was far from over.

Chapter 5

The next morning, Jay hesitated at the edge of his bed, unsure whether he wanted to step outside. The events of the previous night played on a loop in his mind, making sleep an elusive luxury. He rubbed his tired eyes and stared at the muddy sweatshirt crumpled on the floor next to his bed, a stark reminder that the night's horrors weren't just a bad dream.

"Nope, it was not a dream," he muttered to himself, his voice echoing in the stillness of his room. His stomach churned with unease as he imagined the SUV still lurking outside, waiting for him.

'What if this guy is still out there...waiting for me? What the hell does he even want?'

His room was dimly lit by the early morning light seeping through the blinds. Posters of his favorite bands and sports teams covered the walls, but their once comforting presence did nothing to ease the dread that had settled in his gut.

Jay took his time getting ready, each motion slow and deliberate, as if stalling would somehow make the day less daunting. Every few minutes, he'd glance out the window, his heart pounding with each look, but the street remained empty.

Jay knew he had to talk to Will. Whoever was in that SUV knew something, and Jay was certain that Will had the answers he desperately needed. But should he tell Darren and George? What could they do even if they knew? The question nagged at him as he dressed, his mind a jumble of fear and uncertainty.

By the time he pulled up to Darren's house, he had made up his mind. He'd talk to Will first. He needed answers, and Will was the only one who could provide them.

"What's up, dickhead?" Darren greeted as he hopped into the car, completely unaware of the turmoil brewing inside Jay. "You have a good time yesterday or what?"

"Yeah, it was fun," Jay replied absentmindedly, his thoughts still locked on the events of the previous night. He knew he had to keep his true thoughts hidden from Darren, at least for now. The last thing he needed was Darren pestering him about Ms. Davenport or prying into the truth Jay was so desperate to keep buried.

"Well, I, for one, had a great time. What are you doing tonight? Wanna go catch a movie or something?"

"No," Jay muttered, his attention elsewhere.

"Well, who the hell pissed in your Cheerios this morning?" Darren cracked, trying to lighten the mood.

Jay just sat in silence, as Darren rambled on, barely registering his friend's jokes. His mind was too occupied with how he would approach Will. Something was definitely wrong, and Jay was determined to find out what it was. The memory of Will's puffy, tear-streaked face haunted him, and the more he thought about it, the more he realized how little he knew about what was going on in Will's life.

Jay was so lost in his thoughts that he almost ran a red light.

He slammed on the brakes just in time as cars buzzed by, honking and flashing their lights.

A few drivers yelled obscenities and flipped him off as they sped past.

"What the hell?" Darren shouted, dramatically curling into a fetal position in the passenger seat.

"Sorry," Jay mumbled, his voice hollow.

"Sorry? You almost killed us, man! What the hell is your problem this morning?"

"Nothing," Jay replied, wishing he had skipped picking Darren up today, or at least picked up George first to avoid being alone with Darren. As he backed out of the intersection, he glanced in the rearview mirror just in time to see a black SUV slam into the back of their car. The impact jolted them forward into the oncoming traffic.

Jay frantically tried to shift into reverse, but the car was no match for the force of the truck behind them. They were now stuck in the middle of the road, with cars screeching to a halt around them, trying to avoid a collision.

An old mustard-colored station wagon was rear-ended by a metallic green Jeep just ten feet away from where Jay and Darren were trapped. Jay turned to look at the SUV, straining to see through the downpour. His heart pounded as he tried to make out the driver's face, desperate for any clue as to who was behind this relentless pursuit.

The seconds dragged on like hours, and Jay's mind raced through the possibilities. The connection to the previous night was unmistakable—whoever was in that SUV was the same person who had chased him in the park.

Darren's panicked screams barely registered as Jay's thoughts spiraled. 'Why was this person after him? What did they want?'

He looked out Darren's window and saw a red Mustang skidding toward them, the driver gripping the wheel so tightly that Jay could see the whites of his knuckles. The car stopped inches from Darren's door, giving the boys a brief moment of relief.

But it was short-lived.

Another earth-shattering crash hit the passenger side as the Mustang was shoved into them from behind, slamming Darren's side of the car and sending it spinning. Jay's head snapped to the side, slamming into the window, and the glass shattered around him.

Suddenly, everything went dark.

...

Surprisingly, Darren seemed to have no serious injuries, although if you heard him panting frantically, you would have thought he was giving birth in the front seat. The chaotic crash that took place in a matter of 30 seconds felt like a lifetime to the boys.

Jay lifted his head, feeling something warm and wet trickling down his face. His head was dripping with blood, and he could faintly hear Darren yelling and cursing in the background, his voice a mix of panic and anger. Jay looked into the cracked rearview mirror, only to see the SUV gone, as if it had vanished into thin air.

He let his head fall back against the headrest, trying to make sense of everything through the pain. The dull ache in his skull pulsed with each heartbeat, and he shut his eyes, overwhelmed by a wave of dizziness and exhaustion. For a moment, he allowed himself to drift off, just to escape the madness.

The next thing Jay knew, he was surrounded by flashing lights and the muffled voices of police officers. The scene felt surreal, like he was watching everything from a distance. The police were already taking statements from witnesses. It all seemed to have happened too fast for many of them to concretely be able to confirm that the boys had been pushed into the intersection.

Jay sat on the edge of the ambulance, getting his head checked by a paramedic. He couldn't even remember the authorities arriving on the scene.

"Hold still now," said the paramedic, a middle-aged woman with kind eyes. "This might hurt." She gently but firmly pulled a small shard of glass from the side of Jay's head, leaving a cut about an inch long that immediately started to bleed.

"Ow!" Jay yelped, wincing as the sharp pain shot through his skull. He clenched his fists, his frustration building as the adrenaline started to wear off. He didn't know what to do, but anger simmered beneath the surface.

He was mad at himself for not being more aware, for not noticing the SUV behind them.

He was mad at Darren for his dramatics, treating the whole thing like some action movie.

But most of all, he was mad at Will.

Will knew something—Jay was sure of it—and yet he hadn't warned him or even hinted that there was something to worry about. How could Will let him walk into danger like that? They could have been killed!

As the paramedic bandaged his head, Jay debated his next move.

Against his better judgment, he decided not to tell the police about the previous night. What good would it do? They either wouldn't believe him, or they'd think he was just some paranoid kid making up stories for attention.

"So, like I said, we were chillin' at the—uh, I mean... the light, and WHAM," Darren was saying, his voice loud and animated as he re-enacted the events the way Jay described them to the police. He slammed his fist into his palm for emphasis. "Some black truck slams into the back of us, pushing us into the intersection. We didn't even do anything, man."

"Did you get a license plate number?" asked one of the officers, his tone serious and probing.

"Hell no, I was crapping my pants," Darren laughed nervously, still trying to play it cool. "But I hope you find out who it is before I do because that was messed up."

"This is not a joke, son. Somebody obviously wanted you two hurt. Do you have any enemies or anything like that?"

"We're in high school, what do you think?" Darren retorted, rolling his eyes as if the officer had asked the dumbest question in the world.

The officer, unamused, continued, "Well, we have a make on the vehicle. Unfortunately, that's about all we have to go on right now unless you guys have anything else you'd like to add." He turned his gaze to Jay, who was still sitting on the curb, his jaw clenched as he struggled to keep his emotions in check.

"No, sir," Jay replied automatically, his voice void of emotion. He didn't dare mention anything to the officer.

"Well, why don't you two go home and get some rest? If we find out anything, we'll give you guys a call." The officer gave them a final nod before walking back toward the other policemen who were still collecting statements from the scene.

Jay stayed seated on the curb, oblivious to the steady rain that soaked through his clothes. The bright yellow police parka draped over his shoulders did little to keep out the cold. His focus remained locked on the wreckage, the mangled cars scattered across the intersection like discarded toys.

Darren was still babbling on, saying something about how "that was the coolest thing that's ever happened to me," but Jay barely heard him.

His eyes wandered to the open door of the ambulance parked a few feet away. Inside, he could see a little girl from the station wagon, lying unconscious on a stretcher. Her small body looked so fragile, her face pale and motionless. Jay's heart sank as he wondered what grade she might be in if she could have even seen over the dashboard at what was happening around her.

Anger flared in his chest, hot and unrelenting.

He felt guilty. He felt guilty for not noticing the SUV sooner, for not preventing this disaster. Even though he knew there was little he could have done, the guilt gnawed at him as the paramedics shut the ambulance doors, breaking him out of his trance.

He was torn, his emotions pulling him in different directions. Half of him wanted to march over to Will's house and demand answers, maybe even shake the truth out of him. The other half felt like collapsing on the spot, letting the pain and exhaustion take over. His head throbbed, a constant reminder of the danger they'd narrowly escaped. He couldn't understand why someone was after him or how Will could be involved. Will was his best friend—despite everything that had happened, nothing could change that.

"I can't wait to tell everyone..." Darren continued to babble, his excitement in stark contrast to Jay's turmoil.

"Darren...don't tell anyone about this, OK?" Jay said suddenly, his voice low and urgent as he glanced around to make sure no one was listening. He wasn't sure if he should tell Darren about the night before, but the pressure of keeping it to himself was too much. And after the SUV showed up again, he couldn't hold it in any longer.

"Well, it's gonna be kinda hard to keep this a secret, Jay," Darren replied, gesturing to the wreckage around them. "I mean, this is a major intersection, and I'm sure George is wondering where we are. Let alone Jen and Em."

Jay ignored Darren's comments, his voice tense as he finally let the truth slip. "Whoever did this was after me last night. I was..." He paused, the words catching in his throat. He didn't want to drag Will into this.

"You were what, Jay?" Darren's face twisted in shock.

"I was out late, and someone in that same SUV chased me through the park," Jay confessed, the weight of the secret lifting slightly as he spoke. "Some guy in a pickup truck saved me. I know it sounds crazy, and I don't understand it either, but I swear to God, man. This is freaking me out."

"What the hell are you talking about? What SUV? What truck? And what were you doing in the park in the middle of the night...especially when it was storming like it was last night?" Darren demanded, his bewilderment unable to catch up with everything Jay was saying.

Jay knew this was coming. He didn't want to bring Will's name into it until he had a chance to talk to him himself. He knew Darren wouldn't hesitate to confront Will if he found out he was involved. "I don't know," Jay lied, his voice shaky.

"You don't know? You obviously know what the hell you were doing. And why the hell wouldn't you tell the cops?"

"They don't need to know, Darren," Jay insisted, his voice firm despite the doubt gnawing at him.

"Like hell they don't! Look man, I don't even know what the hell really just happened here. I'm kinda freaking out. And you say someone was after you last night and that it relates to this somehow! Why would I not want to bring this to the cops attention?" Darren's anger was palpable, his voice rising with every word.

Jay could only think of one good reason, but there was no way he could bring himself to tell Darren. He had to talk to Will first. "Just let me take care of it, Darren," was all Jay could manage to say.

"Well, what the hell, dude," Darren exclaimed, shaking his head in frustration. "What are you going to do about it? Hunt this bastard down and say, 'Hey, remember me, you tried to kill me...TWICE...I was just wondering if you could give me a good reason.' Gimme a break. You've been acting pretty damn sketchy the last couple of months, you know that?"

"I don't know what I'm gonna do, Darren. But we have to keep this quiet, OK? I don't want everyone knowing about this...not even Em or Georgy, OK?"

"Whatever, man. You're being real weird about this whole thing, and I don't know why. I should do you a favor and tell the pigs myself. But whatever you say," Darren replied sarcastically, throwing his hands up in mock surrender. "You're the boss here, but I'm telling you, this is gonna get out either way."

Jay looked at the scene that Darren was pointing at. It really was horrible. He knew he had to act quickly. The chances of Darren keeping his mouth shut were slim, but maybe he could convince him to stay quiet just long enough to talk to Will and get some answers. But then again, Will had acted so strange the night before—almost like he was hiding something.

Jay looked back at Darren, who was now on the phone with his mother, explaining why he wasn't in school. "Ma, we got in a car accident...No, I'm fine...He's fine too...Ma, look, ma, I'm just gonna go home...You don't have to leave work early...No, I'm not going to the hospital...Because I'm not hurt...Would you calm down...No, we weren't drinking, it's 8 in the damn morning...I'm sorry, I'm a little upset...Because ma..." Darren went on with the conversation, finally giving Jay a chance to piece some things together in his mind.

Jay considered trying to call Will while Darren was occupied, but thought better of it. Knowing Darren, he would hang up on his own mother if he knew Jay was trying to sneak something behind his back. He decided to call Will when he got home. When no one was around.

The boys sat on the curb for a few more minutes until Jay's mother showed up. After she calmed down and got everything explained to her by the police officers, she led the boys to her car. The ride to Darren's house was surprisingly silent, but Jay didn't even notice. He was more concerned about his inevitable talk with Will, and his excruciating headache.

Darren got out of the car and thanked Mrs. Galentino for the ride. "I'll call you later, bro, we still gotta talk," he said to Jay as he turned and walked towards his house. Jay would have preferred to sit through an entire album of the pop-punk bands Darren liked than have that conversation, but he knew Darren wouldn't back down until he had some answers.

"Are you OK, Jay?" his mother reached towards his cut head.

"I'm fine, can we just go home?" he shooed his mother's hand away.

"Of course, honey," replied his mother as she backed out onto the street. "Who hit you in the first place, Jay? The police officer said that whoever it was, was trying to hurt you boys."

"I don't know, ma. Can we talk about it later? I'm a little upset now."

"Sure," sighed Mrs. Galentino. The rest of the ride was outwardly silent, yet the inside of Jay's mind was racing too keep up with itself.

"Yo, you'll never believe what just fucking happened to me and Jay," Darren proclaimed into his phone, ignoring his friend's plea to keep things quiet.

"Are you OK?" George asked after Darren finished his dramatic recount of the accident. "Is Jay alright? Are we still going this weekend?"

Darren pulled the phone away from his ear, shaking his head in disbelief. "You've gotta be kidding me, right? Two of your best friends were almost killed, and you're worried about this weekend? You're out of your damn mind, George."

"I didn't mean it like that," George replied, feeling a pang of guilt as soon as the words left his mouth. "Of course, I'm worried about you guys. I just…I don't know. I'm glad I drove myself to school when you two didn't show up. I figured you were ditching again. But I'll come over after class, check up on you guys. Gotta get to class before Harold catches me."

"You're such a moron," Darren chuckled, but there was no real humor in it. "Alright, I'll see you later. And hey, don't tell anyone about this, alright? Jay wants to keep it quiet."

After hanging up, Darren looked into the mirror and suddenly froze. The memory hit him like a ton of bricks. Was that the same SUV he'd seen outside Jay's house? The one that had given him the creeps?

It couldn't be.

Could it? Was it some kind of warning? The thought gnawed at him, but exhaustion was already weighing him down. He decided he'd figure it out later. Right now, he needed sleep. He walked through the garage door into the kitchen, automatically kicking off his soggy shoes. The kitchen was filled with the familiar sight of his mother's Precious Moments figurines, neatly arranged on every available surface. He'd always teased her about collecting "dolls," but deep down, he found them comforting in a way he'd never admit.

Darren and his mom were close—closer than he let on to anyone. He knew she'd be home soon to check on him, even though he'd assured her he was fine. He might have the exterior of a tough jock, but he was a "momma's boy" at heart, though he hid it well.

He trudged up the stairs, his body aching with every step. His right shoulder throbbed, and his neck was stiff from the whiplash. The sight of Jay slumped over in the car, even if only for a few seconds, had rattled him more than he cared to admit. Reaching his room, he collapsed onto his bed, the weight of the day pulling him under almost instantly. His eyes closed, and within moments, he was out cold.

"Jay..." The bedroom door creaked open slightly, the sound almost lost beneath the steady patter of rain against the window. Jay sat up in bed, rubbing his temples. He hadn't slept at all, the pounding headache from the accident only made worse by the unsettling memories of the previous night. "Jay, are you awake?" The whisper drifted through the cracked door, tentative and almost afraid.

"Yeah, I'm awake," Jay replied, squinting into the dim light. He couldn't quite place the voice at first, but then Will stepped into the room, his face shadowed and somber. The sight of his friend made Jay's stomach tighten. Will looked like he hadn't slept in days—dark circles under his eyes, shoulders slumped as if weighed down by something far heavier than exhaustion.

Will's expression was one of deep grief, almost as if he were carrying the blame for what had happened that morning. Jay couldn't help but wonder if he was right—maybe Will had known something all along, something that had put Jay directly in harm's way. The small desk lamp by Jay's bed cast long shadows on the walls, distorting the familiar posters and memorabilia from their high school years into something almost sinister. The rain outside was relentless, its tapping against the windowpane adding to the eerie atmosphere.

"Look, man," Will began, his voice low, "I heard about what happened earlier. The whole school's talking about it. Are you OK?" He shifted uncomfortably, his gaze never quite meeting Jay's.

"How does the whole school know?" Jay deflected, not ready to dive into the conversation he knew was coming. He was still trying to figure out why Will was even here. He noticed the way Will's eyes darted around the room, never settling on Jay for too long, as if he couldn't bear to face him directly.

"Jen told me earlier at school," Will continued, his tone forcedly casual. "So I left to come check on you. Plus, you know how it is—everyone needs something to gossip about." He attempted a laugh, but it came out hollow. "So, are you OK?"

"Yeah, I'm fine," Jay lied, though he knew Will wasn't really asking about his physical state. There was an underlying tension in the room, something unspoken that Jay could feel simmering just

KILLER SECRETS BURIED TRUTH

beneath the surface. He could sense that Will wasn't here just to check on him—there was something else, something that Will wasn't saying.

"That's good," Will said, his voice lacking any real conviction. "Listen, I know I've been acting different lately, but you're still my best friend, Jay. I don't know what I'd do without you." The words felt rehearsed, like something out of a Hallmark card, and Jay couldn't help but feel that they were leading up to some kind of apology—or confession.

"So, do they know who was after you? I mean...who hit you?" Will's question was almost offhand, but the way he shrugged and let his eyes drift over Jay's head told a different story. He was trying too hard to seem disinterested.

"No," Jay replied, his irritation growing. He could feel the tension in the room thickening, the air heavy with everything they weren't saying. Why was Will being so evasive? What was he hiding?

"Well, whoever it is has to be pretty messed up to do something like that," Will said, trying to keep his tone light. "I mean, pushing your car into an intersection? They've got to be nuts."

"Will..." Jay started, but his words were cut off by the sharp ring of his cell phone. He sighed, "Hold on... Hello?"

"Oh my god, are you OK, baby?" Jen's voice was a welcome relief, her concern palpable even through the phone.

"I'm OK, just a little banged up, that's all."

"I just heard—your mom called me and told me."

"What? Where are you?"

"I'm in school. Do you want me to leave and come stay with you? I can bring you something to cheer you up..." Jen's voice was soft, but Jay could hear the worry beneath her words.

"No, that's OK. Will's here with me right now."

"Will?" Jen's voice took on a note of confusion. "Oh, babe. Let me come over, please."

Jay glanced at Will, who was pretending not to listen in on the conversation. The room felt even smaller now, the tension between him and Will almost suffocating.

"Listen, buddy, I'm gonna get going...you need your rest," Will said suddenly, tapping Jay's leg as he made his way towards the door. "Let me know if you need anything, bro."

"Wait...hold on a minute, babe... Will...hey!" Jay called after him, but Will had already disappeared out the door, the sound of it clicking shut behind him echoing in the dimly lit room.

"Jen, you didn't talk to Will this morning?" Jay asked, turning his attention back to the phone.

"Babe, why did you not go to the hospital?" Jen's tone was scolding, seemingly ignoring his question. But Jay could tell it came from a place of genuine concern.

"There's nothing they could have done that I can't do here."

"Well, I'm coming over."

"No, I'm going to sleep right now. Just call me after you get out of school."

"Fine...get some rest, baby," Jen relented, though Jay could tell she was still worried. "I'll see you later."

"OK, I love you."

"Love you too, baby."

Jay hung up the phone, his frustration boiling over.

He wanted to chase after Will, demand answers, but his body felt heavy, drained of energy. His head throbbed, a constant reminder of the day's events.

He collapsed back onto his bed, trying to force his eyes shut. He was exhausted, but his mind refused to quiet down, thoughts of Will and the mysterious SUV swirling in his head. Finally, fatigue won out, and he drifted into a restless sleep, the rain outside continuing its relentless rhythm against the window.

Jay woke up to the soft sound of footsteps approaching, his mind still foggy from a restless sleep. The room was now bathed in the muted glow of the setting sun, casting warm hues over the cluttered desk and the familiar posters on the walls. The rain had finally slowed to a drizzle, the rhythmic tapping against the window adding a soothing, yet melancholic, backdrop to the scene.

"Hey baby," came Jen's gentle voice, pulling Jay further from the remnants of his dream. She approached him with her arms outstretched, as if trying to comfort a wounded animal.

"Hi," Jay mumbled, still half-asleep, blinking to focus on her concerned expression.

Jen sat down beside him, her eyes widening as she took in the sight of his bandaged head. "Oh my god, look at your head. Why didn't you go to the hospital?" Her voice was a mixture of concern and frustration, her hands gently brushing his hair away from the bandage.

Jay had momentarily forgotten about his injury until she mentioned it. The dull ache in his skull came rushing back, reminding him of the morning's events. "Your mom told me you were pretty banged up," Jen continued, her tone softening. "Let me take you to the emergency room."

"I'm fine," Jay insisted, waving away Jen's hands as she tried to inspect his wound. "Will came here-" he started.

"I know..." Jen looked as though she were trying to assure Jay, as she fought through tears. The conversation and the site of her boyfriend was very overwhelming.

"He's all alone now Jen," Jay muttered, more to himself than to her. He shifted uncomfortably on the bed, the unease from earlier creeping back into his thoughts.

"He'll always have you," a tear rolled down Jen's cheek. "You'll always be his best friend, Jason." Jen used his full name, which she only did when she was being serious. Jay hated it, but there was a truth to her words that he couldn't deny.

Jay's frustration, which had been simmering all day, finally boiled over. He couldn't hold in his thoughts any longer, not after everything that had happened. "He is not the Will I know anymore," Jay began, seeing the confusion flash across Jen's face. "There is something wrong with him."

"Jason, please..." Jen pleaded.

"No!" Jay snapped, sharper than he intended. He immediately regretted the tone, but he was too far gone to stop now. "He called me last night."

"Jason," Jen sobbed silently, trying to keep her voice calm despite the growing tension.

"He called me at 2:30 in the morning. Told me he had to see me right away in the park, so I went to meet him, only...he didn't show," Jay's frustration was palpable as he tried to make piece it together himself.

"So I went to his house, and he slammed the door in my face. It looked like he was crying. When I got there, there was a black SUV in the driveway, and when I turned to leave, it chased me. Whoever was in that car chased me through the park. I know it sounds crazy, Jen, and I thought I was dreaming it, until I woke up this morning and looked there," he pointed to his muddy clothes, still bunched up on the floor next to his bed.

"OK, Jay, this isn't making any sense, babe. You got hit in the head" Jen's voice was laced with disbelief, though she tried to mask it with concern.

"No!!!" Jay's exasperation grew, the pain in his head intensifying with every word. "I don't know. But whoever it was would have gotten me, but some guy picked me up and brought me home. When

I got out of his truck, the SUV was at the other side of the street," he explained, his voice trembling slightly. "You don't believe me, do you?"

"Of course I do, baby," Jen replied, though the uncertainty in her voice revealed the truth. She was struggling to make sense of what Jay was telling her.

"Well, whoever was in that SUV, whoever was chasing me in the park, and was at the other side of the street when I got home...was the same person that pushed me and Darren into the intersection and drove off," Jay explained, his voice pleading for her to understand. "Then all of a sudden, Will starts talking to me like he has had a huge epiphany or something. I don't know. Something's not right. And I'm gonna find out what it is."

"OK, calm down. You're obviously stressed about what happened," Jen tried to soothe him, reaching out to place a comforting hand on his arm.

"I knew you wouldn't believe me!!!" Jay snapped, pushing her hand away more forcefully than intended. The sudden movement startled Jen, her eyes widening in shock.

"I never said I don't believe you," she replied, her voice shaking slightly. She stood up, hurt and frustration clear in her expression. "And you have no right to be an ass to me right now just because you got in an accident!" Her voice quivered as she started towards the door, her back rigid with tension.

"Jen..." Jay called after her, his voice softening as regret washed over him. "Jen, please."

She stopped, tears rolling down her face as she turned back toward him. Despite the relief of finally sharing his burden, Jay couldn't shake the guilt he felt for hurting her.

"I'm scared, baby. Someone is after me, and whether Will has something to do with it or not..." Jay's voice cracked as he finally let the tears fall, the overwhelming emotions spilling out. "I'm not crazy."

Jen's expression softened, and she walked back to him, sitting down on the bed. She gently pulled his head to her chest, her fingers running through his hair, avoiding the bandaged area.

"I know you're not," she kissed his forehead, her lips lingering for a moment before she pulled away. Jay, exhausted and emotionally drained, let his head sink into the pillow as he drifted back to sleep.

Jen watched him for a moment, her own mind racing with conflicting thoughts.

She couldn't help but wonder what was real and what was the knock to the head.

She decided to lie down next to Jay, wrapping an arm around him protectively. No one would mess with him now. He was safe, at least for tonight.

"Jay..." The voice on the other end of the phone was shaky, strained with panic. Jay immediately recognized it, but something was wrong. Will sounded...broken.

"Will? What's going on?" Jay asked, sitting up in bed. His heart pounded in his chest as he heard ragged breathing on the other end of the line. The clock on his nightstand read 2:24 AM, and a sense of dread gripped him.

"They're...all gone, Jay," Will's voice cracked, the words coming out between sobs. "I...I watched it happen. I couldn't move. I just froze."

Jay's mind raced. "What? Who's gone, Will? What are you talking about?"

"I couldn't stop it," Will's voice grew weaker, the sobs almost choking him. "Oh God...Katie... I just stood there. I just—" His words cut off abruptly, and Jay could hear nothing but his friend's desperate breaths on the other end.

"Will! What happened? Where are you?" Jay was out of bed now, pulling on his hoodie, adrenaline pumping through his veins. "Will? Stay on the phone, man! I'm coming over. Just tell me what's going on!" Jay ran downstairs, grabbing his keys off the kitchen counter, not caring about the noise. His parents were asleep, but they didn't matter right now. Will mattered. Whatever was going on, Jay needed to be there.

As he slammed the side door behind him, the cold air hit him like a punch, and the snow fell in thick, blinding sheets. He jumped into his old Camry, fumbling with the keys in his haste. "Talk to me, Will. I'm on my way."

"I...I don't know what to do, Jay," Will's voice sounded distant, almost detached. "They're gone...all of them. My mom...my dad...Katie." He whispered the last name, and Jay's blood ran cold. Katie. Will's little sister. "I didn't do anything... I didn't stop him."

Jay's heart pounded in his chest, his mind spinning as he swerved around the icy roads. He had no idea what he was walking into, but Will's tone terrified him. "Will, who did this? Where are you? Are you hurt?"

The only response Jay got was a low, gut-wrenching sob. He pressed harder on the gas.

When Jay turned onto Will's street, the flashing lights of police cars reflected off the snow-covered trees, casting an eerie glow in the night. His stomach dropped. "What the hell?" He parked the car haphazardly at the curb, barely turning off the engine before throwing open the door.

"Will, I'm here. Where are you?" Jay shouted into the phone, scanning the chaos in front of him. The front lawn was littered with emergency vehicles, and police officers were trying to hold back the growing crowd of neighbors. The flashing lights illuminated the white snow, making the whole scene feel surreal, like something out of a nightmare.

"Jayyy!" Will's voice cracked through the phone, and Jay spotted him, running from the house, dodging the officers who were trying to restrain him. Will's face was pale, his eyes wide with terror.

"Will!" Jay rushed over, and Will collapsed into him, his whole body shaking. Jay barely caught him as he stumbled, his weight heavy against Jay's chest. "What happened, man? Talk to me."

Will's words came in frantic gasps. "He killed them, Jay! He killed them all...Mom, Dad, Katie...all of them! I saw it...I saw everything." His sobs grew louder, more frantic. "I just stood there. I didn't stop him! I didn't do anything!"

Jay's mind raced as he struggled to process what Will was saying. He gripped his friend's shoulders, trying to calm him down. "What are you talking about? Who did this? Who was in the house?" Jay asked, but his own voice felt distant, hollow. He turned to see a gurney being rolled down the driveway, a white sheet draped over the still form beneath it.

"Oh my God," Jay whispered, his throat tightening as the horror of the scene hit him full force. Will's family—his whole family—was gone.

Will's grip tightened on Jay, his body wracked with sobs. "I didn't do anything, Jay. I just stood there... I couldn't move... I couldn't... I—"

Jay's mind whirled. "If Will was there, why would the killer leave him alive?" he wondered. The thought gnawed at him, but there was no time to dwell on it. "Will... you're safe now, okay? I'm here. We'll figure this out."

But even as Jay said the words, a strange chill settled over him. Something about the way Will spoke, the way he was clinging to Jay—it felt...off. Jay shook the thought away, focusing on his friend who was crumbling in his arms. "You're gonna be okay, man."

But deep down, Jay wasn't sure either of them would ever be okay again.

"Jay," he jumped up in a cold sweat, seeing his mother at the end of his bed and his girlfriend looking at him from beside the bed. "Jay, you were having a bad dream. You wouldn't wake up...I had to call for your mother."

"Are you alright, Jason?" Mrs. Galentino looked at her son with concern.

"I...I...just had a bad dream. That's all," Jay gasped.

"What was it?" Jen prodded, not sure she wanted to know what was going to come out of her boyfriend's mouth. "You were thrashing around all over the place."

"Nothing, I'm sorry," Jay didn't want to bring up the past anymore than he had to. Yet his dream did give him a question that had never previously occurred to him. "How could Will have not known who killed his family if he was there, and saw it happen?"

The question took both women by surprise as they exchanged worried glances. Finally his mother turned and started downstairs, seemingly ignoring her son's question.

"Dinner will be ready in a few minutes, you staying over Jenny, we're having sauce?" "Yeah Mrs. G, if that's OK with you."

"Oh, you know you're always welcome here, honey," Mrs. Galentino disappeared down the stairs.

Jen frowned as Jay sat there, visibly shaken from his dream, "Are you sure you're OK baby?"

"Yeah, I'm alright. But don't you think that's a little weird?"

"Jay..." Jen started. Her concern for her boyfriend growing by the minute. How hard was he hit on the head?

"Yeah, but for it to be still unsolved. I don't get it. If he was there..."

"Come on...you need to relax," she ignored her boyfriend's thoughts and started to kiss down his neck, unbuttoning his pants. She lifted his shirt and started kissing his bare chest, inching her way down his torso. She knew he needed something to take his mind off of things. And she also knew that he would not fight her on this. The room filled with a sense of fleeting peace, a temporary distraction from the chaos surrounding them.

Chapter 6

"Jason, I really think that you should stay home this weekend. I mean, after what happened and everything," Mrs. Galentino said, her voice filled with worry as she looked at her son.

The dining room was dimly lit, with the soft glow of the chandelier casting a warm light over the table. The family usually ate in front of the TV, but tonight they were sitting at the polished wooden table, the clinking of cutlery on plates the only sound breaking the silence. Jay noticed how his mother had set the table with the good china, the delicate floral pattern rarely seen outside of holiday dinners. It was clear she was trying to impress Jen, though Jen had been over countless times before.

Jay shifted uncomfortably in his seat, feeling the tension in the air. He glanced at his mother, noting the lines of concern etched on her face, and then at Jen, who sat quietly beside him, her hand resting on his. "Where's Dad?" he asked, deciding to avoid his mother's comment about the weekend.

"I don't know. He called and said he'd be late tonight and that we should go ahead and eat without him," his mother replied, her eyes flickering with a hint of worry.

"Oh," Jay responded, trying to keep the conversation light. He desperately wanted to change the subject and steer his mother's thoughts away from the weekend. There was no way he was going to miss the trip, especially not Jen's Senior Prom. She had been dreaming about it since grade school, and when they started dating seriously, she had eagerly started planning their matching outfits.

"Did you hear me, Jason?" Mrs. Galentino's voice took on a sharper edge, reminiscent of a teacher catching a student daydreaming.

"Ma, I'm going. That's it. I'm not gonna miss this trip, and definitely not the prom. Jen has been looking forward to it since birth, ma," he exaggerated, hoping to lighten the mood.

"Jay, I am more worried about you than the prom," Jen said softly, squeezing his hand.

"Besides, we had all the other dances. Maybe you should listen to your mother."

Jay couldn't believe his ears. This was the same girl who had pestered him endlessly during their sophomore year about what their senior prom would be like, debating every detail from the theme to the food to the color of her dress. They had been crowned king and queen at both Homecoming and the Jingle Ball, but those events paled in comparison to the Senior Prom. He was sure they were destined to be crowned king and queen again.

"Let's just see how tomorrow goes. Could you pass me the sauce?" Jay said, trying to steer the conversation away from another one of his mother's scolding sessions. He reached for the tomato sauce, its rich aroma filling the room.

"Well, I at least think you should go to the hospital, Jason. Your head is disgusting. I think you might need stitches," his mother insisted, her voice trembling slightly.

"Well, get your sewing kit," Jay joked, attempting to lighten the mood, but his untimely humor fell flat. No one laughed.

"I think you should go too, Jay," Jen pleaded, her eyes full of concern. "And I know some of your friends think so too."

"Like who?!" Jay shot a glance at Jen, as if warning her to tread carefully.

"Well, Jason," his mother began, "Darren was pretty banged up too. What did he think you should do?"

Jay's frustration bubbled to the surface. All he wanted was to sit down, relax, and eat without the constant overthinking that made his head feel like it was about to crack open.

"I have to talk to Will," Jay blurted out, shocking himself almost as much as his mother and girlfriend.

The room went silent.

Jen's eyes widened slightly, and his mother stared at him, her expression unreadable.

Mrs. Galentino's face fell, her eyes filling with tears. "Well, I think you need to get checked out," she said, her voice shaking.

"Ma, I'm sorry. I didn't mean to get upset. It's just that things have been so weird, and I told you about my dream…"

"Of course things have been weird, Jason!" his mother interrupted with an uncharacteristic yell. "How could they not be!"

"Okay, Ma, look I'm sorry. I just need to clear some things up. Can I be excused from the table?" Jay glanced at Jen, signaling that it was time to leave his mother alone. Jen had been sitting there the whole time, too afraid to interject and too frustrated to eat her dinner. "I am sorry, Ma," Jay said once again as they moved quietly away from the table and into the living room.

"Look, Jen, I need to take care of a few things on my own, okay? I will call you after I finish. I just have to do this."

"Jay, if you don't want to go to prom, I will understand," she said, ignoring his previous statement.

"No, we are going to prom. And camping. I just have to go talk to Will. Clear my head. He has to talk to me…tell me something," Jay said, trying to convince himself more than his girlfriend. He knew he was right, in part. He had to talk to his friend if he wanted any chance at this weekend being normal. At least as normal as reality allowed for it to be.

"Jay, please. You have to stop…"

"No, I need to talk to him…alone. He won't be the same if you or anyone else is there. As a matter of fact…could you do me a favor? Could you call Liz and maybe the other girls and ask them to come over or go to a movie or something? That way, I know I will be able to talk to him

alone."

"Jason. Please. Stop."

"Please Jen. Just call them," Jay pleaded.

"Uhh, fine," Jen finally relented. She didn't want to upset her boyfriend after he had clearly gone through so much trauma. She picked up her phone to call the girls.

Jay looked at the clock as he got ready in his room. 8:37.

He decided not to call Will first. He just wanted to go over there and talk to his friend. He decided that he wasn't going to confront him with any accusations, although he did want answers.

Answers that only Will could give him.

He crept down the stairs, not wanting to alert his mother after their argument at dinner. He definitely did not want to tell her where he was going since she almost jumped down his throat for bad-mouthing Will earlier.

That was another thing that concerned Jay. Why had his mother been so quick to defend Will and not her own son? He guessed she didn't know the whole story, but he got the eerie feeling that even if she had, she wouldn't have believed him anyway.

He was almost at the side door now. He felt like a burglar, or better yet, a convict trying to escape a death sentence. He looked over his shoulder and headed out the door. That was

almost too easy. Was his mother even there? She must have been. Probably into her Wednesday night TV lineup.

Jay glanced at his father's Jeep parked outside. Why was it there if he wasn't home? He thought about taking it but figured it would be just as easy to walk through the park, almost forgetting about his experience from the other night. As he made his way down the driveway, he could hear his next-door neighbors' children laughing and running around as their parents tried to get them settled down for bed. He longed for that age of innocence, when nothing in the world mattered except for friends, family, and yourself.

He shook off the thought as he reached the park. The rain had not let up, pattering against the wet pavement as Jay walked through the slick grass. The trees loomed around him, casting long shadows in the dim light. There was an unnatural silence, only the sound of his shoes squelching through the mud. His clothes were soaked through by the time he exited the park. Even though the cold air chilled him, it was the thought of seeing Will that made him shiver.

Jay reached Will's street, half expecting the SUV to be in his friend's driveway again, but it was as vacant as usual. Not a car in the empty driveway. Will rarely drove, anyway.

As Jay reached Will's house, he hesitated at the door, debating whether to knock. His head throbbed. He could see a shadow behind the lace curtains. He opened the door slowly, memories of their childhood flashing in his mind. Jay used to just walk in without knocking, the door always open, no boundaries between them.

"Will, that you?" Jay's voice echoed in the stillness of the house. He could see Will sitting on the couch, motionless, almost blending into the shadows.

"Hey, Jay," Will's voice was monotone, emotionless, barely breaking the silence. It was like he hadn't moved for hours.

"What are you doing sitting here in the dark?"

"Just thinking." Will's voice was flat, a dull edge to his words. Jay shifted uncomfortably, the room heavy with tension.

"Well, can I talk to you for a little bit?"

"Why not, Jay?" Will didn't even turn to face him. His eyes stayed fixed on the dark screen of the TV. The air smelled faintly of smoke and stale beer.

Jay hesitated, his stomach knotting. "Look, Will... I need to know. Who was at your house last night?"

Will's silence was deafening. Jay could feel his pulse in his ears, waiting for an answer, but none came.

Jay's voice cracked slightly, "Please, Will. Whoever it was chased me through the park and hit my car today. You have to know something."

For a moment, the only sound in the room was the quiet tapping of the rain against the windows. Then Will spoke, his voice distant, as if he were somewhere else entirely. "You ever look back and wish you could've done some things differently, Jay?"

Jay froze, caught off guard by the question. "Yeah... of course."

Will exhaled heavily, like the weight of the world was pressing down on him. "Yeah, but we can't go back, can we? The past... it's already written, isn't it?" "Will..." Jay tried to interject, but his friend cut him off.

"You're here though, aren't you? Still standing."

Jay took a breath, sensing where this conversation was heading. Will had said things like this before, but this time there was something darker in his tone.

"I guess we are still here..." Jay said softly.

"How do you know?" Will's voice sharpened suddenly, his eyes flicking toward Jay for the first time that night.

Jay stood silent, his mind spinning. He was here because he wanted answers, but Will's cryptic responses were pulling him deeper into uncertainty.

"You ever think... maybe if I hadn't gone out that night... maybe if I had stayed home, things would be different?"

Jay was suddenly transported back to that night—their laughter echoing through the house, the sound of Will's drunken confession of friendship still ringing in his ears.

"Jay...are you listening to me?" Will's voice snapped him back to the present, sharper now.

"Yeah, I hear you, Will," Jay said softly, his own voice tight with tension.

Will continued, "Maybe if I hadn't gone out, maybe if I was coherent, things wouldn't have happened like that..."

The room felt suffocating, the tension thickening with every word. Jay wasn't sure if he should keep pushing, but he knew this was his only shot at getting the truth from Will.

Jay stood frozen in place, taking in Will's cryptic words, trying to find the right way to respond. He had come here for answers, but Will's words were pushing him further into confusion. Jay decided he needed to keep his friend talking, even if it was difficult to follow Will's thoughts.

"Will, what are you saying?"

Will shifted on the couch, his eyes dull and distant, like he wasn't even in the room anymore.

"It's...it's about being there... being aware. Being able to...stop..."

Jay swallowed, his throat dry. He hadn't expected Will to open up like this. He could hear the guilt seeping through every word his friend spoke, the way Will was carrying the weight of that night on his shoulders. "Will, don't do that, man. You can't look back on it like that."

Will shook his head, lighting another cigarette with shaking hands. "You don't get it, Jay. I was right there. I was sober enough to see what was happening. The killer looked right at me, and I didn't do anything. He could've taken me out too, but he didn't. Why not?"

Jay felt an oddly familiar chill run down his spine as Will's words hung in the air. He had never heard this part of the story before, never realized how close Will had been to the whole thing. "Maybe he didn't see you," Jay offered, though even he wasn't convinced by his own words.

Will snorted bitterly, exhaling a cloud of smoke. "He saw me, Jay. He saw me and left me alive. I don't know why, but I know he did. I didn't even have the balls to call the cops until it was too late. By the time they got here, it was over."

Jay could feel the weight of Will's guilt pressing down on him now, too. The more Will talked, the more Jay realized how broken his friend really was. "Will, you were in shock. Anyone would've reacted the same way. You didn't do anything wrong."

But Will wasn't listening. His eyes were focused on something far away, lost in the memory of that night. "People think I'm a suspect, Jay. People who knew me my whole life, and now they look at me like I'm a monster. Like I did all this.."

Jay felt a knot tighten in his stomach. "No, Will. I don't think that."

Will laughed, a hollow, bitter sound. "You're the only one, then. You have no idea what it's like, walking amongst everyone thinking I did this."

Jay wanted to say something, anything to make this better, but the truth was, he didn't know how. He couldn't imagine living with that kind of guilt, but now he was starting to understand why Will had been so distant.

"Will, that's why you need to come with us this weekend," Jay said finally, breaking the silence that had grown between them. "We all need to get away, clear our heads. Get back to normal. You've been through so much, but you're still our friend. Nothing's changed."

Will looked up at Jay, his eyes red-rimmed and haunted. "You really think I can go back to normal? After everything?"

Jay nodded, determined. "Yeah, I do. We've all been through stuff, but we're still standing. We've got each other."

For the first time, Will seemed to consider the possibility. His shoulders relaxed a little, the tension easing just a bit. "Maybe," he muttered, more to himself than to Jay.

Jay leaned forward, trying to make his friend see the truth. "Will, you're not alone in this. We've been friends our whole lives. We're still here for you, no matter what. But I need you to be honest with me, okay?"

Will looked up, his expression guarded. "About what?"

Jay hesitated. This was the moment he had been building up to. "The SUV. You didn't tell me who was at your house last night, and I know someone was there. Whoever it was chased me through the park, and they almost killed me and Darren today. Please, Will. I need to know what's going on."

For a long moment, Will just stared at him. The tension in the room was thick, the weight of Jay's question hanging between them like a storm cloud ready to break. Will's eyes flicked toward the window, the rain continuing its steady tap against the glass.

"I... I don't know who it was," Will said finally, his voice barely above a whisper. "But you're right, someone was here last night. I didn't think they'd come after you, Jay. I swear."

Jay's heart pounded in his chest. "Who was it, Will?"

Will looked down, his hands shaking. "I don't know. But whoever it is... they're not done yet."

Jay's stomach dropped. There was more to this, more than he had ever realized. And now, he wasn't sure if he was ready to hear the rest.

"But Will...who was it that was at your ho—"

Jay was interrupted by the doorbell. He hadn't even noticed the lights dancing off the walls as a vehicle pulled into the driveway. Will noticed. He was already standing up, making his way to the door.

"Will, wait...who is that?" Jay's nerves rushed back all at once. "Is that..." He got up and started walking backward toward the back door. He did not want a repeat chase through the park. Not in the state he was in. His head still hurt, and he was still a little weak.

"It's Darren. I thought we were all going to the movies?" Will looked back at his friend who was visibly shaken, his face cast in shadow by the flickering light from the streetlamp outside.

"What?" Jay demanded as Darren opened the door.

"Bro...what...the...fuck...is going on?" Darren looked at Jay with a level of concern that startled him. He was worried for his friend's well-being. And he wanted to approach the conversation with caution.

Jay looked at Darren. Then at Will who didn't even raise his head. He turned back to Darren.

"What do you mean?"

Darren looked towards where Will had been sitting, then back to Jay. "Bro, I don't know if you got hit a little too hard. But we need to leave. The girls are waiting at the movies."

"Um...ok," Jay shot another confused look towards Will, who finally looked up for the first time. Darren was busy looking around the house as if it were an exhibit.

"Jen called Liz and the other girls and said they were going to the movies. Liz asked if I wanted to go because George and Darren were already going. I figured that's why you came here, right?" Will raised his eyebrows as if he already knew the answer, his eyes momentarily catching the dim light from the hallway, making him look almost ghostly.

"Um...yeah..." Jay answered back, trying to mask his disappointment. The silence that had cloaked their previous conversation was now replaced by Darren's energy, but it left Jay feeling more unsettled than ever.

Of course. Just when he was finally getting somewhere with Will. "Let's cut the fucking bullshit and get the fuck out of here," Darren exclaimed. "This is fucked!"

Jay tried to ignore Darren's insensitive comment as he followed Will out the door. He glanced back at the house, noticing that Will hadn't bothered to lock the door, as if inviting the darkness back inside. It struck Jay as odd, but he decided not to push things right now, especially since Darren was there. The opportunity to talk to Will seemed to be slipping further and further away, and Jay wondered when he would ever get the chance to finish their conversation... if ever.

Darren interrupted Jay's thoughts, "How's your head, bro? Jen told Em it was pretty bad. Look at this shit," he said, pulling down his shirt collar to reveal a massive bruise on his right shoulder as he backed out of Will's driveway.

The interior of the car was dimly lit, the dashboard lights casting a soft glow on their faces. The smell of stale fast food wrappers mixed with Darren's overpowering cologne, making the air in the car feel thick. "It's not as bad as it looks, though. Are you still bleeding?"

"No, I'm fine," Jay tried to dodge his friend's questioning. His mind was still on the interrupted conversation with Will. The streetlights flickered past the car windows, casting fleeting shadows on their faces, adding to the tense atmosphere. The rain seemed relentless, each drop hitting the car like a distant drumbeat, adding to Jay's growing sense of unease.

He thought about how their current situation had come about. Jen knew that he wanted to talk to Will alone. How could she let them all get roped into going out like this? The car's engine hummed steadily, the noise becoming a background buzz to Jay's racing thoughts. It seemed like no one wanted Jay to have a chance at getting near the truth. A truth that he was starting to believe was heavily stacked against him. Too many things in the past two days had painted him as the target. He couldn't help but wonder if Will and Jen both knew something and were trying to keep it from him. He had to trust Jen, though. She was all he could rely on right now. Besides, Darren was the only other person who seemed to be caught in the middle of this mystery.

Darren carried on in the driver's seat, almost to an empty audience. Jay was sitting in the passenger seat and looked back to see an expressionless look on Will's face, indicating that he had checked out of Darren's ramblings too. Jay felt alone with his thoughts. He stared out the window, watching the city lights blur into streaks of color as they passed through the wet streets. The rain tapped steadily against the windows, the rhythm almost hypnotic, though it did little to calm the storm of thoughts in Jay's mind. He wondered if he should confide more in Darren, tell him what he had just learned about Will. But he knew if he did that, Darren would only implicate Will further, making everything more complicated.

He thought back to the distant look in Will's eyes earlier in the evening, that hollow, detached stare. It was something Jay couldn't shake, no matter how much he tried. Will had been distant with everyone, but tonight had felt different—more personal. That look spoke louder than any words ever could. Jay knew something was off, but he didn't know how to address it without pushing his friend further away.

The boys drove on, the rhythmic sound of the windshield wipers keeping time with Jay's spiraling thoughts.

"So, did you tell anyone else what you had told me about earlier?" Darren asked, his voice slicing through the thick tension in the car.

"What are you talking about?" Jay lied, glancing over at Darren from the passenger seat. He shifted uncomfortably, hoping to avoid this conversation, especially with Will sitting silently in the backseat. The rain outside seemed to intensify, each drop striking the car harder, as if echoing the growing unease inside.

Darren's eyes flicked to the rearview mirror briefly, as if checking for something—or someone. Jay followed his gaze for a moment, but quickly looked away. He could not believe Darren would bring this all up as if Will wasn't even there. His emotions shifted from rage to panic as Darren pressed further.

"You know, about the other night," Darren said, a hint of irritation creeping into his voice. "The whole thing you told me about the park."

"Um... no," Jay was trying to avoid the issue as much as possible. He shifted uncomfortably in his seat, feeling the weight of both his friends' stares. The rain outside seemed to grow heavier, the tapping on the windows becoming more frantic.

Darren scoffed. "Whatever, man. You're acting sus as fuck."

From the backseat, Will's voice came low and steady. "What about the other night, Jay?" he asked, leaning into Jay's ear. Jay stiffened at the sound of Will's question, but he kept his gaze forward, not daring to turn around.

Jay swallowed hard, trying to find a way out of this. "I mean, it's not a big deal. Just some stuff, you know?" His words felt hollow, and he could feel Darren's suspicion growing in the silence.

"Right..." Darren replied, unconvinced. "Well, I don't know what's going on. But you really should get checked out man. You're all over the place."

Jay flinched slightly, but he forced a weak laugh. "Yeah, maybe." He could almost feel Will's presence shift behind him, as if he was leaning in closer, but Jay kept his eyes on the road ahead, focusing on the passing headlights through the rain.

The silence that followed was thick with unspoken tension, and Darren finally spoke again, his voice lighter, as if trying to break the awkward mood. "Anyway, you noticed how pumped George is about this trip? Dude's like a kid at Christmas."

Jay could feel some of the pressure lift with Darren's change of subject, but the unease still lingered. Will, though silent now, felt like a cold shadow looming in the backseat.

"Yeah," Jay said with a faint smile, "he's been all over it. I think he's more excited about the food than anything."

"Yeah, sounds like Georgy," Darren laughed, though the mood in the car remained tense. Jay could feel Will listening intently, almost suspiciously.

How had things changed so dramatically between them since they were those carefree kids playing football in the park? Would things ever get back to normal? Jay's thoughts raced as they pulled into the movie theater parking lot. The neon lights of the marquee flickered through the sheets of rain, casting an eerie glow on the wet pavement. The atmosphere felt almost dreamlike, with the bright lights and reflections dancing across the ground.

The girls were waiting for them by the entrance, with George already at the concession stand.

"What, Tubby couldn't wait anymore?" Darren joked as they all walked in, the familiar smell of popcorn and butter filling the air.

Jen caught Jay's eyes immediately. She looked at him, seeing the tension still written across his face. She mouthed, "I'm sorry," to him as they held hands and made their way into the theater. Jay gave a small nod in response, grateful for her acknowledgment but still feeling the weight of his unresolved questions.

The dim lighting of the theater created a hushed, almost intimate environment. The quiet chatter of other moviegoers and the sound of the projector rolling only added to the surreal mood. Jay knew this night wasn't going to bring him the answers he desperately sought, but he hoped, maybe, that he could pretend everything was normal for just a little while longer. He tried to focus on Jen beside him, squeezing her hand as the movie started.

"This movie better be fuckin' awesome," Darren exclaimed as Emily gave him a playful pinch, pulling him back to reality.

Jay just nodded again. At least for now, he could escape into the darkness of the theater and leave the questions for another time.

"Yo, that fucking movie sucked!" Darren announced loudly to the usher as they walked out of the theater. "It was so obvious. Can there ever be a scary movie where you have no fucking clue who the killer is? Ow. I'm sorry... an effing clue." Darren's exaggerated tone broke through the tension, though it did little to ease Jay's mind.

"You OK, babe?" Jen asked, taking Jay's hand as they walked out into the cool night air. The breeze was refreshing but couldn't push away the unease creeping back into Jay's thoughts.

"Yeah, I'm fine. Hey... I know it's a school night, but do you want to stay with me tonight? I could really use the company." He squeezed her hand, hoping to focus on her instead of his racing thoughts.

"Sure, babe, just let me call my mom and tell her." Jen smiled, always ready to support him when he needed her.

Jay smiled back, though the weight on his chest still lingered. He glanced over at Will, who was walking behind Liz in front of them. The shadows cast by the dim streetlights made Will seem more distant, like a figure Jay could no longer reach, despite their years of friendship.

As Jen pulled out her phone to make the call, Jay caught Darren's smirk and the inevitable joke that followed. "Playin' the pity card to get some pussy... I am so fuckin' proud," Darren whispered, his voice dripping with faux sincerity.

"Fuck you," Jay muttered, giving him a playful shove. He looked toward Will and Liz again, and with a sense of urgency. The unfinished conversation still fresh in his mind.

Jay quickened his pace to catch up, making sure Darren and the others were out of earshot.

"We really need to talk. You wanna meet at the arches for breakfast or something?"

Will hesitated, glancing at Liz, who seemed oblivious to their conversation. "Yeah, that's fine, I guess. What time?"

Jay was relieved to get the response he needed. "6:30. We can talk before class. No one will know." He hoped the early hour would give them some privacy. He needed answers, and he couldn't risk anyone overhearing this time.

"Okay," Will agreed with a small nod. He turned back toward Liz's car, but not before Jay noticed something flicker in his eyes—an unease that mirrored his own.

Jen approached after finishing her call, slipping her hand into his. "My mom said it's fine. I told her I had to take care of my baby." She pouted playfully. "She's really worried about you too. Do you think I can stop at my house to grab some things for tomorrow?"

"Yeah, that's fine," Jay said, his mind already shifting to tomorrow's conversation. He'd finally get to the bottom of things. He kissed Jen on the forehead, trying to focus on the moment with her, but his eyes couldn't help but dart toward the parking lot, scanning for something.

As Jen hugged her friends goodbye, giving each of them their typical long embraces, Jay started to feel like he was being watched. The hair on the back of his neck stood on end, and he felt that familiar tightening in his chest. His eyes shifted nervously, scanning the dimly lit street. The sound of laughter and muffled conversation faded into the background as his focus narrowed.

And then he saw it.

Parked at the far end of the lot, half-hidden in the shadows cast by the towering trees, was a black SUV. The same one from the night in the park. His heart raced, pounding against his ribcage as he stared at it, unable to tear his eyes away.

"Jay? You ready to go?" Jen's voice broke through his trance.

"Huh? Yeah... yeah, let's go." Jay glanced back at the SUV one last time, but it hadn't moved.

Was someone inside watching him? Or was it just his imagination playing tricks on him again?

As they got into Jen's car, Jay kept his gaze trained on the rearview mirror, watching for any sign of movement from the SUV. Nothing. But the sense of dread lingered, heavier than ever. He knew tomorrow's talk with Will wouldn't be enough. Whatever was going on, it wasn't over—not by a long shot.

As they pulled out of the parking lot, the SUV's headlights blinked on.

Jay's stomach dropped.

Chapter 7

Suddenly, a loud crash of thunder shook the entire bedroom, knocking the alarm clock off the nightstand. Becky Davenport awoke immediately, startled by the clattering sound. "Shit," she groaned, realizing the storm had knocked the power out. The room was plunged into an eerie silence, save for the drumming rain against the window and the distant rumble of thunder. "Of course... had to be the last fucking week of school," she muttered as she stumbled over to her bedroom door, wiping her tired eyes with her knuckles.

The darkness was thick and oppressive, making the familiar layout of her bedroom seem foreign and menacing. The air felt heavier than usual, saturated with moisture from the storm. Every creak of the old wooden floor under her feet echoed unnaturally loud in the void. Her eyes struggled to adjust to the blackness, but it was like the shadows were actively resisting her gaze. She reached up for her robe, which hung on the back of her thick bedroom door, fumbling clumsily with the belt in the dark. A huge bolt of lightning lit the room suddenly, casting eerie, elongated shadows that seemed to dance menacingly along the walls. It was followed almost instantly by a booming clap of thunder that rattled the windowpanes, as if the storm were pressing against the walls of her house.

The sudden brightness had illuminated the chaotic state of her room: clothes strewn haphazardly across the floor, papers scattered across her desk, and her unmade bed, a tangle of sheets and blankets. Her reflection in the mirror had flashed briefly in the lightning, a pale, wide-eyed silhouette before the darkness swallowed her image again. Ever since she could remember, Becky had hated the dark. There was something primal about it, something that triggered an ancient fear deep within her. Even at twenty-eight, she still had a nightlight in every room of her small house, a habit she had developed from childhood that had never gone away.

She knelt down next to her bed, probing the floor blindly in the darkness as she braced herself with her right hand against the soft mattress. The air in the room felt thick, humid, and oppressive, carrying the scent of damp earth and rain that crept in through the slightly open window. Her fingers fumbled across the floor, brushing against the rough edges of the flashlight she always kept nearby. She had no idea what time it was, but judging by the inky blackness outside, it wasn't anywhere close to dawn. Another flash of lightning lit up the room again, this time almost immediately followed by an earsplitting crack of thunder, loud enough to make her heart skip a beat.

As the thunder rumbled on, fading into the distance, she finally found the flashlight, the cold metal smooth in her hand. Standing up and clicking it on, she watched as its weak beam sliced through the darkness, illuminating small patches of her room. Just as she was about to step toward the door, she heard it—a noise from downstairs, like something heavy collapsing to the floor. Her head whipped toward the door, her breath catching in her throat. Her pulse quickened.

It was probably just the storm. The wind must have knocked something over, or maybe the old house was settling in the damp air. But this sound had been too distinct, too clear. The familiar rush of fear crept up her spine.

"Relax," she whispered to herself, her voice thin and unconvincing. "Just a little thunder."

Still, she couldn't shake the feeling of unease as she cautiously made her way toward the stairs. Every step creaked beneath her, the old wood groaning with each footfall as though warning her of something. She gripped the flashlight tighter, the beam trembling in her hand, casting shifting shadows that seemed to flicker and move on their own. Lightning flashed outside once more, briefly turning the hallway into a strobe-lit tunnel. As the thunder boomed, she nearly lost her balance, the force of the storm rattling the whole house. Her heart was pounding by the time she reached the bottom of the stairs.

The kitchen came into view, illuminated by the erratic beam of her flashlight. Half-unpacked boxes and hastily arranged furniture cluttered the space, making it feel even smaller and more cramped than usual. Her eyes darted around the room, searching for anything out of place. But everything seemed undisturbed, except for the unease gnawing at her gut. She moved toward the kitchen table and grabbed her watch, checking the time in the dim light. 5:39. She was running a little late, but not disastrously so.

She tried to shake off her nerves as she made her way over to the stove. The gas should still work, even with the power out. The storm outside was still in full swing, the rain hammering against the windows, the wind howling like a wild animal trying to claw its way inside. She struck a match, the small flame casting flickering light across the stove. The smell of sulfur mixed with the already present scent of damp earth, filling her senses. But just as she was about to light the burner, she froze.

There it was again—a noise from the basement. It was faint but unmistakable, a soft rustling, like someone moving down there. Her breath hitched in her throat, the small hairs on the back of her neck standing up. Every instinct screamed at her to leave it alone, to go back upstairs and wait out the storm. But curiosity and fear pushed her forward.

Slowly, she turned away from the stove, creeping toward the basement door. Her hand shook so badly that the flashlight beam wobbled erratically along the floor and walls, sending shadows leaping across the room like dark phantoms. She swallowed hard as she reached for the doorknob, trying to steady her breathing. It's nothing, she told herself. Just your imagination running wild. But as her hand touched the cold brass knob, she hesitated.

The door creaked open with a long, drawn-out groan, sounding almost theatrical in the quiet house. She stared down into the pitch-black basement, the stairs descending into an abyss. The flashlight beam barely penetrated the darkness, revealing only the first few steps. Just as she was about to step onto the staircase, she felt it—a hand clamping down hard on her shoulder, yanking her back.

She screamed, the sound tearing through the silence as the flashlight tumbled out of her hand, spinning wildly across the kitchen floor.

"Relax, Beck. It's me."

The familiar voice cut through her panic, and Becky's heart slowed as she registered who it was. Her father. She let out a shaky laugh, turning to face him as relief washed over her. "You scared the shit outta me, Daddy," she gasped, trying to catch her breath. She bent down to pick up the flashlight, now lying on its side and casting a dim glow across the kitchen tiles.

"What are you doing here so early? It's only quarter to six."

"I just wanted to make sure you were OK," he replied, his gruff voice tinged with concern. "I know how much you hate when the power goes out."

Becky exhaled deeply, shaking her head. Of course, he'd come over. She had bought the house next door to her father's, not just because it was convenient, but because she wanted to stay close to him. Her mother had left when she was young, leaving her father to raise her alone. He'd always been her rock, even if he could be gruff and overly protective. Since they worked at the same school, it wasn't unusual for him to come over for breakfast before work.

"I think a tree might have hit Ms. Clayton's house. Sounded like a bomb went off," he added, pulling out a chair and sitting down at the kitchen table.

"Well, that sucks," Becky muttered, still trying to calm her racing heart. She couldn't shake the feeling of unease from earlier, but now that her father was here, the house felt less...ominous. "You want breakfast early since you're here?"

"Why not," Harold said with a shrug, unfolding the newspaper he had tucked under his arm. He squinted at it in the dim candlelight as Becky started moving around the kitchen, lighting more candles. The storm outside roared on, a constant backdrop of howling wind and rain that rattled the windows.

"You OK, Beck? You seem a little shook up," he asked, looking up from the paper.

"I'm fine," she lied. "Just hate storms." She didn't want to tell him about the noises. He'd just laugh it off, call her a scared little girl. She'd heard it all before. Growing up with just her father, she'd never had the luxury of coddling or sympathy. He was tough, and he expected her to be the same.

She cracked an egg on the skillet, watching it sizzle and bubble in the flickering light of the candles. Harold took a sip of the instant coffee she'd made him and immediately grimaced.

"Ahhh...what the hell is this shit?" he spat.

"It's instant coffee, Dad. Power's out. Can't make your normal stuff," she replied, smirking as she flipped the French toast.

"This shit is terrible! I'd rather drink my own piss!" Harold exclaimed, his voice loud in the small kitchen.

"That's real classy, Dad," Becky said, rolling her eyes. The smell of cinnamon and sugar began to fill the air, blending with the musty scent of the storm outside. The warmth of the kitchen and the familiar routine helped to ease the tension she'd felt moments before. But that feeling of unease still lingered in the back of her mind, like a shadow she couldn't shake.

"Well you wouldn't be so scared if you still had a man of the house," Harold knew this would cause a stir, and regretted the words as soon as they came out.

"Yea, well we can't all be blessed by Cupid like you, dad!" Becky pointed out, indicating that her father had no room to criticize her in the romance department.

"All I'm saying, Beck, is-"

"I know what you're saying, dad," she interrupted. "You say it as often as you can. I know I fucked up. I fell for a guy who was a piece of shit. I married the wrong guy. I get all of it. But what I don't get, is why my father, who couldn't keep his own family together, gets to constantly point shit out to me!"

"I didn't mean to-"

"Didn't mean to what, dad?" the veins in her forehead were pulsating. This was a tension that had been building up for years. Normally, she would let his comments go. But not today. She was too worked up to let it pass this time. She stormed out of the room.

Becky's footsteps faded as she ascended the stairs, the old wood creaking under her weight. The rhythmic tapping of rain against the windows and the occasional rumble of thunder filled the silence left behind. Harold sat at the kitchen table, the flickering candlelight casting long, dancing shadows across the walls. The storm outside was relentless, its power rattling the shutters and sending gusts of wind that whistled through the cracks of the old house.

Harold grimaced as he took another sip of the bitter instant coffee, setting the cup down with a thud. He hated mornings like this—everything felt off-kilter, and his daughter's words echoed in his mind. Becky had always been headstrong, just like her mother, but she was different now.

She had grown up, left behind the tomboy she once was, and turned into a woman who attracted attention, attention that made Harold uncomfortable.

He picked up his paper again, but the words swam in front of his eyes, his thoughts still tangled in the earlier conversation. Becky was right in some ways. He had been harsh, especially about her love life, but he couldn't help it. He just didn't want her to get hurt again, not after the way things had ended with that other guy. He had been so sure that Becky would come out of that relationship unscathed, but the way it had unraveled had left scars that Harold knew still festered beneath the surface. He crunched down on a piece of bacon, staring at the candle flame flickering on the table.

The storm outside picked up again, the wind howling louder, and Harold could hear the distant rumble of thunder growing closer. He glanced at the window, squinting at the rain lashing against the glass, the faint outlines of the trees outside swaying in the wind. For a moment, he thought he saw a shadow pass by, but he chalked it up to the moving branches.

He sighed deeply, tossing the paper aside. His daughter had always been a bit of a mystery to him—so tough and resilient, yet with a soft, hidden side that few got to see. He wished he could protect her from everything, but he knew that wasn't possible. He also knew that as much as they bickered, he loved her fiercely. She was all he had left.

The sound of water running upstairs snapped him back to reality. Becky was showering, getting ready for another day at school, probably with a million things on her mind. Harold leaned back in his chair, listening to the rain continue its assault on the house. The unease he had felt earlier, about the storm, about his daughter's safety, lingered like the bitter taste of coffee on his tongue.

"Maybe I am getting too old," he muttered to himself, rubbing his face with his hands.

He heard her rummaging around upstairs, the sound of drawers opening and closing echoing down the stairs.

"Probably looking for more fucking candles," he muttered to himself as he took his final, giant bite of French toast. The sweet taste of cinnamon and sugar mingled with the bitterness of the coffee, a strange contrast that matched his current mood. He folded the paper and tucked it under his arm as he stood from the table, stretching his stiff shoulders and blowing out the candles that had dimly lit the room. The small kitchen, now dimly illuminated only by flashes of lightning through the window, felt oddly comforting despite the tempest raging outside. The smell of breakfast still lingered in the air, but it barely masked the damp chill that had crept into the house.

He ambled toward the back door, his mind drifting to his daughter and the mistakes she had made—mistakes he himself had no right to scold her for. His past was full of missteps, after all, and he knew he had hardly been the perfect example for her. Still, that didn't stop him from worrying or feeling a sense of responsibility for her choices.

Just as his hand wrapped around the cool metal of the doorknob, a loud crash echoed through the house. It wasn't the familiar rumble of thunder that had plagued the town for days. No, this was different. This sound came from inside the house. The basement.

Harold froze for a moment, his brow furrowing. Becky had been staring down those stairs earlier—had she heard something too? Maybe she hadn't wanted to admit it to him, knowing how quick he was to dismiss her fears. "Probably nothing," he muttered to himself, but his curiosity got the better of him. He turned away from the back door and moved toward the basement steps, the old wood beneath his feet creaking ominously with each step.

The air around him grew colder as he opened the groaning basement door, the scent of earth and mildew hitting him instantly as he began his descent into the dark, damp space below. The dimness swallowed him up, the faint light from the kitchen above barely penetrating the gloom.

Meanwhile, upstairs, Becky was still fuming about her father's lecture. He had no idea what she had gone through, the lengths she'd gone to just to keep things secret, including the fact that she was his daughter—a detail no one at the school knew besides the principal.

It wasn't that she was ashamed of him. Not at all. But the rumors that swirled around her at work, combined with the way some of the kids treated her father, made her keep that piece of information to herself. She'd decided it was easier that way.

The beam of her flashlight flickered as she pointed it toward the bathroom door. Another loud crash of thunder shattered the eerie silence in the house, making her jump. The wooden floorboards beneath her feet creaked with every step as she hurried down the narrow hallway, almost chasing the beam of light as it bounced ahead of her. The hallway seemed to stretch longer in the darkness, the familiar walls closing in around her like the night itself.

When she reached the bathroom, she flung the door open and stepped inside, the weight of her father's earlier words still heavy on her mind.

"Fuck him," she whispered into the dim room, the words hanging in the still, humid air. "He has no right to tell me how to live my life." The frustration bubbled up in her chest as she moved toward the closet. Her hands still trembled slightly as she rummaged through it, searching for the candles she knew were buried among the towels and toiletries.

As her fingers closed around the cool wax of a candle, her thoughts drifted—back to a time when things were simpler, when she had felt truly loved. The memory of his arm draped across her waist in the quiet hours of the night still lingered in her mind, the warmth of his body pressed against hers, the safety she had felt in those fleeting moments. Now, that love felt distant, a ghost that haunted her in her loneliest hours. She missed him more than she'd ever admit to anyone, especially her father. The bitterness of that loss made her stomach churn.

"Why does he have to constantly bring it up?" she murmured to herself, setting the candles on the bathroom counter. Her father's words stung more than she'd let on, reopening old wounds that had never truly healed.

The darkness in the house was oppressive, clinging to every corner of the bathroom like a thick, heavy fog. She glanced at the window, hoping to see the first signs of dawn breaking through the storm, but the sky remained an unrelenting wall of darkness. The storm wasn't letting up anytime soon, and the idea of stepping into the dim, shadowy bathroom filled her with unease. She hated the thought of showering in near darkness, especially after hearing the damage the storm had already caused in the neighborhood.

As another crack of thunder reverberated through the house, Becky took a deep breath, trying to calm the racing thoughts in her mind. She reached into the closet, the flashlight shaking in her hand as she grabbed two more pillar candles. The beam from the flashlight flickered again, casting long, eerie shadows that danced across the bathroom walls. The room, normally her sanctuary, now felt more like a cave, the shadows creeping in from every angle, making her feel as though she wasn't alone.

The storm continued to rage outside, the wind howling like a distant scream, while the rain pounded against the windows with a relentless fury. Despite the warmth of the house, Becky couldn't shake the chill that crawled up her spine.

Her heart was still heavy with the lingering memories of her former love, a relationship that had left her with more questions than answers. Would she ever find that kind of love again? Or was she doomed to be haunted by the ghost of a man who had once meant everything to her?

She lit the candles on the bathroom sink, watching as the small flames flickered to life. The soft, warm glow offered a small sense of comfort against the raging storm outside, but it did little to ease the knot of tension in her chest.

All of a sudden, Becky heard a loud crash from downstairs, like the crack of a bat against glass. She whipped her head toward the door, her breath caught in her throat, half expecting to see her father coming in to apologize for breaking something. The crash echoed up the stairwell, reverberating in the silence. Her pulse quickened, but she convinced herself it must have been him, probably knocking over a glass in the dim candlelight that barely illuminated the kitchen. She knew he could be clumsy sometimes. Still, an uneasy feeling nagged at the edges of her mind.

Already undressed, with the water running and steam filling the bathroom, she hesitated. The thought of stepping into the comforting shower won out, and she decided not to inspect the noise.

She took the lit candles, placing them carefully on the edge of the sink, their flickering flames casting eerie shadows that danced across the tiled walls. The steam thickened, curling up toward the ceiling and fogging the mirror, adding to the already oppressive atmosphere. Becky reached a hand into the shower to check the temperature, adjusting the water with a quick flick of her wrist. The warmth of the steam was comforting, and she welcomed it, allowing herself to relax a bit. But the silence pressed in again, save for the rhythmic drumming of the rain on the roof, a distant rumble of thunder, and the sound of running water.

As she stepped into the back of the tub, easing her body in with cautious movements, she suddenly heard another sound—a faint but distinct creak from somewhere down the hall. Footsteps.

Her heart leaped into her throat as she fumbled for the flashlight she'd left on the sink. Her damp fingers slipped against the handle, and the beam of light flickered weakly before steadying. Her breath quickened, and for a moment, she thought she could hear her pulse pounding in her ears, louder than the rain, louder than the thunder. The footsteps had stopped.

She stepped out of the shower, her bare feet splashing against the wet tile floor, the cold immediately biting into her skin. The thick scent of the damp air filled her nostrils as she moved toward the bathroom door. The hall lay in darkness, the faint glow of her flashlight barely penetrating the murky blackness that stretched down to the stairs. For a few moments, she stood frozen, listening intently.

Nothing.

No more footsteps, no creaking floorboards. Just the sound of the water behind her, cascading into the tub, and the steady rhythm of her own heartbeat.

"Relax," she whispered to herself. "It's just your imagination."

With a nervous glance back toward the hallway, she shut the door. The shadows seemed to taunt her from the corners of the room, lurking in the periphery of her vision, always just out of reach. She closed her eyes, forcing herself to calm down as she stepped back into the hot shower. The water felt good against her skin, its warmth relaxing her tense muscles. She let the water beat down on her, closing her eyes and letting it soothe her, the sound of the droplets like a comforting white noise, drowning out the storm outside.

But the tension in her chest wouldn't dissipate. She could still feel it, like a heavy weight pressing down on her ribs, keeping her on edge.

The water poured down over her head, washing away her unease bit by bit. She lathered up, allowing herself to melt into the rhythmic beat of the shower. The candles on the counter flickered, casting their warm light across the misty bathroom, making her feel cocooned in safety. She welcomed the warmth that spread across her body as she stood under the steady stream. Eyes closed, Becky let the heat seep into her bones, trying to forget about the storm, the power outage, and the strange noises that had rattled her.

And for a moment, she did forget. She drifted into the solace of the steamy shower, her thoughts blanking as the water washed over her skin, carrying away her fears.

Then, suddenly, she jumped back in shock.

The bathroom was plunged into darkness.

Her eyes flew open, wide with terror. The candles had gone out. The comforting glow that had enveloped her was gone, leaving her in pitch black. The sound of the water was now deafening. The steam felt stifling, oppressive, choking the air around her. She blinked, trying to adjust her eyes, but it was useless. She couldn't see anything.

She stepped cautiously out of the tub, pulling the shower curtain aside with trembling hands. Her wet feet slapped against the cold tile floor as she reached for the flashlight on the sink, but in her panic, her fingers brushed against it too hard, knocking it to the ground with a heavy thud. The noise reverberated through the bathroom, making her flinch.

"H-Hello?" Her voice shook, echoing eerily in the bathroom. "Anyone there?"

Silence. No response, except for the persistent sound of water splashing against the empty tub.

She crouched down, her hand groping across the floor until her fingers found the handle of the flashlight. Her breathing grew faster, more erratic. She clutched the flashlight tightly, flipping the switch on. The beam flickered to life, bouncing off the mirror, casting shadows that twisted and writhed across the bathroom walls. She swung the light toward the sink, finding the candles reduced to smoldering wicks, thin trails of smoke rising toward the ceiling.

"I'm losing it," she whispered, forcing a nervous smile. Her reflection stared back at her in the mirror, her wide eyes betraying her fear. She shone the light on her face, but her heart froze when she saw something behind her—just a faint shadow, larger than her own.

Someone was in the room.

She spun around, shining the flashlight toward the figure, but it was too late. Before she could react, a hand shot out from the darkness, grabbing her wrist with crushing force. The flashlight slipped from her grasp and shattered against the tile floor, plunging the room into blackness once again.

Becky struggled, but the grip on her wrist was ironclad. She let out a choked scream, but the sound barely left her throat before it was stifled. Her other hand flailed uselessly, trying to push away her attacker, but the figure was too strong. She felt rough fabric brush against her skin as she writhed in the darkness, tears streaming down her face, mixing with the water that still poured from the shower.

Another flash of lightning illuminated the room for a split second, and in that moment, Becky saw the glint of something metallic raised above her. Her heart slammed against her ribs in pure terror. She opened her mouth to scream, but no sound came out.

Then came the pain.

A sharp, violent stab directly into her chest, just above her left breast. The pain was white-hot, searing through her body. She gasped, trying to cry out, but her lungs failed her. Her body convulsed, and she was released from the grip, collapsing to the floor. The thud echoed in her ears as she lay there, unable to move. Her vision blurred as she stared blankly into the darkness.

Then, another sharp pain. This time, there was no heat, no sensation. Her body had gone cold, the shock dulling everything. She could smell the distinct scent of copper, thick in the air, mixing with the damp steam of the bathroom.

Her body felt heavy. Numb. She couldn't lift her arms, couldn't even blink. As the last traces of warmth left her, Becky Davenport's world faded into blackness, and the last thing she felt was the cold, unyielding steel buried in her flesh.

Jay glanced at the clock on his phone. 6:48. He hated being late. His thoughts had been racing since last night's conversation with Will, and now, with every passing minute, the feeling that Will wasn't going to show for breakfast was only growing stronger. Sitting alone in the bustling diner, he felt out of place. The usual sounds of morning—coffee brewing, orders being called out, and people chatting—felt distant, like they were happening in another world.

The waitress had already come by twice to ask if he wanted to order, but he kept putting it off, waiting. 6:54. He set his phone down on the laminated table, tapping his fingers nervously as he looked out the window. Something was wrong. Will had been acting strange for weeks now, but after their conversation last night, Jay had hoped things were starting to make sense. Why wasn't he here?

Suddenly, his phone buzzed on the table, jolting him out of his thoughts. It was Will.

Jay picked up the phone quickly and stood up, stepping out the door for privacy. "Hello?" he said, his voice filled with expectation.

"Jay, I'm not gonna be able to make it to breakfast. Something... came up," Will's voice sounded off. Flat. Almost rehearsed.

Jay frowned, stepping outside the diner into the cold morning air. "Are you serious? What came up, Will?"

"I promise I'll tell you later," Will responded, his voice still unnervingly calm. "I just... I can't make it. I'm sorry, bro."

The chill in the air seeped into Jay's bones as he processed what Will was saying. "Will, I'm freakin' out here, man," Jay pleaded, leaning against the brick wall of the diner. "We really need to talk. I don't know who else to turn to."

There was a pause on the other end of the line, and Jay could almost hear Will weighing his words. "I know we do, Jay. I promise we will. I just gotta take care of something this morning. I'll call you after school today. OK?"

Jay clenched his jaw. Something wasn't right. "I'm supposed to pick up my tux with Jen," Jay said, trying to keep Will on the phone. "Are you still going this weekend?"

"Yeah, I'm going. Why wouldn't I?" Will's tone sounded almost irritated now, but it was the casualness that bothered Jay. Like Will didn't care. Like this whole thing—everything they had gone through—was just background noise.

"I dunno," Jay muttered. He glanced at his reflection in the diner window, watching the rain trickle down the glass. "Well, I'll call you after I pick it up, and maybe we can go out to dinner or something. We really need to talk about things," he said again, emphasizing the urgency.

"I know we do, Jay," Will's voice was a little sharper this time, like he was growing impatient. "I told you, I've got some shit I need to take care of. I'll try to be done by dinner, but I can't promise anything."

Jay felt his frustration boiling over. "You're not going to school, are you?"

There was another pause. "No... not today. I can't. I told you... I've got shit to do," Will repeated, sounding distant again. "Listen, I've gotta go. I'll call you later." "Wait, Will—" Jay started, but the line went dead.

Jay stared at his phone for a moment, the sinking feeling in his gut growing stronger. He knew Will wasn't telling him everything. What the hell is going on? He shoved his phone into his pocket, rubbing his forehead as he tried to collect his thoughts.

Just as he was about to head back into the diner, a loud thud against the window startled him. Jay whipped around to see Darren standing there, glaring at him through the rain with his arms crossed.

George was a few steps behind, looking into the diner with a bemused expression.

Jay rolled his eyes, his heart still racing from the abrupt knock. He opened the door to the Jeep and stepped out into the cold drizzle, the air biting at his skin. "What are you doing here?"

"So this is why you couldn't pick us up, huh?" Darren said, his voice dripping with suspicion. "You're sitting here, hiding out?"

Jay blinked in surprise, glancing back at George, who was still fixated on the diner's breakfast menu posted outside. "I was supposed to meet someone here, Darren," Jay muttered, annoyed that Darren had caught him at such a vulnerable moment.

"Yeah? Who?" Darren shot back, not letting it go. His intense gaze bore into Jay, his frustration evident. "You couldn't even tell us what's up?"

Jay felt the knot in his stomach tighten as he tried to deflect Darren's questions. He didn't want to lie outright, but he also wasn't ready to explain what had just happened with Will. The last thing he needed was for Darren to get more involved. "It doesn't matter," Jay said, avoiding eye contact. "The person didn't show up. Can we just go inside and eat?"

Darren's stare hardened. "Bullshit. You don't just bail on us and come here for 'no reason.' You're hiding something."

Jay clenched his fists, his patience thinning. "I'm not hiding anything, Darren. I just didn't feel like explaining every little detail to you."

"Right. Like you're not being weird as hell right now?" Darren stepped closer, his eyes narrowing. "You've been acting off for days, Jay. We all see it."

George, still lingering behind them, glanced between the two, his face contorted with confusion and concern. "Hey, maybe we should just—"

"No, George, stay out of this," Darren snapped, cutting him off before looking back at Jay. "You're keeping something from us. You always do this. Keeping secrets, acting like you're better than the rest of us. What is it this time? What the fuck were you doing here alone?"

Jay's anger flared. "You think I'm better than you?" he shot back, his voice raising despite the icy drizzle falling around them. "I'm just trying to figure things out, man! Not everything revolves around you!"

Darren took another step forward, his chest puffed out. "Oh, so it's about you now? Big surprise.

What a shocker."

Jay knew this was spiraling out of control, and it wasn't the time for this. Not now, not with everything else he was dealing with. He took a deep breath, trying to calm himself down. "Look, I'm sorry. I just didn't want to get into it, alright? There's stuff going on. I'm trying to handle it. I don't want anyone else getting hurt."

That stopped Darren in his tracks. His eyes flickered with surprise. "Jay...Why do you always have to do it alone? We're here. That's all I'm saying, man."

"Yeah. I know," Jay muttered, feeling the tension ease just slightly. "Shit's been so weird. I wanted to...I dunno. Get answers," Jay was trying to not implicate Will any more.

Darren's expression softened, but suspicion lingered in his eyes. "Why didn't you just tell us that?"

"Because I didn't want to make it a big deal," Jay said, his voice still strained. "I'm trying to figure out what's going on. That's all. Just needed some time."

Darren crossed his arms, thinking for a moment before speaking. "So, what then? Have you figured it out, Detective?" he mocked.

Jay smirked. He was happy that Darren had relented with his joke, but he didn't want to let his guard down too much. For his sake, or Will's. "I don't know anything," he answered bluntly.

There was a long pause as the rain continued to fall around them. George finally spoke up, his voice tentative. "Well, maybe we can all figure it out together?"

Darren looked over at George, then back at Jay. He sighed, some of the hostility draining from his face. "Yeah, okay. But next time, don't keep us in the dark, Jay. We're all in this shit together."

Jay nodded, relieved that Darren had finally backed down. "I know. I'm sorry."

Darren clapped him on the back, the tension between them dissipating. "Alright, let's get inside.

I'm starving."

As they walked toward the diner, Jay couldn't shake the uneasy feeling gnawing at him. Will had bailed on him at the last minute, and now Darren was onto him. Something wasn't right, and no matter how much he tried to push it down, Jay couldn't stop the growing fear that Will's secret was more dangerous than any of them realized.

But for now, he had to focus. Keep things together. Keep Darren and George from suspecting anything more. He could deal with Will later.

They stepped into the warmth of the diner, and the smell of sizzling bacon and freshly brewed coffee filled the air. George headed straight for the counter, eyeing the menu like he hadn't eaten in days, while Darren trailed behind, still looking lost in thought.

Jay took a deep breath and followed them, hoping that somehow, this day wouldn't unravel any further than it already had. But deep down, he knew it was only a matter of time before everything came crashing down.

Chapter 8

Jay walked up the stairs towards the cafeteria, the rhythmic clunk of his shoes bouncing off the cold, metal stairwell. The sharp scent of disinfectant lingered in the air, mixed with the faint odor of cafeteria food creeping up the steps. Each step felt heavier than the last as Jay's stomach twisted in nervous knots, a mixture of anxiety and anticipation. The dull hum of voices grew louder with each step, blending into an indistinguishable roar by the time he reached the top. He paused at the door to the cafeteria, peering through the narrow glass window.

The cafeteria itself was a blur of movement—students chatting, trays clattering, laughter echoing off the tiled walls. The fluorescent lights overhead flickered slightly, casting a sickly yellow hue on everything. It was a place that usually buzzed with life, but today it seemed oppressive, almost suffocating. Jay scanned the sea of students, his eyes immediately landing on Darren, who sat hunched over, his face illuminated by the faint glow of his phone. The distant murmur of voices seemed to grow quieter as Jay locked eyes with him, his heart skipping a beat.

"What's up, bro?" Darren's voice broke through the haze, louder than the background noise. His voice carried with it a strange undertone, a sharpness that cut through the usual cafeteria clamor.

Across the table, George was oblivious, stuffing his face as usual. His fork scraped loudly against the plastic tray, the sound blending into the din of the cafeteria. "The girls left school early," George grunted between bites, a drop of sauce falling onto his shirt, unnoticed. Jay usually found George's carefree nature somewhat comforting, but today it only added to the suffocating tension in the air.

Darren gripped on Jay's shoulder with an uncomfortable firmness, fingers digging into his skin just hard enough to make him flinch. "Everything OK?" Darren's voice was dripping with suspicion now, laced with an edge that made Jay's pulse quicken.

Jay tried to maintain his composure, forcing a tight smile. "Yeah, I'm fine...you mind if I sit down?" He gestured awkwardly toward the chair, trying to slide into his usual spot by the wall.

But the atmosphere was thick, stifling, and there was no escaping Darren's laser focus. The air felt sticky, weighed down by something unspoken, and Jay could feel his throat tighten as he picked at his tray, avoiding Darren's relentless stare. The greasy pizza in front of him glistened under the harsh cafeteria lights, but it had lost its usual appeal. The room buzzed around them, yet it felt as though time had slowed, the moments dragging on uncomfortably as Darren pressed for answers.

"Why were you at Will's last night?" Darren's voice cut through the low hum of the cafeteria, the directness of the question catching Jay off guard. His heart pounded in his chest, matching the frenetic energy in the room. The sound of trays being slammed onto tables and forks clattering on plates seemed to grow louder, creating an overwhelming sense of chaos around them.

Jay glanced down at his tray, unable to meet Darren's eyes. "I dunno...I...," he muttered, trying to sound as casual as possible, though his insides twisted with unease. Darren didn't move, didn't blink—his gaze was piercing, probing, and Jay could feel the sweat beginning to bead on the back of his neck.

The tension mounted as Darren leaned in, his voice dropping to a low whisper that seemed to vibrate in Jay's ear. "Jay! You need to tell me why you were at Will's house last night."

The cafeteria's fluorescent lights flickered slightly, casting unsettling shadows on Darren's face, deepening the lines of frustration etched across his brow. Jay's pulse quickened, a lump forming in his throat as the room seemed to close in around him.

He clenched his fists under the table, the knuckles turning white as he struggled to keep his composure. "I said I needed some answers, Jesus Darren, what's with all the fucking questions?" His voice cracked slightly, betraying the anxiety simmering beneath the surface.

A deafening screech of a chair sliding across the tile floor behind them snapped Jay's attention away. He turned to see two classmates squaring off, their faces inches apart, and the cafeteria suddenly erupted into chaos.

"Fuckin' sweet," Darren exclaimed, abandoning their tense conversation. The heavy atmosphere dissipated as quickly as it had formed, replaced by the charged excitement of an impending fight. Darren leaped onto his chair, towering above the crowd as he watched the spectacle unfold. His laughter cut through the noise, a sharp contrast to the anxiety Jay had felt just moments ago.

Jay, on the other hand, felt nothing but relief at the distraction. He slipped away from the table, weaving through the students who had gathered around to watch the fight. The cafeteria noise faded into the background as he pushed open the heavy doors and stepped into the cold, quiet hallway.

The silence was almost eerie after the cacophony of the lunchroom. Jay could hear the distant rumble of lockers slamming and the faint echo of footsteps on the other end of the hall. He fumbled with his phone, the screen glowing dimly in the shadowy corridor as he dialed Will's number.

The phone rang once...twice...three times. Jay's fingers tapped anxiously against the cold metal of his phone, his breath shallow and quick. When it went to voicemail, his heart sank. He knew Will never checked his messages, but he had to try.

"Hey, Will, it's me. Just wondering where you are today..." Jay's voice echoed softly in the empty hallway, mixing with the distant hum of the building. "You were supposed to meet me for breakfast. Listen, Ms. Davenport's not here either... Just give me a call back, bro. I really gotta talk to ya."

Jay ended the call and leaned against the cool, tiled wall, his reflection staring back at him from the glass windows of the main office. His mind raced, the unanswered questions swirling like a storm inside his head.

But when he glanced back at his reflection, he froze. Darren was leaning against the opposite wall, arms crossed, eyes narrowed.

"So...it's all a little clearer now," Darren's voice was low, but there was an unmistakable edge to it. His words seemed to hang in the air, heavy and suffocating. The hallway, with its dim lighting and empty lockers, suddenly felt far too small.

Jay swallowed hard, his stomach turning. "What are you talking about, Darren?" His voice wavered, and he tried to keep his expression neutral.

Darren stepped forward, closing the distance between them. His shadow loomed over Jay as he pointed a finger in his chest. "Why are you leaving messages on Will's phone? And besides that, what the fuck does Ms. Davenport have to do with any of it?"

The question hung between them, the tension so thick it was almost tangible. Jay's mind scrambled for an answer, his pulse racing, as he tried to make sense of what was happening.

George was still sitting at the table, oblivious to the frenzy that had just unfolded. His fork scraped rhythmically against the plastic tray, his mouth half full of food as he methodically worked his way through his second plate. The cafeteria noise—the clatter of trays, the raised voices of students, and the ongoing scuffle—faded into the background for George. His focus was purely on the food in front of him, a growing pile of wrappers and cartons building up like a fortress around his tray.

Suddenly, his phone buzzed on the table, interrupting his trance. Glancing at the screen, he saw Amy's name flash across the display. With a small grunt, he put his fork down and swiped to answer the call.

"Hey, George!" Amy's voice rang through the phone, chipper and full of energy. "You'll never guess what I found! You know that place on Maple? They've got a whole rack of suits, and they're on sale! I was thinking, maybe you could check them out before prom?"

George rolled his eyes but couldn't help the slight smile that tugged at the corners of his mouth.

"Suits, huh? Didn't we already talk about getting mine done last week?"

"Yeah, but these are way better than what we saw," Amy continued, her excitement evident. "Plus, I just know you're going to look amazing. You have to at least come see them after school!"

"Sure, sure, Amy. We'll check it out later," George mumbled, glancing around the cafeteria distractedly. He noticed Jay and Darren had disappeared, leaving him to fend for himself in the chaotic lunchroom.

As Amy rambled on about all the things she'd seen at the shop, George half-listened, his eyes scanning the room lazily. His attention drifted in and out of the conversation, but he nodded and made the appropriate sounds of agreement when needed.

"All right, I'll let you go for now. But don't forget, we're meeting up later!" Amy said, her voice taking on a playful edge.

"Yeah, I know. I won't forget," George replied with a small laugh. He ended the call and returned to his tray, his appetite diminished now.

Meanwhile, in the hallway, Jay's pulse was still racing from his confrontation with Darren. His mind was spinning as he tried to figure out what to say next, but there was no time to think. Darren wasn't going to let this go. He could feel the weight of Darren's anger, the tension between them like a coiled spring ready to snap.

"Look, Darren, it's really not a big deal, okay?" Jay tried to keep his voice steady, but there was an edge of desperation in it now. He could feel his palms sweating, his heart pounding in his chest.

Darren wasn't having it. "Well, if it's not a big deal, then you can fucking tell me," he snapped, his voice rising as he followed Jay into the bathroom. The fluorescent lights above flickered, casting long, jittery shadows on the floor as the tension between the two boys grew.

Jay stepped back, trying to put some distance between them. "I don't know why you're getting so pissed. I told you, it's nothing." He could feel the lie on his tongue, heavy and bitter.

Darren's eyes narrowed, his face flushed with frustration. "Bullshit," he spat. "You've been acting weird for days, Jay. Don't think I haven't noticed. You are hiding something. And I'm not gonna sit here and let you shut me out again."

Before Jay could respond, the sound of a toilet flushing broke through the tension, and they both turned to see Robert Veiss shuffle out of the stall, his head down, as if trying to make himself invisible. The sound of his shoes squeaking against the tile echoed awkwardly through the bathroom.

Darren's focus shifted, his temper flaring at the sight of Robert. "Get the fuck outta here, nerd boy!" Darren barked, his voice loud and venomous, the anger that had been building now redirected.

Jay sighed, relieved for the momentary distraction, but his relief was short-lived as Robert turned to wash his hands at the sink, taking his time. The hand dryer roared to life as Robert dried his hands, clearly not in a hurry to leave.

"GET THE FUCK OUT!" Darren lunged toward Robert, and the poor kid practically flew out the door, as he made a quick exit.

Jay used the brief moment to take a deep breath, trying to collect his thoughts. But he knew he couldn't stall forever. Darren wasn't going to let this go.

Darren whipped around, his eyes blazing. "I can't believe you'd keep shit from me, Jay. After everything we've been through? You really gonna let this come between us?"

Jay's mind raced, his heartbeat drumming in his ears. He knew there was no easy way out of this. Darren wasn't just suspicious anymore—he was angry. The narrow, dimly lit bathroom felt like it was closing in on him, and he could feel his back pressed against the cold, tile wall.

"It's really nothing, and to be honest, bro, it's none of your business," Jay's voice cracked slightly as he spoke, betraying his nerves. As soon as the words left his mouth, he regretted them. Darren's face went from angry to incredulous, his eyebrows shooting up in disbelief.

"What?!" Darren shouted, his voice bouncing off the tiled walls. "I can't believe you just fucking said that!" He stepped forward, his chest puffed out, eyes wide with rage. "How long have we been friends, Jay? And now you're keeping shit from me? What the fuck is going on?"

Jay looked down, avoiding Darren's intense gaze. The lights buzzed overhead, casting a harsh, unforgiving glow on the confrontation. He could feel his pulse quicken as he tried to find the words to calm Darren down, but nothing came to mind.

"I know Darren, it's just that some things are better left private, that's all," Jay muttered, hoping to defuse the situation. He glanced around the empty bathroom, the silence between them now thick with tension. He could hear the faint hum of the school's HVAC system, the distant sound of doors opening and closing as students shuffled from one class to the next.

Darren's jaw clenched, his fists tightening at his sides. "Private? Between us?" His voice was quieter now, but still sharp, the hurt evident. "We don't keep secrets, man. We never have. This is the shit I'm talking about. You and Will shut me out 6 months ago, and look what happened."

Jay's chest tightened, the weight of the secret he had been carrying feeling unbearable now.

Darren had always been the type to wear his emotions on his sleeve, and Jay knew that
keeping him in the dark for so long had hurt him deeply. But this wasn't just any secret—it was Will's life, his family. It wasn't Jay's place to spill everything, even if it meant losing Darren's trust.

Darren stepped back, running a hand through over his head in frustration. "You know what? Fuck this. I'm done asking. You wanna be shady, go ahead. But don't come crying to me when something like that happens to you."

Jay flinched at the words. Darren's anger stung, but there was truth to what he said. Will's erratic behavior had been weighing on Jay for weeks, and the strain was starting to show. The guilt gnawed at him, knowing that keeping Darren in the dark was only making things worse.

The conversation was interrupted when the bathroom door creaked open. Jay glanced over Darren's shoulder, and his stomach dropped. Robert Veiss was back, poking his head in cautiously, as if trying to see if the coast was clear. He shot a nervous glance at Darren, who immediately locked eyes with him.

"Are you serious right now?" Darren barked, glaring at Robert.

"I, uh... forgot my bag," Robert stammered, pointing to the forgotten backpack lying near the sink.

Darren rolled his eyes, "Just get it and go."

Robert hurriedly grabbed his bag, avoiding eye contact as he slung it over his shoulder and rushed out again, mumbling something under his breath.

The door clicked shut, leaving Jay and Darren alone once more. The momentary distraction wasn't enough to dissipate the tension between them.

Darren turned back to Jay, his eyes narrowing again. "Look, man, I'm just saying... we've always been straight with each other. I don't get why that has to change now."

Jay sighed, running a hand through his hair. "It's not about changing things, Darren. It's just... this isn't my secret to tell. I know it sucks, and I hate it too. But it's Will's life, not mine."

Darren seemed to deflate a little at that, his posture relaxing slightly, though the frustration was still evident on his face. He let out a long breath, looking away for a moment before turning back to Jay.

"Fine. So then that's it then," he backed up, shaking his head at his friend.

The boys walked slowly down the hall, turning the corner and stopping at Jay's locker. He turned the lock a few times and the locker popped open. "I don't know what to tell you Darren," he finally broke the silence as he tossed his German book in the bottom of his orderly locker.

He had often wondered what freshman would get his locker next year, whose it would be for the next four years of high school. He had thought about putting a note in it...leaving some tips for the young student and attempting to pass on his legacy at the school. He had enjoyed the fact that his locker was directly across from the principal's office, often getting inside information about school business from casually eavesdropping.

"Yeah. Well, I dunno either, Jay. We have never had secrets with us before. It just feels like lately...shit has been so hush-hush that it almost feels like we are fading apart. You know that's the absolute last thing I want."

"I know, Darren. But some things are just not my place to say. I hate keeping shit from you," he tried to be as sincere as possible.

Darren started to plead his case as to why he should not be left in the dark, but Jay was looking past him, towards the window of the principal's office. "Something's going on," he interrupted, pointing past Darren's shoulder, trying to listen in on the conversation going on across the hall.

The principal, Mr. Oswald, was standing there, looking very concerned, as a strange man with a gun on his hip stood explaining something to him.

"Why the fuck is that pig here?" Darren whispered, evidently forgoing his conversation with Jay so he could try to find out what was going on too.

"I dunno, but be quiet so they don't hear us," the boys crept up towards the side of the glass doorway so they could get a better chance at listening in.

"No, Mr. Oswald, we have no leads whatsoever," the police officer shamefully shook his head. "This is an incredible act of violence. We haven't seen anything like this since 6 months ago at the Jeffey's home.

But rest assured we will have every man available on this one too."

"OH a lot of good that did last time, Mike," Mr. Oswald was obviously irritated. "What am I supposed to tell my students? How can I possibly break this to them?"

"I think it's best if you let it go for a bit. Say she's on vacation or had something come up," the officer replied.

The boys just looked at each other, not yet willing to believe what they were hearing.

"I do have to ask you a few questions though, Mr. Oswald. We have to try to get to the bottom of this as soon as possible. Cases like this have a better chance of getting solved in the first forty-eight hours. Now, was she well received at the school? I mean, did she have very many people that didn't like her? Maybe students she had failed, or jealous faculty members, anything like that?"

"No, not that I recall. She hadn't failed many people in the brief time she was here at the school. And she was one of the most popular amongst the faculty. I just can't believe this is happening. Has anyone broke the news to her father?"

"Her father? You mean old Mr. Davenport? The guy who lived next door to her?"

"Yes, Harold."

Darren's grip on Jay's triceps tightened as they both looked at each other in amazement. "No fucking way!" Darren tried to keep quiet as best he could.

"Well, as a matter of fact, no one seems to know where he is..." the police officer trailed off as he looked towards the hallway, seeing two shadows on the floor just outside the door. He nodded at Mr. Oswald to bring his attention to the fact that their conversation was not being kept private.

Jay sensed the lull in the conversation and grabbed Darren's shoulder to get him to follow him before they got caught eavesdropping.

"No way, I'm not fuckin' leavin'," Darren tried to whisper although his excitement was doing it's best in preventing him.

"We gotta get outta here Darren, they are gonna catch us."

Mr. Oswald's footsteps clicked the tile floor of his office as he made his way to the entrance. He looked back at the officer and waved him over to the doorway. "No one's here Mike."

"Well I would just be careful who you go talking to about this. We have to try to do this thing as quietly as possible," the officer didn't seem interested in the old principal's findings.

"Holy fuck, dude!" Darren's eyes were bulging. "I cannot fucking believe this shit. Harold is Ms. Davenport's father! Oh my god!"

Jay wasn't thinking about what Darren was saying. His mind was on the conversation they had just overheard, but not on the part that engrossed Darren. He was walking swiftly down the hallway, shaking his head at the news the boys had just learned. His stomach tightened and he felt sick.

"Jay, why the hell aren't you saying anything?" Darren trotted to catch up to his disconcerted friend. "Hey, Jay. What the fuck, dude. Are you gonna say anything? How can you not be as baffled as I am right now?" Darren cocked his head, trying to get a read off of Jay's silence.

Jay stopped suddenly. He looked up and down the rows of brick red lockers that lined the hallway on both sides. No one was around. He knew he was going to regret this, but he thought it was time to tell Darren. He had a right to know. He thought he could keep this secret all the way through their final two years, since Ms. Davenport showed up, but upon hearing the news that they just had, he knew it was time. He was going to need all the help he could get.

"What's up?" Darren pressed, his voice laced with frustration.

Jay took a deep breath, looking directly at his friend. "Darren, I gotta tell you something, but you have to promise me you're not gonna say a fucking word." His voice was low but firm, the tension between them thick.

Darren's expression shifted from confusion to curiosity. "Dude, what the fuck? If you don't want me to say anything, I won't. Relax."

Jay could feel his heart pounding in his chest. He had kept this secret for too long. "Darren, Ms.

Davenport... she was Will's sister. Well...half sister"

Darren's face twisted in disbelief. "What?! Are you serious?"

Jay nodded. "I've known for a while, but I couldn't tell anyone. Will made me promise."

Darren just stared at him, speechless for once. The hallway around them seemed to grow quieter, the buzz of the fluorescent lights fading into the background as the gravity of Jay's revelation settled over them.

"Holy fuck," Darren finally muttered, running a hand through over his stubbly hair. "This is so messed up."

Jay nodded, his shoulders sagging. "I know, man. This shit is crazy. But we better get back to
George before he has a heart attack"
"But how..." Darren started.
Just as Jay and Darren reached the top of the stairs, George came bursting onto the landing. His face was flushed, his breathing heavy, and his hands were braced on his knees as he tried to catch his breath.

"Where the fuck have you two been?" George gasped, his voice strained.

Darren smirked, glancing back at Jay. "We just had to talk. Why, Tubby, you miss us?"

George shook his head, still panting. "No, it's not that. Amy just called me," he gulped some air, giving Darren time to look at Jay and roll his eyes. "She said there are a ton of police cars outside Ms. Davenport's house."

Jay and Darren froze, the casual banter between them forgotten as George's words sank in.

Jay's pulse quickened, and his stomach turned. "Police cars?"

"Yea," George replied, standing up straight, his face still red. "She didn't say much else, just that something big was going down. There are at least four cars out front."

Darren and Jay exchanged a glance, the tension between them ratcheting up. They realized that the eerie conversation they had overheard earlier was not something that could be kept quiet for long.

Jay swallowed hard, trying to keep his voice steady. "Darren, we gotta tell him." His mind was already on Will, and whether he could get to him before this news did.

Darren nodded reluctantly, his eyes flicking to George. "Yeah, okay," he muttered. "George, we overheard something in the principal's office earlier. Something about Ms. Davenport." George's eyes widened, and he leaned in, clearly alarmed. "What did you hear?"

Jay took a deep breath, trying to steady himself before explaining. "We heard the principal talking to a cop. It sounds like something happened to Ms. Davenport. They didn't have all the details, but...it's bad."

"Bad? Like how?" George's voice was rising, his panic evident.

"They don't know for sure yet, but they think it's like what happened before...," Darren added quietly, his voice tense.

George's face went pale, and he took a step back, his eyes darting between his two friends. "You mean...like a murder?"

Jay nodded grimly, his heart heavy with the weight of what they had just heard. "We don't know all the details yet, but we're going to find out."

George's eyes widened with fear. "Do you think it's the same-?"

"There's no way to know that!" Jay interrupted him abruptly. "We don't know anything yet. But we have to find out. I have to go to Will's to get answers."

"Jay...what the fuck?" Darren pleaded. "Why the fuck do you have to keep going over there, man?"

"We need answers, Darren! I don't know where else to look, ok?" Jay's anger flared as his words lashed out.

"Dude...I just don't know why you have to keep going there alone. What do you think you're going to find?" Darren continued to plead with his friend.

"I don't know. But I have to try," Jay's tone calmed. He knew his friend was right. The last few attempts to talk to Will had not ended well. It was almost like the outside world was trying to keep him from getting to the truth. A truth he was worried would be buried too deep to uncover by the time it came to light.

"Whatever, man. I just don't think any of us should be doing anything alone until we know for sure what is going on," Darren added.

"I won't be alone," Jay said, matter of factly. "Will will be there."

Darren paused. He looked at George for help, who sheepishly looked away, offering no help. "I know, Jay," Darren finally relented. He knew that this was a futile argument. He knew how stubborn Jay was, and that no matter what, he was determined to find answers. If this was the only way he thought he could do it, he had to support him.

"You want me to go over there with you?" Darren offered, his voice more subdued now.

"No, it's alright," Jay replied quickly, waving off the suggestion. "I need to do this alone. I think it'd be better that way." He didn't want to say too much in front of George, who was now looking back and forth between them, clearly confused by the undercurrents of tension he couldn't quite grasp. Plus he knew that he would have a better chance with Will if he was alone. Considering all they had between them.

The bell rang, signaling the end of lunch, and the sound of shuffling feet and chatter filled the stairwell as students began to flood the halls. Jay felt a momentary sense of relief at the distraction, grateful for the break in the conversation.

"Fine," Darren said, clearly not satisfied but willing to let it go for now. He started down the next flight of steps, his sneakers squeaking against the linoleum. "I'll call you later. I gotta get to gym. Come on, Georgey. We can't afford to be late for fat-ass Mazzullo's class again."

"Fuck that guy," George muttered, turning to follow Darren, his backpack swinging as he made his way down the steps, leaving Jay standing alone in the stairwell.

Jay lingered for a moment, staring at the empty hallway before him, the sound of his friends' footsteps fading into the distance. His mind was racing, the weight of the day's revelations pressing down on him like a heavy stone. He knew he had to talk to Will about Ms. Davenport, had to tell him what had happened. But would he be able to get to him before the news did?

What is he hiding? Why hadn't he answered any of his calls? Jay wondered, his chest tight with uncertainty. The more he thought about it, the more questions arose, each one more unsettling than the last.

He sighed, knowing there was nothing he could do about it now. He would have to wait, play it cool, and hope he could get some answers from Will later. For now, he decided to go through the rest of the day, keeping his head down and trying to act casual—just another day in the life.

As the hallways filled with students rushing to their next classes, Jay turned and made his way to his locker, his thoughts heavy. He still had to pick up his tuxedo after school with Jen. He just hoped that afterward, he would have enough time to talk to Will...alone.

Chapter 9

Jen had gotten up even earlier than her usual five-thirty alarm time. She knew she was only taking a half-day today, but her excitement was too overwhelming to let her sleep. It was as if she were a young girl again, staying awake in hopes of catching a glimpse of Santa Claus on Christmas Eve. She sat at the half-desk, half-makeup dresser that Jay had made her for their anniversary the previous year. Her boyfriend was always handy, often crafting things with his father in their garage and gifting them to Jen as surprises. Though he was terrible at keeping secrets when it came to things like that, she cherished every one of his creations.

She decided she wasn't going to bother with her hair today since the girls had appointments at Legacy's to get it done together at noon. Although they hadn't all grown up together like the boys had, the girls were very close, especially Jen and Emily. They had been best friends since eighth grade. Jen was very surprised when Emily started dating Darren. She never thought it would last, knowing Darren as well as she did and recognizing his reputation for running through girls like they were trophies to be collected. Despite considering Darren a friend, she warned Emily about him. But that didn't stop Emily. She was convinced she could change him. "All for show," she would say. "Besides, he's really hot!"

Amy had always been a friend of theirs, but she became closer after she started dating George, another complete shock to Jen. She always liked George and thought of him as a big teddy bear. He was always very nice to her, and she knew he was a good person inside. However, she couldn't see what Amy saw in him as a boyfriend. Jen wasn't superficial, but she couldn't get past George's exterior enough to date him. Still, she was happy for them, seeing how they had found each other.

Liz, on the other hand, was never really close with any of the girls. Jen often wondered what Will saw in her, besides the obvious: Liz was very pretty and had a reputation for being somewhat loose with the guys at school. Jen had never really gotten to know her well before the tragedy with Will's family, and since then, Liz and distant from everyone. Liz acted like she was one of the girls when they were around, but Jen knew it was a façade. Jen hoped that would change this weekend, allowing them to put everything behind them and focus on having a good time for a change.

Jen usually didn't wear much makeup, so she decided to put on her usual amount. Even if the weather messed it up, she knew she'd get it redone after her hair appointment. She loved it when Jay told her she looked most beautiful without any makeup, with her hair undone, and dressed in a hoodie and jeans. Inside, she felt butterflies, even if she would just roll her eyes and tell him to "shut up." She knew he meant it, and it made her feel good.

She took off Jay's football jersey that she always wore to bed. He didn't get all the attention that Darren got for his athletic prowess, but she thought he was just as good. She turned on the bathroom light, connected to her room. When she was thirteen, Jen whined incessantly to her father until he finally gave in and built her her own bathroom. She turned on the water for her morning shower. She could never understand how people could go through their day without a morning shower. It wasn't just to clean up but to wake up. Jen was not a morning person and was known to hit the snooze button repeatedly until she felt ready to start the day, which drove Jay crazy. She turned the water to her normal temperature. The knobs had worn a groove from being set in the same position for so many years. She closed the curtain and sat on the toilet to the left of the sink.

She began thinking about the night to come and how it would all play out. She hoped the rain would stop, at least for a while, so they could take their pre-dance pictures. The constant storm that had riddled the town for what seemed like forever showed no signs of letting up, and Jen worried it might ruin her perfect evening.

Besides talking about her wedding since she was a little girl, her prom was her next favorite event to imagine. She always wondered how their pictures would turn out, hoping they would be their best yet. She kept an album of pictures of her and Jay since they started dating and planned to continue it in college, as they were going to the same school next fall.

She wondered who would be voted what for their senior class. She hoped that she and Jay would be crowned king and queen again, but she also secretly hoped to get some other type of individual award. She had never received one, always sharing her awards with Jay. Her other friends always got them, and Jen wanted to feel what it would be like too. Maybe "most likely to succeed," although if anyone were to get that, she figured it would be Jay. She knew Darren was probably a lock for "most athletic" and "best eyes," which he would likely talk about all weekend. "Best style" would probably go to Emily, as she was the trendiest person Jen knew.

Jen switched her thoughts to the previous day and how strangely Jay had acted while they picked up his tuxedo. He told her it was nothing, but Jen knew him better. She knew something was bothering him and was hurt when he wouldn't reveal what it was. She thought it might be that she hadn't fully supported his theory about Will and the car that caused their accident. But how could Will have anything to do with that? After all this time? It worried her that someone would do something like that to Jay, but she didn't want to let him see her concern, so she let it go. Still, something was on his mind yesterday, and it was beginning to scare her.

She stood up and entered the shower from the back to ease herself into the relaxing water. She didn't usually take long showers, not as long as most girls her age. She was always ready to go in less than a half-hour if Jay asked her to be.

After she finished in the bathroom, she re-entered her bedroom with her baby blue towel tightly tied around her torso. She usually let her hair dry without wrapping it in a towel. She looked at the dress hanging in the corner of her room and smiled. This was going to be the best night of her life, and she couldn't wait. Her dress was a low-cut, strapless red that had a silky feel to the

touch. Her only hope was that her breasts would hold it up throughout the night. After getting it properly fitted at the shop with the girls, she knew it would be fine. She stood in front of the mirror, holding the dress tightly to her body and swaying her hips back and forth, mimicking the motions she would perform later that night. She smiled at her reflection, blushing as if someone had just caught her embarrassing herself. She walked back to the corner and hung the dress up. She was so excited about the evening that she didn't want to wait any longer. She wanted to get her half-day of school over with and start making arrangements for her night. Jay teased her about her elaborate plans, telling her she was putting too much emphasis on one night and going through hours of preparation. He knew how important this was to her and wanted to make it as close to her dreams as possible, but he still thought it was a little too much.

Jen leaned over and opened the top drawer of her dresser. She picked the first bra she saw and let the towel drop, revealing her naked body to the empty room. She clasped her bra on and rummaged deeper in the drawer, pulling out a thong and slipping it up her legs. Her mind was still battling between her excitement for the night and her worry over her boyfriend. Her reflection in the mirror gave a blank stare as she put on a pair of mesh shorts over her thong. Suddenly, her phone started ringing from the table next to her bed, snapping her out of her trance. She took one more look in the mirror and shook her head at herself for being so jumpy. As she reached for her phone, she felt a cold chill creep down her back, almost as if a huge draft had swept through the room, begging her not to answer. The phone stopped ringing as soon as she touched it on the table. She wondered who would be calling at this hour as she picked up her phone and opened it. The caller ID read "unknown."

"Hmm," she wondered aloud, setting the phone back on the table. As she turned toward her empty room, she heard a loud crash coming from downstairs. The sound was not the normal crack of thunder she had grown accustomed to in the past weeks. This was different. Her eyes doubled in size as her chest tightened with fear. She debated whether she should investigate the sound or not. She grabbed the tank top that was thrown over the chair on her way out of the room. "It's probably just a branch or something. This goddamn weather better let up," Jen told the empty room, trying to calm herself more than anything.

As she reached the doorway to her room, she felt another familiar chill and tried to shake it off. She sheepishly made her way to the stairs. The entire upstairs had hardwood floors except for her room, which was carpeted in her favorite shade of blue. With each step, the boards of the old house seemed to groan at her, pleading with her to stop and retreat to the safety of her room.

Around this time, the sun would normally just be starting to come over the horizon, yet the clouds that had enveloped the town for the past two weeks blanketed the house in a gloomy darkness, only overmatched by the random bolts of lightning that briefly ignited in a flash of fluorescent light.

Random bolts of lightning briefly lit up the room in sharp, jagged flashes of fluorescent light. Jen gripped the banister tighter, her bare feet hesitating with each step down the cold wooden stairs.

The steady drumming of rain on the roof mixed with the pounding of her heart, a rhythm that echoed in the silent, empty house. Every instinct told her to turn back. She knew it was silly—childish, even—but something about the stillness below made her skin crawl.

Her thoughts flashed back to Jay. He had been acting strange, more on edge than usual, and now, after all his warnings, here she was, feeling that same creeping unease.

Another bolt of lightning crashed outside, followed by an immediate, bone-rattling clap of thunder. Jen inhaled deeply, trying to steady her breathing, but the storm outside seemed determined to test her nerves. The downstairs was swallowed in darkness, an oppressive void she could barely make out as she crept along the wall, her hand trailing the familiar ridges of the paint. It felt different this time, though. This time, the house felt like it was hiding something.

She stepped into the family room, shivering as a cold breeze washed over her skin. The rain was louder now, like a drumbeat hammering at the walls. For a moment, it felt as though she was standing outside, in the middle of the storm. Her fingers fumbled for the light switch by the entrance, but her hands trembled too much to land on the right spot. She'd lived in this house her entire life; why did it feel so foreign now?

Her fingers finally found the switch. She flicked it up.

Nothing.

Darkness. The chandelier above her remained cold and unresponsive, a shadow against the ceiling.

A flicker of lightning. Just enough to illuminate the room for a fraction of a second. That was all she needed to see the window—shattered, glass glittering on the floor like ice in the pouring rain.

Jen froze, her breath catching in her throat. Her chest heaved in short, panicked bursts, and her grip on the doorframe was the only thing keeping her upright. The window stared back at her, an open wound in the house. Jay had been right. She should have listened. The storm outside seemed to be creeping in, inching its way toward her through the broken glass. All of this suddenly felt too real.

She kept her eyes trained on the window, every muscle in her body tense. Something was out there—something had done this. She started to back up, pressing herself against the wall, her heart thudding in her ears, her skin cold from the fear gnawing at her. She had to get upstairs.

She turned, ready to sprint up the stairs to the safety of her room. But the moment she made her move, her foot caught the lip of the first step. The fall was fast, a jolt of pain shooting through her leg as she crashed to the floor. She scrambled to her feet, pulse racing, her breath quick and shallow. The noise she had made was too loud—it had to have alerted whoever—or whatever—was out there.

She lunged for the stairs again, this time crawling up them, each step a frantic, desperate push toward safety. Almost there. Almost safe. She allowed herself a faint, relieved smile, shaking her head at how irrational she was being.

But then she felt it. A hand on her shoulder. Firm. Unmistakable.

Jen screamed, a sharp, terrified sound that echoed up the stairs. She tried to run, to pull away, but her body refused to cooperate. She crumpled to the floor, tears stinging her eyes as her breath came in shallow, panicked gasps. It was too late.

"Jen!" A voice. A familiar voice. Through her sobs, she heard it again. "Jen, relax...it's me."

Emily. She was standing over her friend, only visible in the brief strobe of lightning from outside. Her expression was a mix of confusion and concern. "What is wrong with you?" Emily crouched down, reaching to help Jen to her feet.

"I...I..." Jen stammered, still shaking, her limbs like jelly.

"Are you OK?" Emily asked, her voice softer now, finally realizing just how rattled her friend was. She knelt down and wrapped her arms around Jen, holding her as the tears fell freely. "All this stuff is really starting to take a toll on us, isn't it? But it's going to be OK. This weekend, we'll get away from all of this. We need to let loose."

"Em, I heard something down here..." Jen began, pulling back, her voice trembling.

"It was probably the storm, Jen." Emily's tone was gentle, but there was an underlying edge. "It's crazy out there. I don't think it's going to let up by tonight."

"No, you don't understand!" Jen interrupted. "Look!" She pointed frantically at the broken window, her voice shaking.

Emily followed Jen's finger, squinting in the dim light. Water streamed in through the shattered glass, pooling on the floor. Shards of glass glistened, reflecting the sporadic lightning from outside.

"Maybe the wind blew a branch or something..." Emily trailed off, her voice uncertain.

"No... I heard something!" Jen grabbed Emily's shoulders, her eyes wide. "I was upstairs, and I got a phone call from an unlisted number. Then I heard the window break! I don't know what's happening, but I'm freaking out, Em."

Emily glanced back at the window. "Yeah...maybe we should just go." Her voice cracked slightly, mirroring the unease that Jen felt. She couldn't quite dismiss the feeling that something was wrong.

The girls ran upstairs, grabbed Jen's things, and bolted outside. The rain came down harder than ever, drenching them as they sprinted to Emily's car, the sound of the storm deafening. Jen's stomach churned as they pulled out of the driveway her fingers frantically attempting to call her father through the trembles. She couldn't shake the feeling that someone—or something—had been watching her from the shadows of

that house.

George's excitement was palpable as he approached the jeep, his wide grin beaming with pure anticipation. The boys were glad they got to skip their first class of the day and take their time getting to school. A Prom Day tradition of laziness! "I can't believe it's finally here!" he exclaimed, his voice bubbling over with enthusiasm, barely contained.

"Just get in, fat ass!" Darren shot back with a grin, nudging Jay. The rain beat steadily on the roof of the jeep, the rhythmic pounding matching their growing anticipation. "I can't believe we're even going to school today," he added, turning to Jay, who sat quietly in the front seat, the weight of the day already settling on his shoulders. "We could definitely get away with ditching today."

Jay shook his head, the usual responsibility gnawing at him. His fingers drummed against the steering wheel, but his mind was elsewhere—on Will, on the dance, on what had happened to Ms. Davenport. "If you don't at least show up to school on the day of the dance, you can't go. You know that."

"Yeah, well that's a bullshit rule," Darren muttered, then yelled back at George. "George, would you get in the fucking car!"

George, struggling with the door handle, yelled back, "I'm trying! The door won't open! Unlock the door! Come on...it's pouring out here!"

Darren's laughter filled the jeep as he watched George fumble. The tension in his voice eased slightly as he teased. "Hahahaha. Look at him out there! What a weirdo!" "Just unlock the door," Jay said, his patience fraying.

As George finally lunged into the backseat, drenched from the downpour, he panted, "Holy shit.

Are you sure we're gonna be OK this weekend?"

"We'll be fine. Can you ever relax?" Jay reassured him, backing the jeep down the driveway, the wipers working overtime against the sheets of rain battering the windshield.

"Yeah, man, you're gonna give yourself a heart attack getting worked up like this all the time," Darren added with a smirk, though there was an edge in his voice.

"They said that the site is secluded. We'll be fine," Jay said, his voice a bit more firm this time. But as he turned onto the main road, the uneasy knot in his stomach twisted tighter.

The rain hammered against the roof, a constant drumming that mirrored his rising anxiety. Darren, lowering his voice, leaned closer. His tone shifted, tinged with concern. "Did you get your answers last night?"

Jay glanced into the rearview mirror at George, who was rummaging through his bag in the backseat. "No, I had to go with Jen to get my tux. Then we went out to eat. By the time I got done, it was too late to go over there."

"Ok?" Darren's question hung in the air, loaded with worry.

"I dunno, Darren. I don't know what to do, ok?," Jay admitted. His grip tightened on the wheel as the nagging doubts clawed at him. Why hadn't Will picked up the phone?

Darren's frustration boiled over. "Well, what the fuck?" His voice grew louder, causing George to look up from his bag, eyes wide with curiosity.

"Nothing, Slim," Darren replied, snapping back into his usual teasing mode. "I think I dropped a

Snickers back there the other day. Why don't you go on a hunt?"

"Fuck you!" George shot back, but he couldn't help sneaking a quick look, even though he knew Darren was just messing with him.

Jay tried to focus on the road, but his mind was miles away—on Will, on Ms. Davenport, on the strange events swirling around them. As they turned onto the road leading to the school, his thoughts drifted to the moment he would have to tell Will about Ms. Davenport. How could he tell him that she was gone? Even though they weren't particularly close, she was still Will's only remaining family. The idea of watching his best friend go through more grief made Jay's stomach churn.

Darren's voice sliced through the murk of his thoughts. "What the fuck is going on? What the fuck are all these people doing here?"

Jay looked up, his eyes narrowing at the scene ahead. Television news vans lined the parking lot like vultures, reporters and cameramen jostling for position under their umbrellas. The swarm of activity around the school was unnatural, unsettling.

His stomach dropped. He knew why they were here, and Darren did too. They had all hoped to keep things quiet, just as Mr. Oswald had promised after yesterday's conversation.

Jay pulled into his usual parking spot, the rain pattering relentlessly on the roof. The moment he stepped out, a thick knot of dread settled deep in his gut. The girls pulled in right behind them as the boys began piling out of the jeep.

"What's going on?" Jen asked, her eyes scanning the chaotic scene before her as she gave Jay their usual morning kiss.

"I don't know," Jay murmured, shooting Darren a knowing look. The tension between them was palpable—he could tell Darren felt it too. "What's going on with you?" His gaze dropped to Jen's face. Her eyes were puffy, and her smile didn't reach them.

"Oh, nothing. I'm fine," she insisted, though her voice wavered slightly. But Jay wasn't convinced. He could sense something was off.

"Let's go see what we can find out," Darren said, tugging on Emily's hand as they headed toward the camera crews.

"Are you sure you're OK, Jen?" Jay held her back from the group, his concern growing. The rain wasn't the only thing weighing on his mind now.

"Yeah, it's nothing, babe. I'll be fine," she insisted again, but Jay could hear the fragility in her words. She was hiding something, but he knew better than to push her right now.

The group finally made their way through the cluster of umbrellas and reporters. The air was thick with tension, a sense of foreboding hanging over the school grounds. The same police officer they had seen yesterday in Mr. Oswald's office was now giving a statement in front of the crowd. "...early yesterday morning. At this time, we do not have any suspects, although we are looking for her father, who right now is just a person of interest. His name is Harold Grimes. He works here at the school as well, and we have been unable to reach him..."

Jen nudged Jay in the ribs. "Who are they talking about?" she whispered. "Who's Harold's daughter?"

"Hold on," Jay hushed her, his full attention locked on the officer's words.

"...again, Ms. Rebecca Davenport was found early yesterday morning in her house. Police showed up when they got a call from Executive Principal Oswald that Ms. Davenport had not shown up and not called in to work. He also informed us that her father had not done so either, which was extremely out of character for both of them. We sent a squad car out to her residence, and that is where we found the body. Like I said before, we do not have any suspects at this time, although we are looking for her father, Harold Davenport. The only thing neighbors

reported seeing out of the ordinary was a black SUV parked all night a few houses down. If anyone has any information about the whereabouts of Harold Davenport or any info about the reported SUV, please contact the police department immediately. Thank you."

The reporters surged forward, shouting questions, but the officer swiftly moved away, heading for the group of officers standing nearby. Mr. Oswald stepped forward to try and manage the press. "That's all we have right now. I'm sorry, but the officers are not able to discuss any details of the case with you at this time. We will let you know anything as soon as we find out, but right now I have a school to run, so please, that will be all for this morning."

Jay's mind raced as he watched the scene unfold. His eyes scanned the group of officers, trying to piece together any hints. He couldn't shake the feeling that something was missing—that there was more to the story than they were letting on.

As he swept his gaze over the crowd again, something caught his eye—a white Grand Am idling near the edge of the school's private road, its windows as black as midnight. A chill crawled up his spine. He recognized that car.

"Will!"

Before his friends could react, Jay darted away from the group, racing toward the car. His feet pounded against the wet pavement, his heart slamming against his ribcage. He approached the crowd at a dead sprint, running into a cameraman and nearly knocking him onto the pavement. In what took a mere moment was enough for Will's car to disappear as if it had never been there. Jay's blood boiled.

"What the fuck?" he gasped for air, bending over with his hands on his knees.

"Yo, what are you doing, bro?" Darren's voice came from behind him. Jay hadn't even realized Darren had followed him.

"I saw Will," Jay said, his voice hoarse. "I saw him..."

"Come on, man," Darren muttered, frowning. "You gotta be kidding me."

Jay's head snapped to face Darren, his pulse still racing. "What do you mean?"

"Just come here."

The boys walked back toward their friends, who had just been joined by Amy. Jay tried to mask his unease, hoping his sudden sprint hadn't raised any suspicion. He forced a smile as they approached the group. "What's going on, babe?" he asked Jen, his voice soft but concerned.

Jen was breathing heavily now, her face pale and her eyes wide with fear.

"Tell him what you told us," George urged, seemingly oblivious to the tension in the air, his words casual despite the situation.

Jen took a shaky breath, struggling with every word as her chest rose and fell rapidly. "This morning... before Em got there..." She hesitated, looking directly at Jay. "Someone was in the house. I mean, I never saw anyone, but I know someone was there, Jay!"

Jay blinked, his mind racing. He had been so caught up in his own problems—his worry about Will, the SUV, Ms. Davenport—that it hadn't even occurred to him that harm could come to Jen.

The revelation hit him like a punch to the gut, and with every word, his anger simmered. Someone had crossed the line. This wasn't just about him anymore.

"...and then, when I looked across the room, the window had been shattered, and the rain was pouring in," Jen continued, her voice breaking as she spoke. Her eyes were glassy, and Jay could see the fear etched across her face. He didn't even realize his fists had clenched until his knuckles turned white.

Without thinking, he pulled her close, his arms wrapping protectively around her. "It's OK now, baby," he whispered into her ear, kissing the top of her head. "Nothing's going to happen to you while I'm here." But even as the words left his mouth, he wasn't sure if he believed them.

Darren stepped forward, placing a hand on Jay's shoulder. "Maybe we should rethink this whole weekend, Jay," he said quietly, his voice tinged with concern. "I mean, with everything going on..."

"No!" Jen's voice broke free, her sudden outburst startling everyone. She pulled away from Jay's arms, her determination cutting through the tension. "No... I am not letting this ruin it for us! No way! There is no chance!"

"But Jen, we have to at least think about it..." Emily tried to interject, her voice more measured.

"No!!!" Jen snapped, her insistence growing. Her eyes were ablaze with a fierce determination. "I am not letting that happen! Maybe it was just a coincidence. Maybe I'm just being paranoid or something, and I just need to relax. It coulda just been the storm, like you said, Em."

"Yeah guys, come on... we can't cancel now," George chimed in, his usual playful tone returning, but it only earned him a sharp glance from Darren.

"George, honestly..." Darren cut him off with a glance, trying to silence his whining.

Jay's head swirled with thoughts, each one vying for attention. His friends' voices grew distant as they bickered back and forth. His mind replayed Jen's familiar words—someone had been in her house. Someone had shattered the window. He could feel the anger bubbling again, but this time, it felt like it was going to explode.

He took a deep breath, trying to pull himself together. "Listen, let's just go on as planned for right now," he finally said, holding up his hand to stop Darren's protests. "For right now," he emphasized, his voice firm. "Jen, you do not go back to your house today, OK?" His tone shifted, the weight of his authority cutting through the cool morning air.

"I won't," Jen nodded, her voice steadier now. "My dress is in Em's car. I don't need to go home for anything else today..." She trailed off, suddenly realizing something. "Except my bags for the trip. Oh no!"

"Don't worry about that. I took those last night after I left your house. It's fine," Jay smiled, trying to reassure her. He had anticipated her forgetting, knowing her too well. The small moment of normalcy, of predictability, helped calm him—if only for a second.

"OK, good..." Jen's mood lifted slightly, her face softening as she clung to the reassurance.

"I need you to do me a favor though," Jay added, his expression growing serious again. "I need you to write me a note."

"A note?" Jen raised an eyebrow, confused.

"I'm skipping class," Jay admitted. "And you know how it is—your handwriting is better than mine when it comes to forging a note from my mom."

Jen opened her mouth to protest, but Darren cut her off. "I'm going with you," he declared firmly.

"Don't even try to say no. Whatever you have planned, I'm going!" "Darren..." Jay started, his tone wary.

"No... there is no way you're doing anything alone!" Darren interrupted, his voice rising.

"Going where?" George piped in, his confusion growing. His eyes darted between his friends, clearly missing the full weight of what was happening.

"I'm not letting you out of my sight right now, bro," Darren insisted, stepping closer to Jay. His jaw was clenched, and Jay couldn't tell if he was genuinely concerned for him, or if he was accusing him of something.

Jay sighed. "You need to stay with the girls," he figured playing on Darren's ego was the only way to get him to agree. He lowered his voice to a whisper, "You know George can't handle this shit. You need to be with them. You need to make sure they're ok."

Darren knew Jay had a point. George was a giant teddy bear. Almost afraid of his own shadow. He knew that if the girls were going to be safe, he had to be with them. "What about Liz?" he questioned.

Jay hadn't realized she wasn't a part of the group. "I'll find her." "I don't like this, Jay," Darren's eyes narrowed.

"I know, me either," Jay admitted. "I hate it. But I'll be fine. Trust me." He sounded like he was trying to convince himself more than Darren.

"Just be careful, babe. Please. We don't know who we can trust right now," Jen whispered, holding onto Jay's hand. Her eyes glistened, a fresh wave of fear rising within her.

"There's nothing to worry about, Jen," Jay said, though his voice was confident. He pulled her in for one last hug, whispering softly, "We'll be fine."

"Let's go inside before we draw any more attention," he announced to the group.

Jay walked into the school, taking the umbrella from Jen and giving it a firm shake, sending droplets flying. He wiped his feet on the soaked carpet mat at the entrance. His mind was racing, already fixated on the conversation he was about to have with Will. Today was going to be a day he would never forget, and not in a way he could look forward to. He tried making small talk with George as they walked, but it was half-hearted, meant only to calm George's worry and distract him from the whirlwind of thoughts swirling in his own mind.

Everything felt disconnected—he barely registered the fact that one of their teachers had been killed, that there were police around, and the press swarming the school. All that mattered was the truth, and he was going to find it.

Who was stalking them? Why?

His thoughts briefly flicked to Will. Did Will even know about Ms. Davenport? Did Will know more than he had let on? The bell rang for first class, snapping Jay out of his reverie.

Today, of all days, class would be nothing but a blur.

Jay gripped the steering wheel as he sped down the rain-slicked road, his knuckles white against the leather. The rhythmic thumping of the wipers barely cut through the pounding storm outside, but inside the Jeep, it was eerily quiet—except for the argument playing out in Jay's head.

"I told you I'm handling it," Jay muttered under his breath, his jaw clenched. "I didn't fucking ask for your help, Darren." His eyes darted toward the empty passenger seat as if expecting to find Darren sitting there, glowering at him like always. But of course, there was no one. Just Jay, alone.

"What, you think I don't know what I'm doing?" Jay snapped, his voice rising as though Darren had just accused him of something. "You don't think I've thought this through?" He exhaled sharply, shaking his head. "You never understood. You think everything is just black and white, like I'm supposed to just let this shit go. But you weren't there. You didn't see what I saw."

The Jeep swerved slightly as he clenched the wheel tighter, his pulse quickening. "Of course I didn't tell you. You don't get it, Darren. You never did. You'd just fuck it all up, like you always do." His words were dripping with venom, the anger bubbling over. "I don't need you questioning everything I do."

He slammed his foot down harder on the gas, the engine roaring in response as the Jeep barreled down the road. Rain streaked across the windshield, the wipers struggling to keep up, but Jay barely noticed. His mind was locked in the argument, his heart racing.

"And what do you even know about Will, huh?" Jay continued, his voice rising, almost shouting now. "You think you're so fucking smart. You don't know what's going on! You don't know him like I do. You never did." His chest heaved as he forced the words out, his gaze flickering again to the empty seat beside him. "I told you… I told you I'd handle it."

For a moment, the only sound in the Jeep was the pounding rain and the roar of the tires on the wet pavement. Jay's breath was coming in shallow, ragged bursts, his pulse thudding in his ears. The world outside blurred into a streak of gray, the storm swallowing everything in its path.

"Goddamn it, Darren," Jay growled through clenched teeth. "You don't get it. I have to do this. You don't see what I see." His eyes narrowed as he leaned forward, his hands gripping the wheel even tighter. "Will's just confused, that's all. He's got shit to deal with too, and you don't know what that's like. You'd just make it worse."

Jay's head jerked to the side as if he was listening to Darren's imagined response, his brow furrowing in frustration. "No, I'm not letting it go," he snapped. "I have to see this through. Will's the only one who understands. He's the only one who knows what really happened."

A sudden, hollow laugh escaped his lips, filling the Jeep with a brittle, unsettling sound. "You think I'm losing it?" he barked, his voice filled with mockery. "You think I don't know what's real?" His eyes widened as he stared out at the road, his mind racing, the accusations echoing louder in his head. "Fuck you, Darren. I'm not crazy. I'm not."

The windshield wipers thumped rhythmically, the storm outside raging harder, but inside, the air was thick with tension. Jay's mind spiraled, memories flashing in fragments—Will's house, the SUV, Ms. Davenport, the shattered glass in Jen's house. It all felt disconnected, like pieces of a puzzle he couldn't quite fit together.

He slammed his hand against the steering wheel, his voice cracking. "Will's not involved. He couldn't be! You think I haven't thought about that?" Jay's voice trembled now, the doubt creeping in. "He's my best friend... He wouldn't... He couldn't..."

His breathing grew heavier, and his hands shook against the wheel. "But then why didn't he tell me about Ms. Davenport?" he whispered, almost to himself. "Why wouldn't he just say something? It doesn't make sense..."

Jay's grip loosened slightly as his mind reeled, a sense of unease settling deep in his gut. He glanced at the empty passenger seat once more, his expression softening for just a moment, as if looking for reassurance.

"You don't get it, Darren. None of this makes sense," Jay muttered quietly. "But I'll figure it out. I just need to talk to him... I just need him to explain." His voice trailed off, almost pleading now. "I need to know what's really going on. I'm not losing my mind. I'm not."

The storm raged on outside, but inside the Jeep, Jay's world was spiraling out of control. The lines between reality and his imagination blurred as he sped toward Will's house, his mind fraying at the edges, the shadows of doubt creeping in.

"I'm not crazy," Jay whispered one last time, but even he didn't sound convinced.

Darren sat on the edge of the bench outside the gym, staring at his phone. Jen walked over, her brow furrowed, and sat down beside him.

"Any word from Jay?" she asked, her voice edged with worry.

Darren shook his head, sighing. "Not yet. He's been going to Will's place a lot lately. You'd think he'd want to talk to one of us about it by now."

Jen bit her lip, glancing at Darren. "Yeah, I don't get it either. It's...not healthy, right? I mean, after everything that's happened." She hesitated, choosing her words carefully. "He's been really distant with us."

Darren's eyes narrowed as he leaned back, resting his arms on the back of the bench. "Yeah, it's weird. I don't know what he's looking for over there." He lowered his voice, glancing around to make sure no one else could hear. "But every time he comes back, it's like he's more wound up. Something's eating at him, and I'm starting to think it's worse than we realize."

Jen nodded, her fingers twisting the strap of her bag nervously. "I know...I've noticed it too. He doesn't talk about it, but I can tell something's changed. It's like he's hiding something. Do you think it's just the accident, or...is it more than that?"

Darren rubbed his face, looking frustrated. "It's gotta be more than just that. He was never this messed up before." He paused, staring at the ground for a moment before speaking again. "I think he feels guilty or... I dunno, like he's still looking for answers. But why go over there? There's nothing left to find."

Jen looked at Darren, her concern deepening. "Maybe he's holding onto something. Or someone." She glanced down, as if weighing her next words. "Do you think...maybe Will has something to do with all this?"

Darren tensed, shifting uncomfortably. "I don't know, Jen. I mean, Jay's convinced there's more to what happened...but if there is, he should be coming to us. Not locking himself away, running off to Will's like that."

"I just don't want him getting caught up in something he can't handle," Jen whispered, her voice strained. "I can't shake the feeling that it's all connected...whatever happened back then."

Darren nodded, but his eyes were distant. "Yeah, same. Whatever it is, we need to figure it out before he does something he regrets."

"Jesus, it's been forever," Jay muttered to himself as he stepped out of his Jeep, the rain hammering down relentlessly, soaking through his jacket in seconds. He had parked just down the street from Will's house, hoping the rain would let up a little, but the sky seemed determined to drown the town. He stared at the house, his thoughts a swirl of confusion, guilt, and anxiety. He had to get answers, but the closer he got, the more uncertain he became.

His mind was a battlefield, racing between the events of the past few days—Ms. Davenport's death, the SUV, Jen's fear—and the nagging questions about Will. Jay had always trusted him, but now, doubt gnawed at him. He needed to confront Will, but he dreaded what he might find out.

Jay finally made his way to the door, shaking the water from his hair. His hand hovered over the doorbell for a moment, hesitation creeping in. He had rehearsed this conversation a hundred times in his head, but now that he was here, face-to-face with the possibility that his best friend might be involved in something terrible, he wasn't sure if he was ready.

He rang the bell. Nothing. He rang it again, the shrill sound cutting through the rain. Still nothing. Jay felt his heart pick up speed, anxiety turning his stomach into knots. He pounded on the door this time, harder than before, the hollow sound echoing in the quiet neighborhood.

Finally, after what felt like an eternity, the door creaked open, revealing Will. He stood there, his face half-shadowed in the dim light, his hair damp as if he hadn't bothered drying it after being caught in the rain earlier. There was something off in his expression—a mix of exhaustion and something Jay couldn't quite place.

"Jay?" Will's voice was low, a hint of surprise in it. He blinked at him as if seeing him for the first time in days. "What're you doing here?"

Jay swallowed hard, forcing himself to stay calm. "Will, we need to talk. I have to get some things straight. Can I come in?"

Will hesitated for a second before stepping aside and letting Jay in. The air inside the house felt cold, heavy. Jay glanced around the living room, which looked the same as it always had, but somehow, the familiarity of it made the tension worse.

They walked into the room, and Will sank into his usual spot, lighting a cigarette and leaning forward, elbows resting on his knees. He looked at Jay with a tired expression, his eyes red-rimmed and puffy as if he'd been crying. The sight of his friend's disheveled state hit Jay hard. Was this about Ms. Davenport? Or had Will been dealing with more than Jay knew?

Jay cleared his throat, unsure of how to start. "Will... I don't even know where to begin, man." His voice wavered, betraying the nerves he tried to suppress. "I need to know what's been going on."

Will raised an eyebrow, taking a long drag from his cigarette. "What're you talking about?"

"Everything," Jay said, his words tumbling out in a rush. "The SUV... the accident... the other night when I came by, I saw it parked in your driveway. I know it's the same one that chased me through the park. And now, with Ms. Davenport... it's all connected somehow, and I have to know if you know anything about it."

Will's face darkened, his expression turning defensive. "Jay, I told you before, I don't know anything about any SUV." His voice was sharp, his patience clearly wearing thin. "You're chasing ghosts, man. I didn't even see it. I don't know why it was there."

Jay's heart sank, but he pressed on. "I'm not accusing you of anything, Will. I just need to know what's going on. Something's off, and I'm trying to piece it together. I'm not saying you're involved, but if you know something, anything, you have to tell me."

Will exhaled slowly, smoke curling around him like a protective barrier. He didn't answer right away, staring at the floor as if deep in thought. Finally, he shook his head. "I don't know what to tell you, Jay. I'm not hiding anything."

Jay clenched his fists, frustration bubbling to the surface. He wanted to believe Will, but the pieces didn't fit. "Will, come on. You've been acting weird. And now, with what happened to Ms. Davenport... I mean, you know, right?"

Will's eyes flicked up to meet Jay's, a flash of confusion crossing his face. "What about Ms. Davenport?"

Jay felt a lump form in his throat. He hadn't wanted to bring this up like this, but there was no turning back now. "Will... she was found dead yesterday morning. Murdered."

The words hung heavy in the air, the silence that followed almost deafening. Will blinked, his expression unreadable. He didn't react the way Jay expected—no shock, no anger, no grief. Instead, he just stared at Jay, his face blank.

"She's... dead?" Will repeated, his voice flat.

Jay nodded, trying to gauge his friend's reaction, but Will's expression remained unsettlingly neutral. "Yeah. They don't have any suspects yet, but they're looking into it. Will, this is serious. And I'm worried about you."

Will leaned back in his chair, his fingers drumming against the armrest. "Huh," he muttered, almost to himself. "I barely knew her, you know? She was my half-sister, but we weren't close."

Jay's stomach twisted. He had expected more emotion, more... something. But Will's detached response left him feeling cold. "Will, it's OK to be upset about this. You don't have to act like it doesn't bother you."

Will shrugged, taking another drag from his cigarette. "I don't know, Jay. I guess I just don't feel much of anything these days."

The words sent a chill down Jay's spine. This wasn't the Will he knew—the guy who used to be so full of life, so protective of his friends. Something had changed in him, something deep.

Jay sat forward, his heart pounding in his chest. "Will... I need you to be straight with me. Are you in some kind of trouble?"

Will's eyes flicked toward him, narrowing slightly. "What kind of trouble are you talking about?" Jay hesitated, choosing his words carefully. "You know what I mean. I'm talking about the SUV, the accident, everything that's been going on. I just need to know if there's something you're not telling me."

Will shook his head, a small smile tugging at the corner of his mouth. "You're overthinking this, man. There's nothing going on."

Jay stared at him, searching for any sign that Will might be lying, but he found none. His friend's face was calm, composed—too composed. "Will... I don't know if I can believe you."

Will's smile faded. "I told you the truth, Jay. There's nothing more to say."

Jay stood up, his heart racing. He couldn't shake the feeling that something was terribly wrong, but he didn't know what else to do. "Are you still going this weekend?" he asked, desperate to shift the conversation away from the growing tension.

Will nodded. "Yeah. Liz and I are heading up early to set things up. You guys will meet us there,

right?"

Jay hesitated, glancing at the map on the coffee table. Something about this trip felt wrong now, but he couldn't back out. "Yeah. We'll be there."

Will stood and walked Jay to the door, his expression softening slightly. "It's gonna be good, man. You'll see. We'll clear our heads and get away from all this shit."

Jay forced a smile, though his gut twisted with doubt. "Yeah. I hope so."

Will clapped him on the shoulder, a fleeting gesture of familiarity that felt hollow now. "See you up there, Jay."

Jay nodded and stepped out into the rain, his mind spinning. As he climbed into his Jeep, he couldn't shake the feeling that Will wasn't telling him everything. And as he drove away, the pit in his stomach only grew deeper.

Jen, Emily, and Amy decided to drag Darren and George out with them while Jay searched for his answers, hoping to distract themselves from the recent turmoil. They gathered at their usual hangout, a cozy local café nestled on the corner of Maple and 3rd, where the warm lighting and soft hum of conversation always seemed to ease their minds. Despite the rain pattering persistently against the windows, inside the café was a world away—soft amber tones reflecting off polished wood tables, the air thick with the scent of freshly brewed coffee and baked pastries.

Jen sat closest to the window, watching the raindrops streak down the glass, her fingers idly tracing patterns on her latte cup. Emily, across from her, absently stirred her own drink, the clinking of the spoon oddly soothing.

"I can't believe everything that's happening," Emily said, her voice low as if afraid of breaking the temporary peace. "It's like we're living in some sort of nightmare."

Darren and George sat in silence. This was not a comfortable environment for them. George needed Amy to decipher the menu for him. And after finally being convinced that he would like a scone, even though it sounds like a disgusting word, he sat down and relinquished the attention.

Darren, on the other hand, was taking it all in. Something wasn't sitting right with him. Something wasn't making sense. He sat in his chair, observing.

Jen's lips pressed into a thin line as she nodded, her expression troubled. She had tried to keep up appearances all day, but inside, she felt like she was unraveling. "I know... It's been really hard to focus on anything else. I barely slept last night."

Amy, always the one to keep the group grounded, chimed in with a gentle smile. "Well, let's not let it ruin our day. We have the dance tonight, and we need to enjoy ourselves." She reached across the table, squeezing Jen's hand. "We all deserve a break."

Jen managed a smile in return, grateful for Amy's steady presence. Emily nodded, her shoulders relaxing slightly as the tension eased out of the group. The café's warmth seemed to cocoon them, and for a brief moment, the outside world faded away.

They spent the next hour dragging Darren and George while they did some browsing through last-minute accessories and trying on earrings and necklaces, laughing over old inside jokes that managed to lift their spirits. The rain poured on outside, but inside, the girls created a bubble of lightheartedness, refusing to let the weight of their worries steal the entire day.

Darren even lightened up when he got to put some earrings up to George and make him pretend to be a pretty princess. That got a laugh from everyone, even a few patrons at the store.

"Remember the summer we all went to the lake and had that huge picnic?" Emily mused, her smile returning as she remembered. "It feels like forever ago."

Jen's laugh bubbled up, genuine this time. "Oh my gosh, yes! And George ate almost the entire watermelon by himself. We had to drag him away before he devoured the whole thing!"

Amy grinned, shaking her head, poking George's belly. "He's always been like that. It's amazing he hasn't turned into a watermelon by now."

They all laughed, the memory a brief and much-needed escape from the heaviness that lingered over them. As they strolled through the mall, the rain continued its relentless beat on the rooftop, but the girls felt lighter, if only for a while.

Passing by a small jewelry shop, Jen paused, her eyes catching on a display of delicate bracelets. "Let's get something to remember tonight by," she suggested, her voice bright with excitement that had been missing earlier. "Something small, like a charm or a bracelet. You know, something to mark tonight."

Emily and Amy exchanged a look and nodded, smiling. They all knew this night would be important, not just because of the dance, but because of everything they had been through together.

They spent the next half hour in the shop, carefully selecting matching bracelets—dainty silver chains with tiny charms that glittered in the dim light. As they fastened the bracelets around their wrists, a sense of unity settled over them. It was more than just an accessory; it was a promise that no matter what happened, they would face it together.

As Jay drove, his mind wandered back to happier times. He remembered a summer day a couple of years ago, when he, Will, Darren, and George had spent the entire day at the lake. The sun was shining, and their biggest concern was who could make the biggest splash from the diving board.

It was one of those perfect summer days where the sky was a brilliant blue, dotted with the occasional fluffy white cloud. The heat of the sun was tempered by a gentle breeze that rustled the leaves of the towering oak trees surrounding the lake. The water sparkled like a thousand tiny diamonds, inviting and refreshing under the scorching sun.

The boys had arrived early, eager to make the most of the day. Jay could still hear the sound of their laughter as they raced to the water's edge, each trying to be the first to dive in. George, with his larger frame, had predictably been the last, but he made up for it by cannonballing in with such force that he drenched them all with a tidal wave of water.

"Man, George, you're gonna empty the lake!" Darren had laughed, shaking the water from his hair.

"Just trying to cool you guys off," George had retorted with a grin, floating lazily on his back.

Will, always the daredevil, had climbed up the rocky outcrop that jutted out over the deeper part of the lake. He stood there for a moment, silhouetted against the sky, before executing a perfect dive, slicing through the water with barely a splash.

"Show-off!" Jay had called, though he couldn't help but admire Will's grace.

After swimming for a while, they had spread out a blanket on the grassy shore and dug into the lunch they had brought. George, of course, had outdone himself with his double-decker sandwiches, each one packed with enough meat and cheese to feed a small army. They had feasted like kings, washing everything down with ice-cold beers from the cooler.

As they lounged in the sun, their bellies full, the conversation had turned to their plans for the future. Darren, ever the dreamer, had talked about becoming a professional athlete, while Will had shared his aspirations of traveling the world. George had been more practical, discussing his desire to open a restaurant one day. Jay had listened, soaking in the camaraderie and dreaming of his own future, though he hadn't yet decided what it would be.

"Hey, let's play water polo!" Darren had suddenly suggested, jumping to his feet.

The idea had been met with enthusiastic agreement, and soon they were dividing into teams.

The game had quickly devolved into a chaotic splash fight, with more laughter and shouts of mock outrage than actual play. Will had surprised everyone by scoring the winning goal with a spectacular underwater maneuver, popping up behind Darren and tossing the ball into the makeshift net formed by their cooler.

Exhausted but happy, they had sprawled out on the blanket again as the sun began its slow descent towards the horizon. The sky turned shades of pink and orange, the colors reflecting off the still surface of the lake. It had been a perfect end to a perfect day.

"Remember that time we stayed out here until it got dark?" Will had asked, his voice a soft murmur in the gathering dusk.

"Yeah, and we made a campfire and told ghost stories," Jay had replied, smiling at the memory.

George had chuckled. "And Darren tried to scare us all with that dumb story about the lake monster."

"Hey, it wasn't dumb! You were the one who screamed when a fish brushed against your leg!" Darren had protested, laughing.

As the first stars had begun to appear in the sky, they had reluctantly packed up their things and headed home, each of them carrying a sense of contentment and the feeling that they had just experienced something special.

Back in the present, Jay felt a pang of nostalgia for those simpler times. The weight of recent events pressed heavily on him, but the memory of that perfect summer day gave him a moment of solace. He longed to recapture the carefree joy of those days, hoping that somehow, they could find their way back to that place of untroubled friendship and happiness.

As he turned onto the road leading to the school, Jay made a silent vow to himself. No matter what it took, he would protect his friends and restore the sense of peace that had been shattered. He glanced at the passenger seat, imagining Darren sitting there, lost in his own thoughts. They had been through so much together, and Jay was determined to see them through this as well.

The memory of that summer day lingered in his mind, a beacon of hope and a reminder of what truly mattered. With renewed resolve, he parked the jeep and stepped out into the rain, ready to face whatever challenges lay ahead.

He wouldn't let the darkness creep any further into their lives. Not if he could help it.

"Those were the days," he murmured under his breath, the bittersweet smile still lingering on his lips. But those days weren't gone—not yet. He would fight to protect them, to bring back that sense of unbreakable camaraderie. No matter what it took.

Chapter 10

The flashes of Mrs. Galentino's camera almost rivaled the lightning that cracked through the dark, rain-streaked windows. Inside the cozy living room, the group of friends forced smiles, their expressions a poor mask for the tension that pulsed beneath the surface. The air buzzed with a discomfort that even their parents' cheerful encouragement couldn't shake.

Jen was making small talk with everyone while they waited for Jay to finish getting ready. It wasn't like him to take such a long time, but she knew he was under a lot of pressure lately. And still sore from the accident. She imagined herself entertaining the guests as if she were the hostess at a dinner party while they awaited his Royal Highness to grace them with his presence. The thought made her giggle to herself.

Jay finally strolled down the stairs. He looked like he had just gotten out of the shower and forgot to dry himself off before putting his tuxedo on. Jen went over to him to fix his hair. "Hey, baby! Everything OK?" she asked.

"Yea, all good," Jay panted.

Why was he out of breath? This whole week had really taken a toll on him. Jen was wrestling with the thought of cancelling everything and just watching a movie with everyone at Jay's house. At least they would all be safe! But she knew how much the prom meant to all of them. There's no way anyone would go for it.

"OK," she winked at him. Something was off with him. With all of them. She told herself it would be OK once the night got underway. She gave him a kiss and led him in with the others.

Darren leaned in close to Jay between the rapid-fire bursts of the camera. "What are we gonna do?" he whispered, his voice strained but low. "Are we really goin' up there tonight?"

Jay barely turned, his smile faltering only for a second as he gently rubbed Jen's back. "Why wouldn't we?" he asked, his voice calm but firm, his eyes fixed on the camera lens as his mom snapped another photo.

"Bro, I'm freaked out. This is serious."

"I told you, we have nothing to worry about." Jay's jaw tightened, but his voice remained steady.

"Whatever, man. We'll talk later."

Jen's ears caught the hushed exchange. Her eyes flicked between Jay and Darren as she tried to make sense of their tension. She'd been asking Jay about their trip ever since arriving at his house, but every time, he brushed her off with a casual "It's fine." She wanted to trust him, but her body betrayed her, still trembling from that morning's scare. She tried to hide it, but Jay always knew when something was bothering her. She had suggested they cancel the trip after the dance, but Jay wouldn't hear of it—insisting that getting away was the perfect remedy for their frayed nerves.

"Smile, Jen!" Mrs. Galentino's voice broke through Jen's thoughts, pulling her back to the present.

"Oh, sorry," she muttered, flashing a quick, apologetic smile toward the camera.

Finally, after a few more forced poses, the group started to loosen up. Darren insisted on a goofy picture of George and Jay hoisting him into the air like a Persian princess, which sent the girls into fits of laughter. For a brief moment, the tension in the room seemed to dissipate, replaced by the excitement of the night ahead.

"I wonder what they're serving for dinner," George said as they piled into the limo, shutting the door with a soft thud as rain continued to drum against the roof.

"Of course you do!" Darren teased, drawing more snickers. "I just wanna know if me and Em are gonna beat the Great Galentinos for king and queen!"

"Oh, stop it," Emily swatted his arm playfully, her laughter warm but laced with mock seriousness. "Besides, you know we'd never beat the First Couple of Northstar." The group erupted in laughter, exaggeratedly bowing toward Jay and Jen.

"Whatever," Jay rolled his eyes, but the warmth of their teasing pulled a smile from his lips.

The rain continued to pour relentlessly as the limousine made its way through the soaked streets toward the school. Inside the car, the mood shifted between excitement and lingering unease. The girls, still fussing over their slightly damp hair, shared light-hearted banter while George was busy predicting what would be served for dinner.

"I hope they have steak," George declared, running a hand over his stomach as if anticipating the meal. "Maybe some lobster, too. You know, a proper prom feast."

Emily leaned over, rolling her eyes playfully. "You and your stomach. What are you gonna do when you're king and too full to dance?"

"I'll manage," George grinned. "Can't let a full belly stop me from being the best dancer in the room."

Darren gave him a side-eye. "You mean the worst."

The group laughed, and the sound felt like a small moment of normalcy amidst everything else going on. Even Jay, who had been quieter than usual, cracked a smile. The limousine's interior lights flickered on as they approached the school, casting warm glows on their formal attire. It was almost time to put everything else behind them, at least for tonight.

Jen glanced out the window at the rain streaking against the glass, trying to keep her own apprehension hidden beneath the surface. She still couldn't shake the tension from earlier in the day, and Jay's evasive attitude wasn't helping her nerves. She wondered if he was thinking the same thing, though she hadn't dared ask again.

Bill Oswald hated Prom Night.

It was, without a doubt, his least favorite of all the duties that came with being principal at Northstar High School. The night was always filled with teenagers dancing far too provocatively, sneaking alcohol or drugs past the chaperones, or disappearing into bathrooms to indulge in behavior he didn't want to imagine. It was the one night he truly despised his position, knowing full well that behind the dresses and tuxedos, students were up to their usual antics—just dressed fancier.

Tonight, though, his usual irritation was laced with something deeper. There was a gnawing unease in his stomach, a tension that had been growing since the news of Ms. Davenport's murder. Rebecca, a beloved teacher, had been found dead, and her father, Harold Davenport, a longtime faculty member, had gone missing. Bill couldn't get the image of Rebecca's lifeless body out of his head, nor could he stop wondering about Harold. Had Harold done the unthinkable? He didn't want to believe it, but there was a tiny, dark part of him that whispered maybe.

Bill had known Harold since their school days at Northstar, though they were never particularly close. Harold had been quiet, keeping to himself most of the time. They had remained acquaintances over the years, nothing more. When Harold had come to him for a job all those years ago, Bill hadn't hesitated, but he'd never really gotten to know the man on a deeper level. Still, the thought of Harold being capable of something so heinous made Bill feel sick. And now, Harold was missing.

He stood in his bathroom, staring at the fogged mirror, the mist from his shower clinging to every surface. He ran his hand across the glass, clearing a patch just wide enough to see his reflection, though the steam quickly began creeping back. He had been trying to shave, but his hand trembled with a tension he couldn't shake. The water from the shower rained down into the empty tub, hot and steady, but the warmth of the room did nothing to ease the chill that had settled deep in his bones. His thoughts drifted through the day's events—students mourning, whispers in the hallways, the storm outside adding a fitting backdrop to the gloom that had settled over his school.

The shower hadn't helped. It never did these days. There was too much on his mind, and the water did nothing to wash away the anxiety. He stepped out, wrapping the towel around his waist, and stood in front of the mirror again, absently wiping away the mist once more. His thoughts wandered to Rebecca Davenport. She had been one of the most respected and adored teachers at Northstar. A bright, kind woman, loved by her students, admired by her colleagues. And now she was gone. Taken violently, too soon. The thought of it made his stomach churn.

He dried himself methodically, his movements almost robotic. His house was spotless, as always. Everything was meticulously placed. The white walls and sparse decor made his home feel more like a sterile environment than a place to unwind. It was how he liked it. His obsessive-compulsive tendencies had always been a part of him, a fact that drove his mother mad when he was younger. Everything had to be in order. That's how he maintained control—over his home, his job, his life.

And yet, tonight, it felt like everything was unraveling.

Was it a mistake to have let the prom go on? Maybe it was in bad taste, with Rebecca's death so fresh. But what was the alternative? To cancel it and let the students stew in their grief and confusion? He had made the call, and now he had to live with it. The kids needed a distraction, something to take their minds off the tragedy. He repeated this to himself like a mantra, but it didn't settle the knot in his gut.

Wrapping the towel tighter around his waist, he padded out of the bathroom and into his bedroom, where the low murmur of the television filled the room. CNN, as always, giving updates on some political scandal or economic downturn. He paid it no mind. The rain lashed against the windows in steady waves, a constant reminder of the storm raging outside, one that seemed to mirror the chaos in his head.

His house was eerily quiet, save for the occasional boom of thunder in the distance. Bill couldn't shake the feeling of unease that had crept in. He walked over to the bed where his clothes were laid out—black slacks, a crisp white shirt, and his jacket. As he began to get dressed, he heard a faint noise coming from downstairs.

It was subtle, almost swallowed by the storm, but distinct enough to catch his attention. The sound of footsteps? No, it couldn't be. The doors were locked. He had checked them before heading upstairs. The sound came again—soft but deliberate, as if someone were moving cautiously across the kitchen floor.

Bill stood frozen for a moment, straining to listen. His mind raced through possibilities—was it the storm playing tricks on him? He wasn't sure, but an inexplicable chill crawled up his spine. Something didn't feel right.

"Calm down," he muttered to himself, shaking his head. He was being paranoid. He knew it. But even as he told himself this, his feet carried him toward the bedroom door. He couldn't shake the feeling that something was wrong.

The rain battered the windows harder now, and the wind howled outside as Bill made his way downstairs. The hallway was dim, and the shadows seemed to flicker with each flash of lightning. As he reached the bottom of the stairs, another sound reached his ears—a creak, like the groan of a floorboard being pressed under weight.

Someone was there.

His heart rate spiked, and his breath quickened. The cold tile floor of the kitchen felt like ice beneath his feet as he crossed the room, his eyes darting toward the back door. Locked. Just as he'd thought. The windows were closed, too. No sign of a forced entry. But there, near the door, a puddle of water glistened on the floor, a dark, irregular shape that hadn't been there before. The rain? No. It looked like...footprints.

Cold sweat broke out across his skin.

He fumbled for the light switch beside the door and flicked it on. Nothing. The house remained cloaked in darkness.

"Perfect," he whispered sarcastically.

A flash of lightning illuminated the kitchen for a brief second, casting long shadows that twisted and danced along the walls. Bill's mind raced. He wasn't imagining things. He was sure of it now—someone had been here. Someone was still here.

He turned, intending to grab a flashlight, but before he could move, the sound of heavy footsteps echoed from the basement. His blood turned to ice. Bill stood rooted in place, his eyes fixed on the basement door. The footsteps were deliberate, methodical, growing louder with each step.

With every ounce of courage he had left, Bill moved towards the basement door. His hand hovered over the doorknob, hesitating. The pounding in his chest was deafening, but he couldn't back down now. Slowly, he turned the knob and pulled the door open.

The darkness below seemed impenetrable, the faintest outline of the stairs barely visible. He swallowed hard and took a step forward, descending into the unknown.

The first thing he felt was the dampness in the air. It clung to him, heavy and suffocating, as he made his way down. His foot caught on something slippery, and he stumbled, catching himself on the railing.

And then, out of the shadows, a figure moved.

Before Bill could react, the man was on him—tackling him to the floor with a force that knocked the wind from his lungs. Bill gasped, struggling to push the man off, but the figure was too strong. He clawed at the slick floor, trying to gain traction, trying to get away, but it was no use. The figure loomed over him, silent and menacing.

"What do you want?" Bill gasped, his voice barely audible over the storm. The figure said nothing.

In the dim light, Bill caught a familiar glimpse of a face—covered by a hood, obscuring all features. But there was something chilling about the emptiness beneath it, as if the hood itself was a void, swallowing all light and hope.

The blade came next, gleaming briefly in the darkness before plunging into Bill's chest with a sickening thud. Pain exploded through his body, white-hot and all-consuming. He tried to scream, but only a gurgle escaped his lips as blood filled his throat.

His vision blurred, the shadows closing in around him. The figure above him stood still, watching as life drained from Bill's body. The last thing he saw before the world went black was the blade, dripping with his blood, gleaming in the faint light from the basement window.

And then, nothing.

"What the fuck, bro?" Darren followed Jay closely as he tried to escape his friend. "We have to talk about this."

"Talk about what Darren? There's nothing to talk about! Everything is going to be fine" "Bullshit! You know there is, man. Don't try to hide from this shit," Darren persisted.

"Look...I know shit is really weird. I get it. Hell,I admit...I was a little sketched out too...but what are we supposed to do?"

"Look man...I don't know about you...but I know exactly what the fuck we should do!" Darren responded harshly as the two reached the table that had been set out to display all of the drinks.

"OK Darren," Jay said sarcastically. He reached for a can of soda that was in a cooler on the table. He never understood why every sitcom or teenie bopper TV show always made references to a punch bowl. And people always spiking it. In all of the dances that he had gone to over the years, he had never once seen a punch bowl. Although if there ever was a punch bowl, he wouldn't put it past Darren to spike it.

"I'm just saying...something don't feel right, bro," Darren said taking a look around before pulling out his flask and filling a cup of ice halfway with alcohol. "I just don't know, man. That's all I can say. I got a vibe."

"Oh, you've got a vibe," Jay laughed. He could tell that his friend was nervous and he really couldn't blame him. After the way Will had acted earlier that day, he was on edge as well. But after all, Will was their best friend. And at least he was talking now. So maybe he was a little different. Isn't that to be expected considering everything that had gone on? Wasn't he allowed to be a little 'off'?

"You're telling me you're completely OK? There's nothing going on?" Darren continued his interrogation.

"No," Jay admitted reluctantly. "Like I said, I was a little sketched out too. But what are we just going to just not go? Just call and say something came up?" Jay didn't want to admit that the thought had crossed his mind as well. Will had given him his word. And Jay didn't have a reason to doubt that.

Darren bit the inside of his lower lip as he pondered what Jay had just said. He knew that Jay was right. He imagined the thought of calling Liz to tell her they weren't going to meet up with her. Still he couldn't shake the uneasy feeling. Something was eating at him. It was something that he couldn't describe. He had tried to talk to

Emily about it, but she was so wrapped up in the dance that she hadn't really paid much attention to his rant. Besides, they had all looked forward to this weekend for so long. It would be kind of silly to let it go just because he got a weird vibe from one of his best friends.

"I guess. I'm just really freaking sketched out," Darren finally spoke up as he poured half a can of cola into the cup. He was concentrating so much on his conversation with Jay that he hadn't even noticed George walk up behind them. "I mean I guess we should go. I dunno tho..." he trailed off.

"Don't know what? If we should go where?" George stammered. "I knew you were gonna do this shit!" he began, sounding like a five-year-old pouting in the toy store.

"Whoa, calm down," Darren pleaded.

"No," George continued, hyperventilating in protest, "Everything has been set and now you're talking about not going..."

"You don't even know what we're talking about, Georgey," Darren responded, trying to soothe his friend's worries as best he could.

"Yeah, George," Jay tried to chime in, "don't even worry about it." He did not want to have to explain everything to their friend. As excited as George was for this trip, he knew that all it would do is upset him and get him to start worrying and having anxiety.

"Bullshit...I heard you," George looked like he was going to cry.

"Dude, relax, we're going!" Darren looked at Jay for support.

"Yeah, George. Darren's just being a bitch. Let's just go back to the table and get some food." Jay didn't even give George an opportunity to protest any further. He led the way back to the other side of the room, weaving through the maze of tables that were spread out, unevenly on the gymnasium floor. The boys had the discussion earlier that evening how the cliché Proms were always at some fancy place, off school grounds, while their dump of a school had theirs in the first-floor gym. They laughed at Darren's ramblings that you could dress it up as much as you want, at the end of the day, it was still a gym.

The boys got back to the table as the girls were just getting back from their fourth group trip to the bathroom together. Jen snapped a picture of Jay with her phone as she yelled, "Say cheese!"

Darren leaned over George's shoulder, "don't worry bro, I'm not letting anything mess this up," he whispered as he walked around his friend and put his arm around Emily's waist. He looked back at George and gave him a wry smile and a wink.

George just shook his head and mouthed the words, "fucking pervert" to his friend.

The group sat down just as dinner was being served. They talked about how there wasn't as much actual dancing at their last dance of high school as the other dances. It felt more like a banquet than anything else. They were being served baked chicken and ziti with a side of steamed vegetables and dinner rolls. It was a pretty bland dinner, but George was happy with it. He tried to slow down his eating in front of Amy, but he still finished before everyone else in the group.

Small talk engrossed the table as dinner wore on. Jay felt a slight sense of relief come over him. He figured that Darren was finally done with his persistent nagging. He could finally start to enjoy the night. Although he couldn't help his own doubts from creeping to the forefront of his mind. He knew he was right about them still going on the trip. There was no reason for them to change things up on account of everything that had gone on that week. In fact, he was pretty sure that going away was the exact thing that would help the situation. That getting out of town for the weekend would allow the weird vibe to pass, and they could actually concentrate on enjoying themselves instead of living in the constant shadow of fear and doubt that had clouded this past week for all of them.

"Alright...well I gotta go freshen up for my acceptance speech," Darren announced to the table. Dinner was just about done and the ceremonies for Prom King and Queen were set to take place at the conclusion of the dinner.

"Yeah, I might as well go too," Jay ignored his friend's arrogance as he stood up with Darren to go to the bathroom. The girls all stood up as well, not letting another opportunity pass to go have girl talk in the ladies' room. George didn't want to be left alone so he took one last bite of Amy's chicken and stood up as well.

"I'll meet you back here in a little bit my King," Jen whispered in Jay's ear as she gave him a kiss on the cheek. She strolled off to catch up with the girls as Jay watched her. He couldn't believe how beautiful she looked tonight. It never ceased to amaze him how absolutely gorgeous his girlfriend really was. He considered himself to be the luckiest out of all of his friends.

He started walking in the other direction with Darren and George towards the men's locker room. It really was kind of a disgrace that they were using the locker rooms as restrooms for their prom, but it didn't bother the guys. They never really got caught up in trivial things like that, but the girls were disgusted at the idea, thinking that they deserved better.

"So you really think you got a shot, huh?" Darren playfully pushed his friend's shoulder, the sharp contrast between the ominous feelings brewing in their minds and his outward joking unmistakable.

Jay responded with a laugh, shaking his head at his friend. They all knew that Jen and Jay were going to be crowned once again. It was inevitable. They were the "it" couple—Northstar's golden pair. But Darren couldn't help teasing Jay, if only to mask his own anxieties simmering beneath the surface.

As the boys made their way down the dimly lit corridor leading to the locker room, the atmosphere shifted. The dull thud of their footsteps echoed ominously against the cold walls. An all-too-familiar chill ran down Jay's back. He glanced at the metal lockers lining the hallway, their reflective surfaces catching occasional slivers of light and sending faint glimmers across the shadows.

The space felt wrong, as if the air itself was heavy with an unseen presence. Every slight noise was magnified, from the clicks of their dress shoes on the linoleum to the whispered echoes of their breathing. A shiver ran through them as they paused at the top of the stairwell.

"Ok, pussies...I'll fucking go first," Darren finally volunteered, a smirk on his face masking the rising tension in his voice.

Jay and George exchanged nervous glances but said nothing as they followed Darren down the stairs. The descent felt slow, the weight of dread pulling at their feet with each step.

"Take out your phone," Jay murmured quietly, breaking the stillness. "We need light."

"Yeah, man, I can't see shit," George added, his voice betraying his nerves as his eyes darted about.

"You two are fucking pussies," Darren muttered, fishing his phone out of his pocket and turning on the flashlight. The pale beam cut through the darkness, casting long, flickering shadows that danced across the walls. Even Darren, with all his bravado, seemed a little too eager to have the light on now.

The locker room entrance loomed ahead of them, a yawning black hole that seemed to swallow the dim light of Darren's phone. Something felt distinctly off. Darren hesitated, reaching out for the light switch by the door, flicking it up and down a few times.

Nothing.

The oppressive darkness remained, making the room feel even more claustrophobic.

"Okay...this is weird," George muttered, trying to steady his voice. A strange, metallic scent hung faintly in the air, almost masked by the locker room's usual musty odor. His stomach churned.

"What the fuck is going on?" Darren's bravado finally cracked, his earlier cockiness giving way to unease.

George's eyes darted to the floor, his voice trembling as he asked, "What is that?"

Darren directed his phone's light toward the floor, revealing what appeared to be a dark, viscous liquid pooling on the cold white tiles. At first, it was just a small, discolored spot, but as the light illuminated more of the floor, the boys' expressions darkened.

"That's fucking blood, dude," Jay whispered, a sense of urgency tightening his grip on his friend's shoulders.

Darren knelt closer, bringing the phone's beam to the liquid. "Holy shit," he breathed, the light catching the crimson smear. "Look... there's more."

George whimpered quietly, his voice barely audible. "We need to get out of here."

But they couldn't move. Their minds were racing—who could have done this? And why here, on this night of all nights? The other two leaned over Darren's shoulder, fixated on the trail of blood leading deeper into the shadows.

"What are we doing, man?" George pleaded, his breath quickening. "We need to get out, now."

"We have to see this through," Jay insisted, his voice steady. His heart pounded in his chest, but his curiosity outweighed his fear. The string of strange occurrences, Ms. Davenport's death, the SUV—it was all connected. He could feel it.

Darren pushed forward, following the blood trail into the locker room. The room felt alive with tension, the faint drip-drip of water from an old faucet adding an eerie soundtrack to their slow, deliberate movements. The locker room, usually familiar and mundane, now felt hostile, like something was waiting for them in the shadows.

"Goddamn it... what the fuck is this?" Darren whispered as the blood splatters became larger, more erratic. The narrow hallway led them to the tiled shower area where the trail of blood thickened. The smell of iron grew stronger, assaulting their senses.

George swallowed hard, the familiar sense of dread clawing at his throat. Every step brought them closer to an inevitable horror he could feel in his bones.

The boys paused before turning the corner into the first shower stall. The tiles gleamed faintly under the phone's glow, their shiny surfaces amplifying the sense of unease.

"What the fuck is going on?" George's voice cracked with fear.

The blood trail led to the far wall, where something—or someone—was slumped in the darkness. Darren inched closer, raising the light.

They all froze in place.

There, propped up against the tiled wall, was Mr. Oswald. His headless body was posed unnaturally, his arms arranged as if cradling something precious. And in his lap, his own severed head rested, the lifeless eyes wide open, staring back at the boys with frozen terror.

George's stomach lurched violently as Jay's mind raced to process the scene, but his body refused to move.

"What...the...fuck..." Darren's voice quivered, breaking the stillness that had enveloped them.

George staggered backward, his hand flying to his mouth as he struggled not to scream.

Jay's hands shook violently. He looked up and saw the words scrawled above the body in dark red blood.

"Who'z next..."

"What do we do?" George whimpered, panic seizing his entire body.

"Get the fuck out of here. Now," Darren hissed, finally finding his voice. His earlier bravado was gone, replaced by sheer terror. He snapped a picture with his phone, barely able to steady it as he captured the horrific scene.

The boys were sprinting down the dimly lit hallway back toward the gymnasium. The only light came from the erratic bouncing glow of Darren's phone, casting fleeting shadows along the worn linoleum floor. The cold air whistled through the corridor, prickling their skin as they ran.

Darren held back, choosing not to leave his friends behind, though his athletic frame could have easily propelled him far ahead. He figured they'd better stick together—strength in numbers.

George, a few feet behind, was gasping for air, his breath ragged and strained. The sound of his dress shoes slapping against the slick floor echoed like the erratic heartbeat of their collective fear. He was running purely on adrenaline now, his mind unable to process anything beyond the primal urge to escape the terror closing in around them.

Jay's thoughts raced just as fast as his legs. His mind fixated on the image of Mr. Oswald, the blood, the way the life had been ripped from his body in such a grotesque fashion. The memory of it gnawed at his senses, but he pushed it aside, trying to piece together the fragmented puzzle that had brought them to this moment.

They neared the heavy double doors of the gym. The muffled sounds of laughter and music leaked into the hallway, a stark contrast to the darkness they were fleeing. Jay's hand shot out, grabbing Darren by the arm, the fabric of Darren's suit jacket slick with sweat.

"Wait... we can't go busting in there," Jay gasped, struggling to catch his breath.

"Like hell we can't!" Darren snapped, jerking his arm free. His eyes were wild, adrenaline surging through him, urging him forward. George collapsed beside them, doubled over with his hands braced on his knees, greedily sucking in air as if it were the only thing keeping him from collapsing completely.

"We can't cause a scene," Jay insisted, his palm pressing firmly against Darren's chest, holding him back. "What if they're still here?"

The weight of Jay's words hung in the air like the oppressive storm outside. Darren hesitated, his pulse pounding in his ears. Jay was right. Whoever had done that to Mr. Oswald could still be nearby, lurking in the shadows, watching them. Darren's hands clenched into fists as he forced himself to stay still.

"Well, what do we do?" Darren asked, his voice tight with frustration.

"We gotta play it cool," Jay said after a moment, his breath still labored. "Act like nothing's wrong. We get the girls, and we get the fuck outta here." He said the words with finality, the curse adding an edge of urgency.

Darren's shoulders relaxed slightly, accepting the plan. "OK. What do we tell them?"

"I dunno... but we gotta do it quick." Jay threw a glance over his shoulder at the gym doors, then back at his friends. The distant sounds of prom night—the music, the laughter—were a dissonant reminder of the innocence they had just left behind. He stepped forward, pulling the heavy doors open slowly, careful not to draw any attention.

The gym was buzzing with energy. The crowd was restless, students shifting in their seats as someone on stage tried to restore order with a strained voice over the PA system. Jay led the way, weaving through tables draped in cheap plastic covers and half-empty cans. They moved like shadows through the room, their bodies stiff with tension. Jay glanced back to make sure Darren and George were following. Darren's face was a mask of concentration, while George, still sweating profusely, tried not to attract the curious gazes of their classmates.

When they reached the girls' table, Jay immediately grabbed Jen's arm, halting their conversation. His grip was firm but gentle, his eyes pleading. "We gotta go," he whispered, just loud enough for their small group to hear.

Jen looked up at him, confusion furrowing her brow. "What do you mean?" she asked, her voice soft but strained.

"I can't explain it now," Jay's voice was urgent, low. "Just... come with us." He extended his hand, his face pale beneath the dim lighting. The girls exchanged glances, uncertainty flashing between them. They could sense the tension, the urgency, but the announcement for prom court was about to happen—one of the most anticipated moments of the night.

Darren leaned toward Emily, his voice surprisingly soft. "Come on, baby... we really do have to go." George, still flushed, offered a trembling hand to Amy, though his eyes were distant, still haunted by what they had seen.

"Go where?" Emily snapped, her annoyance bubbling to the surface. "They're about to announce the court. Why would we leave now?"

"Please, baby," Darren's voice was gentle but firm, uncharacteristically so. His eyes locked onto hers, pleading for her trust.

Emily looked at the other girls, frustration clear in her expression. She didn't want to miss this.

She knew they weren't going to win King and Queen, but they were sure to be part of the court. Why leave without a good reason? Her patience snapped. "Are you kidding me?" she snapped, yanking her hand from Darren's grip.

Jen, however, was locked in a silent exchange with Jay. His eyes, filled with desperation, told her everything she needed to know. After a tense pause, she nodded, taking his outstretched hand. "Ok," she whispered, standing from her chair. The relief on Jay's face was instant, though the weight of their situation still hung over them like the storm outside.

Emily stood abruptly, her voice loud enough to catch a few glances from nearby tables. "Now you've got to be kidding me!"

"Babe... just settle down," Darren said, his patience wearing thin. "I'll explain everything in a little bit. We just REALLY need to go. Now."

Amy was already behind George, her eyes scanning his face, sensing the unease radiating off him in waves. She knew something was wrong, even if she didn't yet understand what.

Emily shot Darren a glare that could cut through steel. He was ruining one of the biggest nights of her life, and she would never forgive him for it. She stormed past him, leading the way out of the gym and into the foyer. She spun on her heel, demanding answers. "So what is so important, huh? Please, enlighten us as to why we just left one of the biggest nights of our lives!"

Darren ignored her, turning to Jay instead. "You think our driver is still here?"

"I hope so," Jay muttered, squeezing Jen's hand as they pushed through the gym doors and into the swirling storm outside.

Darren felt a wave of relief wash over him when he finally saw their limo pull up to the curb. The sleek black vehicle gleamed under the pale streetlights, the wet pavement reflecting its glossy exterior. He exhaled sharply, grateful that the endless barrage of questions would soon be interrupted.

But even as he moved toward the limo, a knot of anxiety tightened in his stomach. How in the world were they supposed to tell the girls the truth? The gruesome reality of what they had seen weighed on him like a stone. He glanced back at the girls, then at the limo, signaling them with a subtle nod that it was time to make a run for it. Jen caught his look and nodded in return, her eyes wide with a silent understanding.

The cold wind howled as they threw the limo doors open and sprinted through the driving rain.

The droplets hit their skin like pinpricks, soaking through their clothes in seconds as they dashed toward the car. The storm seemed to be gaining strength, as if nature itself was reacting to the terror they had just witnessed.

Jay was the first to emerge from the limo when it pulled up to his driveway. He barely waited for the car to stop before launching into a dead sprint up the slick, rain-soaked blacktop. His shoes slid slightly on the wet surface, but he kept his balance as he rummaged through his backpack for the house keys. His fingers fumbled clumsily over the zippers, slick with rainwater. He knew his mother would already be gone for the weekend. Mrs.

Galentino never liked being alone, and with Jay and her husband both gone, she had taken the opportunity to join her friends on a trip. The house was silent, waiting, with only the sound of the storm pressing against its walls. Behind him, the girls' muffled complaints filled the air, their voices shrill over the sound of the rain pounding the roof of the limo. Emily and Amy hadn't let up since they had left the school. What should have been a short, quiet drive had felt like an eternity,

Jay understood their frustration. After all, they had been yanked out of their senior prom with no explanation. He could sympathize, but the weight of what they had seen silenced him. Jen, on the other hand, had been surprisingly calm. It was as if she already knew what was at stake, even without being told. Her quiet presence was the only thing that had kept Jay grounded during the chaos of the ride. Every question from the girls had been deflected with the same vague promise, "We'll talk about it when we get back to my house." But even as he said it, he knew the words weren't enough to pacify them.

The group reached the side door of the house, the wind whipping at their soaked clothes. Jay violently swung the door open, the hinges creaking as the screen door rattled in the gusts. He held it open for the girls, who scurried inside, holding their small purses above their heads in a futile attempt to shield themselves from the downpour. The air inside the house felt thick, almost oppressive compared to the wild storm outside. The darkened interior seemed to echo with the weight of what they had just experienced.

George was the last to enter, his face pale and drawn. He had been silent the entire time, barely able to process the events that had unfolded. It was as if he were trapped in some sort of daze, frozen in shock. The image of their slain principal seemed to have burned itself into his brain,

refusing to let go. He followed the group into the house like a sleepwalker, his eyes wide with disbelief. He glanced at Jay, his expression one of helplessness—the most vulnerable Jay had ever seen him look.

Darren, standing by the door, gave Jay a knowing look as he held the screen door open, urging him inside. The unspoken exchange between them was brief but powerful. They both took a deep breath, steeling themselves for what was to come. Somehow, they had to find the words to explain what they had seen. But how? Neither of them had the faintest idea how to break the news.

As Jay stepped into the kitchen, he was hit by the overwhelming sense of guilt. He had spent the past week accusing Darren of being selfish, of meddling where he didn't belong. But now, standing in the quiet kitchen, shivering from the cold rain and the terror of the night, he realized how wrong he had been.

"So, is someone going to explain what the hell is going on?" Emily's voice cut through the heavy silence. Her mascara was running in dark streaks down her face, her frustration evident in every word.

Jay turned to face her, hesitating as he looked at her smeared makeup, the stress and fear etched into her features. "Look..." he began, walking toward the light switch on the wall. "I don't really know how to say this..."

"Just say it! What are you guys being so weird about?" Amy chimed in, her voice edged with impatience.

"It's just... not that easy to say..." Jay tried again, his voice faltering.

"Well, there better be a damn good reason..." Amy started, but before she could finish, Jen snapped.

"Shut up!" Jen's voice was sharp, her frustration boiling over. "Just shut the fuck up and let them
talk!"

Jay was momentarily stunned by his girlfriend's sudden outburst. He fought back a small smile that threatened to creep onto his face. Despite the chaos, Jen's fierce loyalty warmed him. He took a breath and continued, "We kind of saw something. Something bad." His voice was low, as though speaking the words aloud would make them too real.

He looked over at Darren, who picked up where he left off. "We knew you guys would freak out if we told you at the school..."

"I'm about to freak out right now!" Emily shot back, her glare fixed squarely on Darren.

Darren shifted uncomfortably but continued. "While we were going to the bathroom in the boys' locker room, we..."

The weight of what they were about to say hung in the air, thick and suffocating. The girls stood frozen, their eyes darting between Jay and Darren, desperate for answers.

"Mr. Oswald's dead," George suddenly blurted out, his voice flat and devoid of emotion.

The words hit the room like a sledgehammer. The girls spun around to face him, their eyes wide with shock. George's gaze was glued to the floor, his body rigid as if he were barely aware of what he had just said.

"What did you just say?" Amy asked, her voice barely above a whisper as she crouched slightly, trying to meet his vacant stare. But George refused to look up, his eyes remaining fixed on the floor.

"That's what we saw," Darren confirmed, turning the girls back around to face him. "He's dead."

"What do you mean, dead?" Jen's voice quivered as she looked at Jay, pleading silently for him to make sense of what they had just heard.

Jay swallowed hard. "We saw it..." he trailed off, exchanging a pained glance with Darren. The terror of the past week had finally caught up with him, crashing down like an avalanche. He didn't want to be the one to say it, but they deserved the truth. They had to know.

"Murdered," Jay finally whispered, the word hanging in the air like a dark cloud, sending a collective shockwave through the group.

The girls stood frozen in place, their faces drained of color as the gravity of what the boys had just revealed sank in. The kitchen, once just a simple backdrop of familiarity, now felt heavy with a new, oppressive weight. The cold air from the rainstorm outside still clung to their damp clothes, but none of them seemed to notice. It was as if time had slowed, the stillness in the room amplifying the sound of their ragged breaths. Each of them was too terrified to be the first to break the silence, their thoughts swirling in confusion and fear. Emily's lip trembled as the brutal reality started to take root in her mind, her eyes glossing over with unshed tears.

"What is happening?" she finally whimpered, her voice barely audible as the tears spilled over. Darren instinctively wrapped his arms around her, pulling her close in an attempt to shield her from the overwhelming fear. The warmth of his embrace was the only comfort he could offer as her body shook with quiet sobs.

After the initial shock passed, the group began to truly feel the implications of what they had learned. The tension in the room was thick, palpable. Jay and Darren moved to the forefront, standing protectively in front of the others as they huddled closely together in the dim kitchen. The room felt too small, too cramped under the weight of everything that had happened.

The rain continued to beat against the windows in a steady rhythm, like a persistent reminder of the chaos outside. George, who had been paralyzed with shock, seemed to stir from his daze and sheepishly joined the group. His face was pale, his movements slow and hesitant, but at least he was present again, however fragile that presence might be.

No one wanted to speak. The silence stretched out, filling every corner of the room like a dark, heavy fog. Jay knew he had to break it. The truth had to be faced, no matter how terrifying. He took a deep breath and looked around at the others, their faces pale and expectant.

"Look, we don't know anything right now..." Jay's voice was steady, though there was a subtle tremor beneath the surface. "All we know is that Ms. Davenport and Mr. Oswald are dead," he said, matter-of-factly, his fingers tapping against his palm to punctuate his words. The bluntness of the statement hung in the air like a cloud, impossible to avoid. "We don't even know if the murders are related at all."

Jen's voice broke the silence, cutting through the tension. "How could they not be?" she asked, her tone carrying the weight of the obvious truth. Her mind flashed back to the strange events earlier that week, the creeping sense that something had been terribly wrong. She had been so relieved when Emily had come over to the house that morning, but now she couldn't help but wonder—what had Emily really heard in her empty house? The thought chilled her.

"I know... I'm just saying," Jay nodded, his voice quieter now as he tried to remain calm. His words were pragmatic, but there was fear behind them, the reality of their situation starting to sink in. "The fact is... we don't know if it has anything to do with what's been going on with us lately," he admitted, his eyes scanning the faces of his friends, wondering if they were all coming to the same, terrifying conclusion.

Emily's breath hitched as panic began to grip her, the fears that had been lurking in the back of her mind suddenly rushing to the forefront. "Well, what if it does..." she said, her voice rising as her breathing quickened. The words that had only been fleeting thoughts moments ago now felt undeniable. "What if they're coming after us?"

The room seemed to grow colder as the thought lingered in the air, the possibility too real to ignore.

"We can't think like that," Jay said quickly, his eyes darting to Darren for support.

"Yeah, baby. We can't think like that," Darren echoed, though his voice lacked the conviction it normally carried. The truth was, the implications were overwhelming, even for him. He felt as though he were standing on the edge of a cliff, unsure of what lay beneath.

"Thanks, Darren," Jay muttered sarcastically, shaking his head. "The thing is, we don't know what's going on. We don't know who is doing this. And we don't know why. What I say we do is stick together... not separate for ANYTHING... and wait this whole thing out. Nothing will happen if we are together." He looked over each member of the group, his gaze lingering on each face as he tried to convey the seriousness of his words.

They all nodded slowly in agreement, their faces a mix of fear and uncertainty.

George, who had been silent up until now, suddenly spoke up, his voice hesitant. "What about the trip?" he asked, shame creeping into his tone.

"Oh, you've gotta be fucking kidding me!" Darren lashed out, his voice sharp with frustration. His outburst echoed in the kitchen, cutting through the thick silence.

"No, no," George said quickly, trying to defend himself. "I'm not saying we go for fun… but shouldn't we get out of here?" His voice trailed off as he saw the doubtful looks from the others.

The group exchanged glances, no one knowing what to say. Each of them was wrestling with the same thought: staying at Jay's house didn't feel safe, but running off into the unknown didn't seem like a better option. The rain pounded against the windows, the howling wind adding to the unease that filled the room. Jay mulled over George's suggestion, his mind spinning with possibilities. On one hand, if there was a connection between the murders and everything that had happened to them, staying at the house seemed like a mistake. But leaving, heading to some isolated location—was that any better?

"I don't know," Jay finally said, his voice uncertain. "I honestly don't know. I mean… I don't even want to go down this route, but…" He paused, knowing his next words wouldn't sit well with the group. "IF there is a connection at all, then the last place we should be is here." His eyes scanned the room, watching their reactions closely.

The weight of his words settled over the group like a heavy blanket, uncomfortable but impossible to ignore.

"The thing is though, we have no clue. And there's really no way of knowing…" Jay's voice trailed off, the uncertainty gnawing at him.

Jen's voice was soft, but it cut through the air like a knife. "But babe," she said, her tone intimate as if they were the only two in the room. "How can we go up there in good conscience?"

Jay ran a hand through his damp hair, letting out a long breath. "I know..." he began to respond, but Darren interrupted him.

"What about Liz...?" Darren's voice pierced the conversation like a sudden alarm. His gaze, which had been fixed on the floor, now rose to meet the group, his expression dark. Jay didn't even hear the rest of Darren's sentence. He was right.

Liz....and Will!!

Jay's stomach dropped as the realization hit him. How could he have forgotten? He spun around, rushing to his backpack that sat slumped on the counter. His fingers fumbled with the zipper as he unzipped the main compartment and frantically rummaged for his phone. His heart pounded in his chest as panic set in. His mind was already connecting the dots that Darren was putting together.

But it couldn't be Will. He couldn't. Could he?

He started playing it over in his mind. Over all of the interactions he's had with Will in the last 6 months. They all seemed distant. Cold. Almost as if Will had ceased to exist that day and had been replaced by something else. Whatever it was, it didn't resemble his friend. And with everything that had gone on. He had to admit that the possibility had already crossed his mind.

But how could it be Will? How could he even allow himself to think that? After all they'd been through together. To think that he would do this. Without Jay knowing? No way.

Darren continued,"...I mean, they never found out what happened. Maybe it's all related"

"What's all related, Darren?" Jay surprised himself with his protective outburst as he awoke from his own trance. "Why does it always have to be Will?"

"Bro, what are you talking about?" Darren tried to keep his tone calm, though the tension was building. "I never said anything about Will. All I said was that it never got solved. Now shit is happening again. Seems like a little bit of a coincidence, don't you think?" his sarcasm was not what Jay needed right now.

"Whatever, man," Jay tried to deflect his guilty conscience. The same thoughts were running through his head that Darren was voicing. But he didn't want to admit it to himself. I mean, there was no way. Was there? His mind raced, fighting against the fear creeping up his spine. Shaking his head, he turned his attention back to his phone. His fingers trembled as he pressed the button to unlock it. Nothing.

"She called," Darren announced to the group, his voice barely above a whisper.

"Put it on speaker," Emily said without hesitation, her voice barely concealing the tension bubbling beneath the surface. George, Amy, and Jen had silently gathered at the end of the counter, drawn in by the escalating conversation. The room felt crowded now, everyone sensing that they were on the verge of something big, something terrifying. No one spoke, the earlier bickering forgotten as the seriousness of the situation sank in.

Darren's hand hovered over his phone for what felt like an eternity as he stared at the blurred icons on the screen.

Jay's thoughts drifted, pulling him through the chaotic web of the past week. The strange phone call that Will had denied making echoed in his memory. The SUV parked in his driveway. The terrifying chase through the park. The crash, Darren nearly being killed, and the visit to Will's house before the movies, his unsettling behavior in the restroom, and the news about his half-sister's murder. It all connected, a sinister thread running through everything, now tangled with the brutal death of Mr. Oswald. It felt like too much, the weight of it pressing down on Jay's chest. The evidence might be circumstantial, but it was overwhelming.

Was it possible?

Could Will really be involved?

Jay didn't want to believe it, but he could see how Darren, how anyone, might come to that conclusion.

Darren's thumb hovered over the voicemail icon for a moment longer before he tapped it, then hit speaker. The tension in the room thickened as the message played.

"Hey baby bro. I know you're at the dance and I know things have been really weird lately. I just wanted to thank you again for...being you, I guess. You really are like a brother to me, and I don't wanna get all mushy and shit. But I love ya. Thank you for sticking by me throughout everything. I'll try to open up and let my feelings about Jay go. I know you're probably right.

Anyway...the site is all set. Just the way Will wanted..." she paused. "Anyway. See you soon."

The message ended, leaving a thick silence hanging in the air like a storm cloud about to break.

Jay slowly lifted his head, his eyes scanning the faces of the group. Then they fell on Darren. "What feelings about me, Darren?" his eyes narrowed.

"Look man, I don't know..." Darren started. "She's had a lot going on recently, ya know."

"What does that have to do with me?" Jay cocked his head as his growl seemed more sinister now.

"Jason!" Jen's voice brought him back to his senses. "We don't have time for this!"

Jay knew she was right. Time was the last luxury they had right now. Jen, sensing the turmoil inside him, stepped closer. "I'm sorry, baby," she whispered softly, guilt threading through her voice. "It's just... we just..." She trailed off, unable to find the words to comfort him, because she knew there weren't any.

Jay sighed deeply, his decision made. "Get your stuff. We're going," he said quietly, his voice steady but firm. His eyes met Jen's, a silent reassurance passing between them.

He didn't blame her for doubting Will. He didn't blame anyone. But he knew what needed to happen next. The group had left most of their things in the Jeep before the dance, but they had smaller bags packed for the night, ready to change out of their prom clothes. They moved quietly into Jay's den to retrieve their bags and get changed.

"Ok," Jen said as she turned to follow the others, but she stopped as Jay tugged gently on her arm, pulling her close to him.

"I love you, babe," he whispered, brushing a soft kiss against her lips. The tenderness of the moment felt fragile, a brief respite in the storm that had become their lives.

"I love you too," Jen replied, her voice just as quiet.

Jay was relieved to be leaving the house. It had become a place of tension, of creeping dread that seemed to seep from the walls. He hadn't felt comfortable there in days, the air thick with unease. The trip might not be what they had planned, but it was an escape. Something, anything, to get away from the chaos that had been building, suffocating them all.

He glanced into the rearview mirror of the Jeep as they started down the road. Amy and Emily were already asleep in the back, exhaustion from the night's events finally catching up to them. George sat behind him, staring blankly out the misted window, his breath fogging up the glass.

The rhythmic patter of rain against the Jeep's roof was hypnotic, a steady lullaby pulling the others into sleep. Jen had given Darren the front seat, claiming she'd likely fall asleep during the long drive. It hadn't taken more than five minutes before her eyes fluttered closed, her head resting against the window as the rain drummed softly outside.

Jay kept his promise to drive carefully, the conditions outside making it impossible to do otherwise. He had always been skeptical of the little switch Jen made him turn on—the one with the icon of screeching tires on wet pavement—but tonight he didn't argue. If it gave her a little peace of mind, it was worth it.

"How long you think it's gonna take?" Darren's voice broke the silence after nearly two hours, a low whisper meant to keep from waking the others. The night felt eerie, the quiet too thick, and Jay had wondered how long it would last.

"I dunno," Jay replied softly, glancing at the dark road ahead. "Will said it was a hike, and it'll probably be longer in this stuff." The rain had only gotten heavier, the high beams cutting through the relentless downpour. The country roads were unfamiliar, winding and narrow, and Jay didn't want to push his luck. He kept a tight grip on the wheel, nerves on edge.

Darren pulled out his phone and flicked through his photos, his voice trailing off as he murmured, "Man...I can't believe this shit."

"Why do you keep looking at it? That's fucking sick!" Jay hissed, trying to keep his voice down. He'd seen Darren glancing at the photo more than once during the drive, but he hadn't said anything. He was relieved that Darren had had the decency not to show it to the girls. They knew Mr. Oswald was dead, but they had no idea how horrific the scene really was. The boys had kept those details to themselves.

"Do you think we're gonna be in trouble?" Darren ignored Jay's rebuke, zooming in and out on the grisly image, trying to make sense of it.

"Why would I be in trouble?" Jay was taken aback.

"We fled the scene of a crime. We didn't report it. Seems like those are always the people who get into some shit," Darren muttered, still staring at the photo.

Jay hadn't thought of that. His focus had been on getting himself and his friends out of there as quickly as possible. The idea of staying behind to explain what they'd seen hadn't even crossed his mind. "They don't know why we left. Plus...who were we gonna tell?"

"I guess," Darren mumbled. The rush of adrenaline from earlier was long gone, leaving only fatigue in its place. But Darren wasn't about to fall asleep. Not yet.

"We'd probably still be there if we had said something," Jay added, more to reassure himself than Darren. "I just needed to get the fuck out."

"Yeah, you're right," Darren agreed quietly, his voice trailing off as exhaustion began to take hold.

"So...what do we do now?" Darren asked, his voice barely more than a whisper.

Jay immediately knew what he meant. The thoughts of what to say had been swirling in his head ever since they left. "I have no idea. I mean...I don't know if he'd really care...well...not that he wouldn't care..."

"What?" Darren interrupted, nodding. "Man, what are you talking about with that?"

"Will."

"Will?" Darren's confusion almost woke up the entire Jeep. He sat for a second, contemplating his friend's choice of words. "So you do think it's related?"

Jay noticed George stirring in the back, listening in on the conversation. Darren continued, "You know...before all this shit went down tonight...we were still kind of iffy on the whole thing."

"Iffy on what?" Jay asked defensively, the tension between them hanging in the air. The conversation might have ended earlier in the night, but this wasn't over.

"Bro the shit never got solved," Darren pushed further.

George leaned forward, joining in for the first time. "I know I wasn't with you guys, and I'm out of the loop on all that has gone on...but in all honesty...how does that happen?"

Jay's level of unease increased. He didn't want everyone to think things were related. After the brutality of what happened at their friend's house 6 months ago. Although, he had to admit, after seeing the scene in the locker room, the similarities were uncanny.

"I know. But how does that have anything to do with us?" Jay tried to shed light onto the situation.

"How does it now?" George pleaded, as he sat up closer to the front so he didn't wake the girls.

"Look, all I know is that shit has ben weird the past 6 months," Darren correctly pointed out.

Jay couldn't tell if he was accusing Jay of being weird, or the situation in general. But he allowed his friend to continue, "I think we have to consider all possibilities at this point. I mean, treat everyone like a suspect. For all we know...everyone is!"

Jay stayed silent, listening intently as the conversation unfolded. Darren had a point—Will's behavior had been strange, distant, even cold. And George was right too. No one really knew what happened 6 months ago. And it didn't make sense to Jay why no one ever suspected Will. He just figured that everyone thought there was no way Will could ever do that to his own family.

But maybe they were wrong. As much as Jay didn't want to admit it. It wasn't the same Will they had grown up with.

The silence stretched out as they let their own thoughts take over. George leaned forward, resting his chin on his clasped hands, his elbows braced against the front seats. The rain continued to pound on the roof of the Jeep, the occasional flashes of lightning illuminating the sky for a split second. They were completely surrounded by trees now, the narrow road snaking through the forest. Jay's imagination began to play tricks on him. The dark silhouettes of the trees seemed to close in on them with every passing mile, like they were being swallowed whole.

"Wait a second!" Darren's sudden outburst startled George and Darren, snapping them both out of their thoughts. "The other message!"

Jay froze. They had forgotten all about the other message. Caught up in the fear, the guilt, the uncertainty, he had completely neglected the second message. He exchanged a wide-eyed glance with Darren as he was pulling out his phone again. His fingers fumbled slightly as he put in the passcode, his pulse quickening. He turned down the speaker volume, careful not to wake the others, and hit

'play.'

"Hey Darren...it's Liz. Just wanted to see if you guys had left yet. It was kinda sketchy getting here, and that was during the day..." They could hear muffled noises in the background. "...but drive careful 'cuz the rain is supposed to pick up. Anyway...that was pretty much—what the fuck—who the fuck is that?" A rumbling noise came through the speaker, followed by a blood-curdling scream. "What the fuck are you doing!!" The sound of a struggle. A loud thump. Then, Liz's voice, strained and terrified: "Darren...please..." And then silence.

The phone's backlight blinked off as the recording ended, plunging the Jeep into darkness. The three boys sat frozen, their minds racing to process what they had just heard. The silence in the car was suffocating, stretching on for what felt like an eternity. Outside, the trees seemed to blur together, the rain streaking across the windshield in endless rivulets.

"What the fuck!" Darren's shocked exclamation was cut short as the Jeep jolted forward, the impact sudden and violent.

Jay's eyes snapped to the rearview mirror, his heart hammering in his chest. Behind them, the grill of a vehicle loomed dangerously close, its headlights glaring in the rain. Before he could react, the vehicle slammed into them again, harder this time. The Jeep skidded, Jay momentarily losing control of the steering wheel as the girls in the backseat woke with startled gasps.

Jay and Darren exchanged a look, no words needed. They both knew who was behind them.

The SUV.

Chapter 11

The clapping thunder echoed violently through the forest as flashes of lightning tore across the night sky, illuminating the narrow passage the road carved through the thick, towering trees. The storm seemed to tighten around them like a predator closing in on its prey. Amy and Emily jolted awake with loud, panicked screams, their voices piercing through the Jeep's cabin. Their frantic movements were chaotic, scrambling to climb over the backseat as though the thin cushion could somehow shield them from the relentless SUV smashing into the Jeep's rear. The entire vehicle shook violently with each hit, the force of the impacts reverberating through their bones.

Jay's foot pressed harder against the gas pedal, but no matter how fast they went, it didn't feel like enough. His heart was pounding in his chest, the adrenaline pumping through his veins in a desperate battle with the terror that had taken hold of him. His mind raced, barely able to comprehend the situation unraveling before them.

Was this it? He thought to himself, panic clawing at his mind. Had the entire week been leading to this terrifying chase?

Even in the chaos, he found himself irrationally trying to make sense of everything—the bizarre events of the past week, the strange phone call from Will, the SUV tailing them, the murder of Mr. Oswald. All of it crashed together like the storm that raged outside. His knuckles cramped from gripping the steering wheel so tightly, bracing for the next inevitable hit from the SUV.

"What the fuck?!?" Darren shouted in the passenger seat, his voice raw with fear and anger, though he wasn't speaking to anyone in particular.

"Jason..." Jen's voice cut through the noise, pleading with him, but Jay didn't dare take his eyes off the road. The narrow bends came quickly, their sharp turns slick with rainwater that splashed up from the tires. He could feel the Jeep struggling to hold the road with every swerve. Their pursuer was ruthless, timing each ram with terrifying precision, pushing them closer and closer to disaster. Every so often, Jay risked a quick glance in the rearview mirror, bracing himself for the next violent jolt that sent the entire vehicle shuddering.

The pattern had become disturbingly familiar—an attack, a moment of reprieve, then another violent crash. Jay could feel the rhythm of it now. Another hit was coming.

"Who the fuck is this douchebag?" Darren yelled, twisting in his seat to look over his shoulder. "This fucking asshole is dead when I get ahold of him!" His face was contorted with rage, but his eyes betrayed a deep, gnawing fear.

In the middle seat, the girls huddled together, their bodies trembling in unison. Tears streaked down Emily's and Amy's faces, their sobs lost in the howling wind and the deafening rain battering the Jeep. Jen wrapped her arms around them, trying her best to comfort them, though her own hands shook with fear. "It's okay. We're gonna be okay," she whispered, though her words sounded hollow even to her. She glanced at Jay, whose jaw was clenched with steely determination. His nostrils flared in anger as he checked the mirror again, bracing himself.

"Throw something out the window!" Darren shouted at George, who was paralyzed with fear, his wide eyes fixed on the chaos unfolding around him. He hadn't spoken since the first hit from the SUV. Now, he sat motionless, clutching the door handle so tightly his knuckles were pale. His gaze met Jay's in the rearview mirror, searching for some kind of reassurance, but Jay was too focused on keeping them alive to notice.

"George!" Darren reached back, hitting George on the leg with a hard smack, snapping him out of his daze.

"Wha...what do you want me to throw?" George stammered, his voice barely audible over the storm.

"Anything...just get this fucking asshole off of us!" Darren barked back, his frustration boiling over.

George glanced at Jay, hoping for some kind of approval, but Jay's eyes remained glued to the road. With no other option, George grabbed his backpack from the floor and rummaged through it frantically. Every second felt like an eternity. Finally, he yanked out a notebook, holding it up like a prize. He looked to Darren for confirmation.

"Do it!" Darren shouted, nodding furiously.

George ripped a few sheets from the notebook, opening the window just enough to let the freezing wind and rain whip through the Jeep's interior. The roar of the storm intensified, and George's hand shook as he held the papers up to the window. The wind immediately snatched them from his grip, the soggy pages fluttering like pale ghosts into the night.

George turned around, watching helplessly as the pages disappeared into the darkness, hoping that they had made some impact. "More!" Darren demanded, his voice cracking under the pressure.

George tore out another clump of papers and tossed them into the gale. The wind howled, whipping the pages into a swirling frenzy behind them. Jay caught a glimpse of the paper confetti in the rearview mirror, the sheets dancing erratically in the storm. For a brief moment, the sight of it was oddly mesmerizing, but he quickly turned his attention back to the road.

Suddenly, the blinding headlights that had been tailing them vanished.

Darren whipped around, his face lighting up with disbelief. "I think you fucking got him, Georgey!" he exclaimed, his voice filled with excitement and relief.

George twisted in his seat, peering through the rain-splattered back window. The girls remained huddled, their faces pale with fear, while the boys strained to see any sign of the SUV. A jagged streak of lightning split the sky, illuminating the road behind them for a split second. Nothing. The SUV was gone.

George turned back around, a smile spreading across his face. He sat back in his seat, pride swelling in his chest. Darren returned the smile, glancing at Jay, whose chest was rising and falling rapidly as he tried to catch his breath. His grip on the steering wheel finally loosened, and he exhaled a long, shaky breath. The terror that had consumed him was starting to ebb, replaced by a cautious relief.

Jay looked over his shoulder at the girls, who were still tangled together in a mess of arms and legs, their breaths coming in short, panicked bursts. He let up on the gas pedal, allowing the Jeep to slow to a safer speed. The forest road, still winding and narrow, seemed less threatening now that the SUV was gone. Jay closed his eyes for a brief moment, trying to calm his racing heart. They had gotten away. For now, they were safe.

No one spoke for what felt like a long time. The only sounds were the steady drum of rain on the roof and the occasional crack of thunder in the distance. The storm outside seemed to mirror the lingering tension inside the Jeep.

Lightning continued to flash across the sky, illuminating the desolate road ahead. Jay kept checking the rearview mirror, half-expecting the SUV to return at any moment, but the road behind them remained empty.

"Holy shit," Darren muttered, breaking the silence. "Liz!" The girls exchanged puzzled looks, but the boys were already contemplating what Darren's outburst meant.

"What do we do?" Jay's voice was quiet but urgent, his eyes wide with realization. They had completely forgotten about the voicemail when the SUV had first attacked. Darren fumbled for his phone in his jacket pocket, the adrenaline still making his hands tremble. "Call her," he answered, matter of factly!

The phone rang once...twice...then the call went to voicemail.

"Hey, it's Liz...leave one."

"Shit!" Darren cursed, hanging up in frustration. He looked over at Jay, who could tell immediately that the call had gone unanswered.

"What's going on, Jason?" Jen asked, her voice tense with worry. "Why do you guys need to call Liz?"

"Dude, what do we do?" Darren questioned impatiently, still scrolling through the phone.

"I don't know..." Jay muttered, turning his attention to Jen, who was staring at him intently through the rearview mirror. "We got a call from Liz..." "And?" Jen interrupted, her voice rising with concern.

"It sounded like she was in trouble," Jay admitted, the weight of his words sinking in.

"What do you mean she was in trouble?" Emily spoke up, her voice shaky as she finally sat up straight, abandoning her huddled position in the backseat.

Darren was already playing the voicemail, his eyes fixed on the girls as they listened, their expressions growing more and more alarmed as the message reached its chilling end.

"We have to go home!" Emily whined, her voice cracking under the pressure. "What are we still doing here? Honestly?"

"Jason...how long ago did you guys listen to that?" Jen's voice was calm but firm, more concerned about being kept in the dark than anything else.

"It was literally seconds before that asshole started ramming us," Jay muttered, his eyes flicking to the rearview mirror again, scanning the dark, rain-slicked road behind them. His heart pounded in his chest, each beat a dull thud in his ears. He searched the surrounding trees for any sign of the SUV, still not entirely convinced that they had shaken their pursuer. The papers George had thrown seemed to have worked, but doubt lingered like a fog in his mind.

"Call Liz from your phone!" George demanded suddenly, his voice cutting through the tense silence. He was leaning forward, his face pale as he directed Amy.

"Here, hang on," she said quickly, fumbling to hand it over. George snatched it from her and immediately started scrolling through her contacts, the glow from the screen casting eerie shadows across his face. The rest of the group watched him, their expressions tight with anxiety, as the phone rang in his ear.

They all waited, breaths held in anticipation, eyes locked on George's face.

"Well?" Darren's voice was a sharp whisper, his eyes wide with impatience.

George lowered the phone, his face grim. "Voicemail," he reported quietly, his voice thick with dread. The news hit them like a lead weight. They sank back into their seats, each lost in their own thoughts, the gravity of the situation pressing down on them like the heavy storm clouds outside. The silence in the Jeep was thick, oppressive, broken only by the rhythmic patter of rain against the roof.

No one wanted to speak. Fear gripped them, coiling tighter with every unanswered question.

"Dude... what the fuck?" Darren finally broke the silence, his frustration boiling over as he slammed his head against the back of the passenger seat. The dull thud echoed through the cabin. He turned to Jay, who was biting his lower lip in thought, his brow furrowed in concentration. "What do we do, bro?"

"I don't know," Jay answered quietly, his voice barely audible over the rain. He didn't want to admit how nervous he was, but he could feel their eyes on him, waiting for him to make the call. The weight of their gazes bore down on him, and he could feel the pressure mounting. His mind raced through the options, but none of them seemed promising.

How could anyone dare chase them?

Deep down, he knew what the rest of the group wanted to do, but he couldn't bring himself to abandon their friend. Not like this. Not when Will was out here, somewhere in the wilderness, potentially in danger. He had to know. He had to find out.

And then there was the SUV—Jay wasn't entirely sure they had seen the last of it. The sense of dread clung to him like the wet clothes sticking to his skin.

Finally, after what felt like an eternity, Jay made his decision. "We have to keep going," he said, his voice firm, though his eyes remained locked on the road ahead. He couldn't bear to look at the others just yet.

To his surprise, no one protested. A collective sense of relief seemed to wash over the group. It was as though they had all been waiting for him to make the call, and now that he had, they felt some small sense of direction.

The tension in the Jeep lingered, but no one argued. Instead, they sat quietly, each lost in their own thoughts as the rain continued to drum against the vehicle, the thunder rolling ominously in the distance. Time seemed to stretch unnaturally, every second feeling like an eternity as they exchanged uneasy glances. Jay's GPS flickered intermittently, losing its signal in the thick forest and stormy weather, but the last reading told him they were only two miles away.

Two miles to Will.

Everyone in the car braced themselves, their muscles tense, knowing that whatever was waiting for them at the end of this road could change everything. The air inside the Jeep was thick with anticipation, each breath feeling heavier than the last. Jay's heart hammered in his chest as he spotted a slight break in the trees ahead. The road curved, and he instinctively eased his foot off the gas, letting the Jeep coast. His hand reached for the switch to turn off the headlights, plunging them into near darkness, save for the faint glow from the dashboard.

They crept forward, the engine barely a hum as the Jeep slowly rolled around the bend. Then, there it was—Liz's white Mustang, sitting still and silent on the side of the road.

They were here.

Jay maneuvered the Jeep beside Liz's car, the vehicle coming to a gentle stop with a soft tap on the brakes. He threw it into park, and the tension in the air spiked again. Everyone held their breath, their eyes fixed on the Mustang, waiting for... something. Anything.

Jay's breath fogged the window as he stared out, his pulse quickening. His eyes scanned the car for any sign of movement, but there was nothing. It was as if the car had been abandoned, left to rot in the middle of the storm.

His gaze drifted beyond the car, toward the narrow path that led into the forest. The trees loomed tall and menacing, their dark silhouettes made more imposing by the flashes of lightning that sporadically lit the sky. Jay's stomach churned. He could feel Darren watching him, waiting for him to make the next move. He turned, glancing at the others in the backseat. Every eye was on him.

"Well..." Jay swallowed hard, his throat dry. He shifted his weight, trying to steady his nerves. "Let's go," he said finally, though his voice sounded more unsure than he intended.

"That's it?" George stammered, his voice rising with panic. "What do you mean 'let's go'? What the hell is the plan? I'm not going out there without some sort of a plan!"

"There is no plan for this shit, George!" Jay snapped, his irritation finally boiling over. He had tried to hold it together, but now the frustration poured out. "I'm going to go outside, follow that path, and see where it leads. I'm not sitting here while who knows what is out there! If you want to stay in the car, then fine. But I'm going to find him."

"Find who?" George shot back, his voice trembling with desperation. He was grasping for any excuse, any reason not to leave the relative safety of the Jeep. "Liz?"

"What the fuck do you mean?" Jay's outburst caught everyone off guard, his voice laced with anger. "You see her fucking car, right?"

The harsh reality of Jay's words settled over the group like a heavy blanket. No one had a response. The truth was undeniable. Liz wasn't in the car, which meant she was out there, somewhere in the dark, rain-soaked woods.

Everyone exchanged uneasy glances, the weight of the situation pressing down on them. The storm raged on outside, the rain slashing against the windows in sheets. Lightning illuminated the dense forest in brief, blinding flashes, casting long shadows across the road. Jay's jaw tightened as he prepared himself for whatever came next.

They had no choice but to go.

"Calm down, Jason," Jen's voice was soft but steady as she tried to console her boyfriend from the back seat. She could see the tension building in him, the strain of the week's chaos etched into his face. She knew how much he was genuinely worried, despite everything they had been through. Her hand rested on his shoulder, a small gesture of comfort amidst the turmoil. "I'm coming with you."

"Yeah, me too," Darren added firmly, his voice cutting through the rhythmic patter of rain on the roof. He glanced over his shoulder at Emily, who was still huddled between Amy and George, her body shaking with fear. "Let's go, Em," he said, his tone more gentle as he looked into her tear-filled eyes. There was no argument from Emily. She wasn't going to let Darren out of her sight.

Jay pushed the door open, the weight of it heavy in the thick, damp air. The cold rain immediately assaulted him, drenching his hair and clothes in seconds. It came down in a steady, unrelenting stream, soaking everything beneath it. The storm felt alive around them, its breath chilling the air, its voice in the thunder rolling across the dark sky. Darren followed Jay's lead, giving Emily a nod before stepping out into the downpour. She scrambled after him, fumbling her way out of the back seat, her shoes slipping on the slick ground as she hurried to his side.

Darren pulled her close, wrapping his arms around her shivering body, his hands running up and down her back in a desperate attempt to soothe her. "It's gonna be okay, baby. I promise," he whispered into her ear, his voice trembling with uncertainty. He held her tightly, feeling her frantic sobs slowly begin to fade, her breathing finally steadying in his arms.

On the other side of the Jeep, Jen made her way through the rain to where Jay was waiting. The cold raindrops dripped down her face as she wrapped her arms around him, pressing herself against his chest. They didn't need words. Jay held her close, feeling her small frame shivering against him. He wished he could do more—wished he could take away the fear that clung to them all like a shadow. But he knew he had to stay strong. For her. For all of them. The weight of their safety rested on his shoulders, and he couldn't afford to fall apart now.

Inside the Jeep, George sat still, staring at Amy. His mind was racing, torn between fear and responsibility. "What do you want to do?" he asked quietly, not wanting to make the decision alone.

Amy glanced out the window at the others, her eyes following Jen and Jay as they huddled together in the rain. She sighed. "It's up to you, babe," she said softly, though her voice wavered with hesitation. "But I'm not so sure I want to go out in that rain..."

"Yeah, I know," George began, but his words were cut off by the sudden sound of the passenger door flying open.

"Get the fuck out of the car, dumbass!" Darren's voice rang out, sharp and commanding. He stood in the downpour, glaring at George through the open door. "We're not splitting up!" Without waiting for a response, he slammed the door shut, his eyes meeting Jay's across the hood of the Jeep. Jay nodded, the silent agreement passing between them: whatever happened, they were in this together.

George scowled at Amy, clearly annoyed. He hated the rain, hated getting wet, and his friends all knew it. But there was no point in arguing. With a heavy sigh, he opened the back door and gingerly stepped out into the storm. The cold rain instantly soaked through his clothes, and he winced as it dripped down the back of his neck. Darren wasted no time, yelling at him to move faster, the urgency in his voice unmistakable.

"I just think someone should stay here..." George stammered, his voice barely rising above the sound of the rain pelting the ground. "In case Liz comes back to the car."

"Are you fucking out of your mind?" Darren shot back, incredulous. "How dumb are you? You know what happens to people who split up from the group—"

"This isn't a movie, Darren!" Jay interrupted, the frustration in his voice surprising even himself. The words had slipped out before he could stop them. He wasn't quite sure why he'd said it, but in the moment, it felt necessary.

Darren looked at him, stunned. He couldn't believe Jay would even consider splitting up, especially after everything that had happened so far. The weight of the night's events hung heavy in the air between them, and Darren struggled to understand Jay's reasoning.

"Have we forgotten what the fuck is happening here?" Darren's voice was louder now, rising above the rain. "Did we forget what we saw in the locker room tonight? And the fucking ride up here?

Someone is definitely fucking with us. If you want to be the one left behind, then be my fucking guest. But I say we stick together!" He was shouting now, his words barely audible over the relentless storm, but the fear behind them was unmistakable.

Jay bit his lip, considering Darren's rant. He knew his friend was right—splitting up was dangerous, especially after everything they had seen. But the thought of leaving Will out there, in the dark, while they waited by his car gnawed at him. What if Will came back while they were out searching? The question bounced around in his head, but deep down, he knew the answer. He felt Jen's cheek pressed against his chest, and the realization washed over him. Whatever happened, she wasn't leaving his side. And that somehow gave him the confidence to make his decision.

"Darren's right, George. We stick together," Jay said, his voice steady as he made eye contact with his sulking friend.

George groaned, his shoulders slumping in defeat. Amy nudged him gently, offering a small smile of encouragement. "It's okay, baby. Let's just go."

"How far is the campsite?" Emily's voice was quiet but tense as she looked warily at the dark path ahead, the trees looming like sentinels guarding the entrance to the unknown.

Darren and Jay exchanged uneasy glances. Neither of them had any idea how far they would have to hike to reach the campsite their friends had chosen. The path ahead was barely visible in the dim light, disappearing into the thick, rain-soaked forest.

Jay swallowed his uncertainty and forced a reassuring smile. "It can't be that far," he lied, hoping to calm the rising tension. The truth was, they had no idea what awaited them beyond the trees.

They gathered at the back of the Jeep, the rain pouring down relentlessly, soaking them to the bone as they rummaged through their bags. The sound of zippers and rustling fabric was drowned out by the continuous drumming of the storm. No one spoke as they hurriedly grabbed a few essential supplies, pulling on ponchos that they smartly packed of clothing for warmth. The cold air seemed to seep through every gap, chilling them despite their efforts. The rain had become a constant companion, an unrelenting force that showed no signs of letting up. They had packed rain gear, but none of them had expected the weather to be this bad. This was supposed to be a getaway—a weekend to enjoy, not survive.

Jay grabbed three flashlights, flicking each one on to ensure they worked. The beams of light barely cut through the dense rain, their glow weak against the suffocating darkness of the forest.

"Are those waterproof?" Darren asked, accepting one of the flashlights with a skeptical glance.

"I honestly don't know. Better keep them as dry as we can just in case," Jay muttered, handing another flashlight to George, who grudgingly took it, his expression one of clear reluctance. George had never been one for the outdoors, and it showed. He pulled his hood tighter over his head, already shivering from the cold and the rain. The last thing he wanted was to be out in this storm, but he knew there was no choice now.

Jay shut the trunk with a dull thud, the sound swallowed by the surrounding weather. He took a long, steadying breath and turned to look at the group, his eyes meeting each of theirs in turn. They were all soaked, pale, and tense, but ready. Without another word, he started toward the path that led into the woods, the beam of his flashlight flickering slightly as the rain dripped down its length. Jen followed closely behind him, her hand gripping the back of his jacket, unwilling to lose him in the shadows. The cold, wet mud clung to their boots as they trudged forward, each step sinking into the soft earth with a sickening squelch.

Emily followed, her breath ragged and uneven, keeping close to Jen. Darren was right behind her, his flashlight sweeping side to side as if expecting something—someone—to leap out from the trees at any moment.

Amy and George lingered behind the group, their movements slow and hesitant, as if each step took more effort than the last. They walked in a single-file line, the narrow path offering no comfort, only the oppressive feeling of being swallowed whole by the towering trees.

Jay's boots sank deeper into the mud with each step, the ground soft and unsteady beneath his feet. The forest was thick, dense with shadows that seemed to move and shift with every flicker of their flashlights. The beams of light did little to pierce the inky blackness ahead. The air was thick, cold, and heavy with the smell of wet earth and decay. The sounds of the storm—rain pelting the leaves, wind whipping through the branches—only added to the tension that hung in the air.

Jay pressed on, though with every step, his nerves frayed further. The tension in his chest was almost unbearable. Every snap of a twig, every rustle of leaves behind him set his heart racing. He could feel the weight of the group's reliance on him, their unspoken need for him to lead them through this nightmare. But beneath his facade of calm, he was terrified. His thoughts churned—Where was Will? Was he okay? And who had been driving that SUV, toying with them? The questions spiraled through his mind, each one adding another layer of dread.

They walked for what felt like hours, though only ten minutes had passed. The rain never let up, but it barely touched them through the thickness of the forest, the cold biting through their clothes and making every movement more difficult.

"Yo, Jay. Hold up," Darren's voice broke the silence, sounding more urgent than before.

Jay stopped abruptly, the tension in Darren's voice sending a chill down his spine. His pulse quickened, and he turned to face his friend. "What's wrong?"

"Where the fuck is George?" Darren asked, his eyes wide with alarm. He whipped around, shining his flashlight into the empty path behind them. The beam of light cut through the rain, but there was no sign of George or Amy. The path stretched out in eerie silence, swallowed by darkness.

"Are you fucking serious?" Jay hissed, his frustration bubbling over. George and Amy had disappeared, leaving the group without a word. His stomach twisted in anger and disbelief.

"I'm gonna fucking kill him myself," Darren muttered through clenched teeth. "Do you think he went back?"

"I don't know. Probably," Jay replied, his voice tight with irritation. George's habit of avoiding confrontation was no secret, and this wasn't the first time he'd bailed. But now, when they needed him most?

"You wanna go back and get him?" Darren asked, his flashlight still sweeping the empty path behind them, searching for any sign of movement.

Jay didn't answer right away. His mind was spinning. His instincts told him to keep moving forward, to find Will and Liz. But he also knew that he couldn't just abandon his friends, even if George had made the choice to split off. The weight of the decision hung heavy on him, each second dragging by as he wrestled with what to do. He felt Jen squeeze his hand, her silent reassurance giving him the strength to make the call.

"Jay!?" Darren snapped, his voice rising as he turned back to face him, the flashlight's glare hitting Jay's eyes.

Jay raised his hand to shield his eyes from the beam. "Let's just go a little more," he finally said, the words coming out slowly, deliberately. "It can't be that much further. We can deal with

George when we..."

"Holy fuck!" Darren's sudden exclamation sent a jolt through the group, his voice filled with pure shock. His eyes were wide, his face pale as he stared past Jay, the flashlight shaking in his hands. His gaze was fixed on something ahead, just beyond the beam of light.

In an instant Jay spun around, his flashlight following Darren's. The knot in his stomach tightened, dread surging through him as his beam never landed on it's intended target. Before he could fully turn he was hit with a forceful blow knocking him back into the thickness of the brush.

"Jaaaay!" Jen screamed as she lunged forward towards where Jay and his attacker had disappeared.

Darren grabbed her arm. Knowing full well what Jay would want him to do. He couldn't let Jen any closer. He had to get the girls to safety. "Jen, no!" he yelled. "We have to go!"

"I'm not leaving him!" Jen's futile attempts were drowned out be the storm.

Emily helped Darren grab Jen and wrestle her back onto the path, "Jenny, we have to go!" she cried to her friend.

They struggled to wrangle Jen, who was putting up a fight to stay and find Jay. But finally Darren picked her up and carried her along the path. He had to get them away somehow.

"We shouldn't have left them," Amy said, glancing nervously at the storm outside. Her voice was barely audible over the rain pelting the roof of the Jeep. She hugged her knees to her chest, curling into herself as if trying to create a shield against the growing unease settling in her stomach.

George, already halfway out of his rain-soaked jacket, grunted in frustration. "I'm not getting lost out there for someone to hunt me down," he muttered, wrestling the jacket off and tossing it into the back seat. The Jeep rocked slightly as he shifted from side to side, his wet clothes clinging uncomfortably to his skin. "I don't know why we're even here. Jay's lost his fucking mind if you ask me."

Amy frowned, sitting up straighter. "What do you mean? What were we supposed to do? Just leave her out there?"

"He's chasing ghosts," George snapped, turning to face her with wide, panicked eyes. "Ever since... well, you know." He hesitated, as if saying it out loud would make it more real. "He's been obsessed. None of this shit makes sense."

Amy chewed on her lip, unsure how to respond. She had noticed Jay's behavior too, but part of her didn't want to admit it. "He's under a lot of pressure, George. We all are."

"That's not pressure," George shot back, shaking his head. "That's paranoia. The way he talks, the way he keeps looking over his shoulder—it's like he's waiting for..." His voice lowered, as if he were confessing something forbidden.

Amy felt a chill run down her spine, the weight of George's words sinking in. She couldn't deny that something about Jay had felt off for a while, but she hadn't wanted to think too hard about it. After all, they were all coping with trauma in their own way. She rested her head against the window, watching the rain streak down the glass. "Do you really think he's... losing it?"

George sighed heavily, finally getting his other shoe off and tossing it to the floor. "I don't know what to think anymore. I mean, you heard Darren. Someone seems to be after him. Maybe Jay is the one they want. Maybe we're just caught in the middle of whatever the fuck this is."

Amy blinked at him, suddenly unsure. George's words hung in the air like a thick fog. *What if he's right?* she thought. *What if this isn't about us? What if we're just in the way?* The idea made her stomach churn. "So you think we're just... bystanders?"

George shrugged, rubbing his face with both hands, exhaustion creeping into his voice. "I don't know. But ever since 6 months ago, Jay's been acting weird as hell. He's obsessed with finding answers and figuring things out. Maybe someone knows something and they're trying to shut him up."

Amy's thoughts raced. George's theory sounded far-fetched, but then again, everything about the past week had been surreal. Ms. Davenport. Mr. Oswald. The SUV chasing them. Could it all be connected to Jay's obsession with Will? She wasn't sure what to believe anymore.

"Well, how do you explain Ms. Davenport and Mr. Oswald?" Amy asked, trying to sound logical.

"Do you think that's just a coincidence?"

"I don't explain it, Amy! That's not my job," George retorted, pulling off his shirt and tossing it aside. "But I'll tell you this: the closer I am to Jay, the more I feel like I'm next. So if staying away from him means we're safer, then that's exactly what I'm gonna do."

Amy sat in stunned silence. George's reasoning was terrifying, but it made a sick kind of sense. She shivered, hugging herself tighter. "So what now?" she whispered, her voice barely above a breath.

CRASH!

The sudden sound of breaking glass filled the Jeep. Amy screamed as shards of glass sprayed across the back seat, sparkling like deadly confetti in the dim light. George jerked violently, hitting his head against the ceiling as he scrambled to turn around. His heart pounded in his chest as his eyes darted toward the broken window behind the driver's seat.

"What the fuck was that?!" George stammered, his voice trembling with fear. His pulse raced as he scanned the darkness outside, but the rain pouring down made it impossible to see anything clearly.

Amy's hands flew to her face, her breath coming in rapid, panicked gasps. "George! What's happening?!"

George's mind was spinning. He desperately tried to rationalize what had just happened, but nothing made sense. "I don't know... I don't fucking know!" His voice cracked as he reached for the door handle. "We need to get out of here. Now."

His jostling in the Jeep made it impossible for them to notice the back hitch slowly rising.

"Get out and go where?!" Amy's voice was rising, teetering on the edge of hysteria. Her eyes were wide, her face pale as she struggled to stay calm. She clutched George's arm tightly, her nails digging into his skin. "We can't just—"

"Ahhhhh!" George shrieked in pain as a sharp point stuck out from his chest. He had been stabbed straight through his back with such force that the blade had come out the front of his chest an inch.

Amy screamed in terror as she her eyes widened. She stumbled to get away, kicking at the floor as she spun her head to try to see who was behind her boyfriend. Shrouded in the darkness of the Jeep, she could barely make out a familiar silhouette as the last thing she saw before the blade met her in the chest in one strong strike.

The Jeep fell silent. As the back door closed quietly in the storm.

Darren had let go of Jen as she finally relented her pursuit of Jay. She knew he was gone. Her sobs didn't help her lungs get air as her legs started to wobble. "Wait!" she pleaded, as she slowed to a stop, gasping for breath.

Emily grabbed Darren's arm, looking back at her friend.

"Come on, Jen! We can't wait!" Darren demanded. He was as distraught as she was over losing Jay, but they had to keep going. Or they would be next.

"What about Amy and George?" Emily looked up at him.

Darren had forgotten all about them in his hasty decision to keep running along the path. "Shit!" he hissed, as the realization hit him.

They had to go back.

"Come on!" Darren grabbed Emily's hand and bolted down the muddy path, his flashlight bobbing wildly in front of him as they tore through the dense underbrush. The beam of light flickered and danced with every frantic step, offering little clarity in the chaotic darkness. Jen was right behind them, struggling to keep up as they raced through the slick, rain-soaked trail.

The branches snapped and whipped against their faces, stinging their skin as they ran. The mud squelched beneath their shoes, sucking at their feet with every hurried step. They could hear the rain above the canopy, which might make for a better setting than the eerie darkness that gripped them in the dense forest.

Ahead, the path began to open up, a faint glimmer of light signaling the clearing where they had left the Jeep. Darren was the first to break free from the suffocating forest, bursting out into the open, his breath ragged and labored. He stopped suddenly, his body stiffening as he stared ahead in shock. Emily collided with him, gasping for air as she looked up, her eyes following Darren's gaze.

"Georgey," Darren half-whispered, half-choked, his voice a broken mix of disbelief and horror. His flashlight flickered, its beam revealing the crimson lines smeared across the windshield of the Jeep, glowing ominously in the rain.

Blood.

Jen's stomach twisted into knots, her pulse quickening as her eyes followed the outline of light provided by Darren's flashlight. The beam illuminated the windshield, where the unmistakable words, written in dark, thick strokes, stared back at them.

"Who'z Next?"

The message was smeared across the length of the windshield, bold and defiant against the rain that pelted down. But the most unsettling part—the part that twisted Jen's insides—was that the rain wasn't washing the blood away. The letters remained, stark and chilling, as if etched into the very glass itself.

As they moved closer, a horrifying realization sank in—the writing wasn't on the outside of the Jeep.

It was on the inside.

The girls approached cautiously, their footsteps slow and hesitant as they followed the Darren toward the Jeep. The sound of the rain drumming against the metal roof mixed with the squelching of their shoes in the mud, adding to the unbearable tension that hung in the air. Every step felt like it took an eternity, the anticipation of what they might find making their movements agonizingly slow. The fear was palpable, thick in the air, making it hard to breathe.

Darren reached the driver's side window first, his hand trembling as he raised his flashlight to peer inside. The beam of light cut through the fogged-up glass, revealing the nightmare they had all silently feared.

George was slumped over in the middle seat, his body completely still. His torso was soaked in blood, a deep, dark stain that spread across his chest. A gaping wound ran the length of his throat, fresh blood still oozing down his front, pooling in his lap. Darren's breath caught in his throat, his chest tightening as his eyes darted to the seat next to him, where Amy was slumped in a similar fashion, her lifeless body hunched over, drenched in blood.

The sight of their friends, brutally murdered, tore through them like a knife.

Darren's knees buckled beneath him, and he sank to the ground with his back pressed against the side of the Jeep. "No…" he whimpered, his voice barely audible over the sound of the rain. His hands covered his face as sobs wracked his body, tears mixing with the raindrops that streamed down his cheeks. Emily knelt beside him, wrapping her arms around him, her own tears falling silently as she held him.

Jen stood frozen in place, her chest heaving as she tried to hold herself together. The lump in her throat was unbearable, and her vision blurred as the weight of the moment pressed down on her. She looked over at her friends, who were slumped in a pile next to the Jeep.

What were they going to do?

The questions tormented her, clawing at her conscience. Maybe if they had gone back, they'd all be dead by now. The thought only deepened the guilt. She squeezed her eyes shut, trying to push the thoughts away. For the first time, she let herself feel the full weight of what had happened. The terror. The loss. The guilt.

Suddenly, her eyes snapped open, a jolt of realization shooting through her.

She nudged Darren with her foot, who looked up from Emily's arms, his tear-streaked face filled with confusion.

Jen didn't say a word. Instead, she nodded toward a spot a few feet away, where Darren's flashlight was now shining. Darren's eyes followed the beam of light, his sobs catching in his throat as he stood up, his face twisting in disbelief.

For the first time, they noticed something chilling.

Liz's car was gone.

Chapter 12

Jen stood looking at the empty space that was once occupied by Liz's car. A million thoughts flooded her head as hope drained her body.

"What the fuck?" Darren's voice snapped Jen out of her thoughts, the words slicing through the rain-soaked air.

Jen glanced at Darren, his face twisted with rage. Darren had seen it coming—he had known something was wrong all along.

"Darren, stop!" Emily's voice was weak, trembling as she tugged on Darren's jacket, trying to pull him back from the edge. "Let's just go..."

"Fuck that, Em!" Darren jerked his arm away, his eyes wild. "I'm done with this shit!"

"Darren..." Jen's voice interrupted, a note of panic in her tone. She pointed to the back driver's side tire of the Jeep, her eyes wide with fear. Darren followed her gaze, and his stomach dropped.

The tire had a long, jagged slash in it, completely deflated.

Darren's heart skipped a beat as cold dread flooded his veins. Instinctively, he turned and shined his flashlight toward the front tire. It was slashed too. He could feel the panic rising in his chest as he raced to the other side of the Jeep. His eyes widened as he saw the same thing—all four tires were slashed, drained of air, leaving the Jeep crippled and useless.

They were trapped.

"W-what do we do now?" Emily whimpered, her voice trembling as she clung to Darren, fear and exhaustion weighing heavily on her.

Jen joined the others on the opposite side of the Jeep, her face grim as she exchanged a look with Darren, who was frantically tapping at his phone.

"No service... Fuck!" Darren spat, shaking his phone in frustration as if it would somehow magically connect.

Everyone else quickly pulled out their phones, each of them checking in vain for a signal.

Nothing. No bars, no hope. They were cut off. The towering trees surrounding them felt

oppressive, like silent sentinels guarding them from the outside world. The forest loomed, dark and indifferent, closing them in and trapping them within its suffocating embrace. The isolation was suffocating.

Was this part of the plan? To leave them stranded, vulnerable, and afraid?

"Something's not right," Jen muttered, his brow furrowed in confusion. The rain dripped down his face, cold and relentless, but he hardly noticed it. "This doesn't make any sense. Why would she leave us here?"

"Who the fuck knows, man," Darren scoffed, still pacing as the rain soaked his jacket. "She probably took off before George and Amy even got back to the Jeep."

The rain intensified, drumming against the Jeep and the ground in a rhythmic, maddening beat. It felt as if the storm was closing in, squeezing them tighter with every passing second. The once distant trees now seemed like towering walls, trapping them in this nightmare.

"Either way, we have to find someplace where our phones will work," Jen finally said, cutting through Darren's tirade. Her voice was calm, but her words were filled with urgency. "Nothing's gonna get accomplished by us sitting here."

"And where the fuck are we supposed to do that?" Darren shot back, his frustration boiling over.

"We're in the middle of nowhere."

"I know that, Darren!" Jen snapped, her own frustration rising. She gestured around them, the oppressive darkness pressing in from all sides. "But we don't have a choice. We can't just sit here and wait for someone to show up. No one's coming. We have to figure this out ourselves. If we want to get out of here, we need to find a way to call for help."

The weight of Jen's words sank in, the grim reality of their situation hitting everyone. They were truly stranded. The towering trees and suffocating darkness felt more menacing than ever, as if the forest itself was conspiring to keep them trapped. Emily and Jen exchanged a fearful glance, their eyes wide with helplessness. Tears welled up in their eyes as the full gravity of the situation hit them. They squeezed each other's hands, then turned to the Darren, seeking any kind of comfort. They were all in this together—if they were going to survive, they would have to stick together.

"I say we follow the road," Jen suggested, her voice more confident than she felt. "See if we can find a clearing or someplace where our phones get coverage. We had service on the way here. It can't be that far off."

"I guess," Darren muttered, though doubt lingered in his voice. "But what if that douchebag comes back?"

Jen didn't have an answer. She avoided Darren's gaze, her eyes fixed on the dark road ahead. "Let's just worry about finding service first," she replied, her voice quieter now.

"So, what? We're just gonna walk down the road?" Darren pressed.

"Do you have a better idea, Darren?" Jen shot back, her irritation flaring. "What else can we do?"

"I don't know, dude... but standing out in the middle of the fucking road just feels like we're asking for—" Darren's voice cut off suddenly, his eyes locked on something in the distance.

Their collective hearts skipped a beat. The girls followed Darren's gaze and saw it too—two headlights approaching from far down the road, cutting through the rain-soaked darkness.

Jen's mind raced, every possibility flashing through her head. Was it Liz? Was it help? The headlights were slowing down, creeping toward them.

But then, without warning, the lights shut off.

The night swallowed them whole once again, the sudden absence of light plunging them into deeper darkness. The rain, which had been a constant backdrop, now seemed to amplify the silence that followed. The sound of their own breathing and the pounding of their hearts filled the void as they strained to hear anything—any movement, any sound that might signal what was coming next. The oppressive weight of the darkness pressed in on all sides, suffocating and thick. The forest, once just a shadowy backdrop, now felt like it was watching them.

Jen's pulse raced as she strained her ears, the rain still drumming relentlessly around them, the leaves rustling in the wind. But no sound from the vehicle, no more headlights. The world had gone eerily still.

"Darren, come on!" Emily hissed, her hand instinctively tightening around his. Darren didn't hesitate. He nodded back as they both followed Jen back toward the mouth of the path, the rain hammering down harder as if urging them to run faster.

The darkness seemed to close in behind them.

Whoever was creeping up on them clearly wasn't friendly. The way the headlights had been turned off, just as Jay had done earlier, was a deliberate move to mask their approach. Jen's heart raced as she reached the small opening in the forest and squinted into the suffocating darkness, trying to see who or what was lurking beyond.

The forest around them felt alive, like it was closing in with every breath as they sat there just into the opening of the path. The trees were packed tightly together, their branches entwined into a near-impenetrable canopy that blocked out what little moonlight the storm allowed. The ground beneath them was treacherous, a slick mess of mud, leaves, and fallen branches that turned each step into a gamble.

A jagged bolt of lightning split the sky, briefly illuminating the scene ahead. In that brief, blinding flash, Jen's breath hitched in her throat.

The SUV.

It was unmistakable, its hulking silhouette creeping around the bend like a predator stalking its prey.

Jen turned sharply to see Darren standing right behind her, his face twisted in fear and recognition. They both saw it. The deep rumble of thunder followed, the sound crashing through the trees like a warning. The group stood frozen in place, feeling the vibration of the SUV as it slowly pulled into the spot where Liz's car had been.

They flicked off their flashlights, plunging themselves into total darkness. Their breaths were shallow, barely enough to keep them alive, as if exhaling too loudly might give them away. The night pressed in, heavy and stifling, the air thick with rain and dread. Every drop that fell from the sky was cold, piercing their skin like icy needles. The oppressive blackness seemed to wrap around them like a shroud, muffling every sound except the rhythmic pounding of the rain.

They couldn't see a thing. They huddled together, eyes wide and straining, ears tuned to every rustle of the forest, every shift in the dark. Jen's mind raced. Who was in the SUV? Her thoughts swirled, twisting into knots of confusion and fear. She couldn't shake the feeling that something wasn't adding up.

The seconds dragged by, each one stretching into what felt like an eternity. Every tick of time was excruciating, amplifying the uncertainty that hung in the air. Darren's muscles were tense, his body ready to spring into action, but his mind was paralyzed by the countless questions clawing at him. They couldn't run. Not yet. If they did, they would give themselves away. But staying in the thick, unyielding darkness felt just as dangerous. The path behind them was slick, treacherous, and filled with obstacles that had slowed them down before. It felt even more foreboding now.

They waited.

Nothing.

Darren nudged Jen, pulling her from her thoughts. She glanced at him, noticing Darren's anxious expression. Darren tilted his head toward the path, silently urging Jen to make a move. But she wasn't ready. Her curiosity gnawed at her.

Jen turned back to the road, eyes narrowing as she tried to pierce the inky darkness where the SUV had stopped. Then, without warning, a sudden blinding flash cut through the night. Jen flinched, her heart leaping into her throat as she instinctively recoiled, crashing back into Darren and Emily huddled behind him.

But this wasn't lightning.

The light had come from the ground. It was deliberate. Targeted.

The headlights.

The SUV's headlights had switched back on, piercing through the blackness like searchlights, sweeping the area where they stood. Jen barely had time to process it before her body reacted on instinct. Without a word, she sprang from her crouched position, her feet already moving before her mind caught up.

Darren and Emily were already tearing down the dark path, their footsteps muffled by the thick mud and rain. Jen pushed forward, the trail narrowing as thorny branches reached out to snag their clothes, scratching and clawing at their skin like unseen hands trying to pull them back.

The trees loomed overhead, gnarled and twisted, their branches whipping violently in the wind. The rain had turned the ground into a slick, treacherous mess, making every step a battle to stay upright. The darkness swallowed them, the trail barely visible under the dim, flickering beams of their flashlights.

Behind them, a car door slammed shut, the sound cracking through the storm. The noise sent a jolt of fear through Jen's veins, fueling her desperate run. Her legs felt like lead, each step sinking into the mud as if it were trying to pull her down, but she kept moving. The cold, wet weight of her clothes made everything harder, each breath labored as they pushed through the storm.

Darren whipped his head around, eyes wide as he made sure the girls were still close behind him. He lifted his forearm, shielding his face from the constant barrage of rain, his heart pounding in his chest. "Come on," he urged, his voice barely above a breathless whisper. His legs burned, his lungs felt like they were on fire, but he knew he couldn't afford to slow down. He was running slower than he normally would, holding himself back for the sake of the girls. A part of him wanted to turn around and confront their pursuer, to end this nightmare once and for all. But instinct overrode anger, forcing him to keep moving. Protecting Emily was his only focus now.

As they plunged deeper into the thick forest, Darren caught another brief flash of lightning, the jagged light illuminating the horrifying path. He pressed forward, his body screaming in protest. They hadn't been this far into the woods yet, and every step felt like it was taking them deeper

into a dark, uncharted abyss. The crack of a snapping branch echoed through the air, sending shivers down Darren's spine. They weren't alone.

Jen could hear it too—the sharp, distinct sound of breaking twigs somewhere behind them. Whoever was chasing them was gaining ground. Her thoughts raced as fast as her legs. She could feel the presence closing in on them, the eerie familiarity of being hunted washing over her. Who was this? And why were they after them? It didn't make sense. She slipped on a wet, mud-covered log, nearly face-planting into the ground, but caught herself just in time.

Darren came back to help her.

"You ever look back and wish you coulda done some things different, Jay?"

Will's words echoed in Jay's mind, his voice a ghost from just a few days ago, now haunting him as his chest heaved with a volatile mix of pure terror and seething rage.

His eyes were wide, locked in disbelief on the empty spot next to the Jeep where Liz's car had been only moments before.

His entire body was sore from whatever blindsided him in the path. He had lost time and came to to this grizzly scene. Tears welled up as he looked at George slumped over and Amy next to him. Part of him felt responsible.

He saw the SUV parked where Liz's car had been. He felt enraged.

He had no idea where anyone else was. He stood there frozen, paralyzed by the flood of emotions swirling inside him, boiling like a dormant volcano ready to erupt. The truth had finally struck him, heavy and undeniable: his suspicions about Will that he had tried so hard to supress had been right all along.

But why? Why would Will—his best friend, the person he'd grown up with—do this? They had been through everything together, every joy and hardship. Jay had stood by him even in the darkest moments. Even helped him with the unthinkable.

Now the storm raged around him, mirroring the storm within. Cold, biting rain pelted his skin, but he didn't feel it. His mind was drowning in memories and confusion.

"Yeah, but we can't go back, can we? I mean, the past is the past, and there's no changing it. It makes us who we are today... and at least we're here today, aren't we, Jay?"

A shiver crawled down Jay's spine, his muscles twitching involuntarily as he remembered Will's eerie words from their conversation. Was Will talking about his family? Had he been guilty all

along? Jay's thoughts spiraled, his heart pounding in his ears. Could it be true? Was he too close to Will, too blind to see the truth? The cold reality wrapped around him like a vice—what had Will wished he could change? Did he murder his family?

The turmoil left Jay numb, his body stiff. He felt the hard plastic of the flashlight cracking under the pressure of his clenched hand. Rage surged through him, twisting his stomach. How could his best friend—the one person he'd trusted without question—betray him like this? Anger at himself bubbled to the surface. He had ignored the signs, the strange behavior, always making excuses for Will. Everyone had been right. This wasn't the same Will they had grown up with.

Something had changed in him, something cold and dangerous, but Jay had refused to see it.

A wave of sadness washed over him, momentarily quelling the anger. How could he feel sympathy for someone who had caused so much pain? Yet, a part of him still wanted to make excuses, to believe that Will was somehow a victim in all of this. The truth, though, was staring him in the face. This was the final break—the moment when Jay had to accept that he had truly lost his best friend. That kid from the park, who used to laugh and play football with them, was gone, replaced by a monster hiding behind a mask of grief.

A jolt of lightning illuminated the clearing and he swore he could see Will's silhouette walking into the clearing of the path.

He didn't hesitate. There's no way he could let Will get to his friends. Not to Jen. He took off down the path after him. His pace quickened, even though his muscles ached with pain. Almost as if he'd already run a marathon that day. The rain lashed at his face, blurring his vision, but it didn't matter. He had to find them. He had to warn them.

Flashbacks of his conversations with his friend started coming back to him.

"You know, through all of this... all the bullshit and fake sympathy, people not knowing what to say... you've always been there," Will's words cut Jay like a knife.

He forged on. His thoughts bounced from Jen. To Will. To how things used to be. To how he used to be. Before it all went wrong.

"You think you could...uh...meet me in the...um...park in a little while? I...gotta talk to you about something," the memory of Will's phone call sent chills up Jay's spine as he ran on. Had Will set him up this entire time? How could he? After all Jay had done for him?

"So, do they know who was after you? I mean...who hit you?" Jay remembered Will's question after his accident. Had he wondered if the cops were onto him? If they knew he was behind all of it.

Was he so desperate to save himself that he would kill his own friend to keep his secrets?

Jay's legs burned as he continued his pursuit.

Where was Will?

How had he not caught him by now?

Another snap—a branch breaking, closer this time. Their pursuer was closing in.

"Hurry up!" Darren shouted, his voice raw with urgency. He pushed the girls to quicken their pace.

Another blinding flash of lightning lit up the sky, revealing a clearing up ahead. Darren's heart surged with hope. If they could make it there, they might be able to regroup or find cover. He lengthened his stride, his legs screaming in protest, the mud clinging to his shoes like wet cement. The clearing was only about fifty yards away, but it felt like an eternity as they ran, the underbrush clawing at their clothes and faces. His skin was warm from the fresh scratches left by the thorny branches, his breath labored as the cold air stabbed at his lungs with every inhale.

Jen strained to hear any sounds from the path behind them. Her ears were sharp, scanning the darkness for the telltale signs of pursuit. But then—nothing. The snapping branches stopped.

Had they lost them? For a brief, fleeting moment, a glimmer of hope surfaced in her chest. Maybe they had escaped. Maybe they were safe.

That hope was shattered as she collided with Darren, who had come to an abrupt stop just as they reached the clearing. Jen stumbled, gasping for air, and looked around. The group had emerged into a small field, surrounded on all sides by a dense wall of trees that loomed like silent giants, their twisted branches casting eerie shadows on the ground. The field didn't seem to belong in the middle of this dark, suffocating forest. It was like a hidden pocket of space, cut off from the outside world.

They were all hunched over, panting, their breaths coming out in ragged gasps, mixing with the relentless drumming of the rain. The cold drops pelted their faces like icy needles, each one a reminder of the unrelenting storm that mirrored the chaos of their situation.

"I think we mighta lost 'em," Darren panted, his eyes locked onto the opening they had just come through. His ears strained for any sound—any sign of pursuit. But there was nothing. Just the rain, steady and rhythmic, tapping on the leaves and ground around them like the ticking of a clock. He straightened up, finally catching his breath. "What do you think?" he asked Jen, still unsure.

"I dunno," Jen whispered, her voice low and strained as she stretched her neck forward, trying to peer deeper into the thick line of trees. Her legs throbbed with exhaustion, her muscles aching from the relentless sprint. Beads of sweat mixed with the rain, dripping down her face as she squinted into the darkness. She couldn't see anything beyond the wall of trees, just shadows that seemed to move in time with the wind. She closed her eyes for a moment, trying to focus on the sounds of the forest.

Silence.

No branches cracking. No footsteps splashing through puddles. Just the steady hum of the storm. Darren's eyes snapped open, a frown creasing his brow as he scanned the trail again. "Where the fuck is he?"

Emily swallowed hard, her mind racing. "I dunno. Let's keep going," she muttered, her voice barely a whisper as she cast a wary glance around the clearing.

Their eyes darted from tree to tree, searching for another path—some way out. They couldn't shake the feeling of being watched, of something lurking just beyond their field of vision. They couldn't go back the way they came. That much was clear. But they didn't know where they were, didn't know how far away they were from anything resembling safety. The sense of helplessness crept up on them, seeping into their bones like the cold rain.

Darren looked back at Jen and Emily. The thought of losing them made his chest tighten with fear. He had to stay strong—for them. For all of them. He had to protect them, no matter what.

"Dude!" Darren's voice broke through the tension, a little too loud for comfort. He immediately cringed, realizing his mistake, and quickly scanned the trees for any signs of movement. Nothing. He turned back to Jen, his eyes wide with excitement. "Look!" he hissed, holding up his phone, shielding the glowing screen from the rain as best he could.

He had a signal.

"Call 9-1-1!" Jen's excitement was barely contained, though her voice was more restrained than Darren's.

Finally, after everything, a break in their favor. For the first time in what felt like hours, hope surged through her. They were going to get out of this nightmare. She could feel it. Help was on the way.

"Yes... I don't know exactly where I am," Darren was pacing the edge of the forest, moving cautiously to find a better signal without stepping into the open. He didn't want to become a sitting target. His phone was pressed tightly to his ear, his free hand raised to block out the relentless downpour. "We came up for a camping trip, and there's some psycho after us..."

Emily gently released Jen from their embrace, her eyes scanning the edges of the field for any sign of movement. Relief flooded her veins, but she couldn't let her guard down—not yet.

Someone was still out there, lurking in the shadows, and they had no idea where they could strike from next. "No, he slashed the tires," Darren's voice grew sharper, tinged with impatience and frustration. "Look, there are dead bodies up here—you better fucking hurry!" he shouted into the phone, his anger boiling over.

Another crack of lightning lit up the sky, casting an eerie, brief daylight over the forest. In that split-second flash, Jen's heart froze. A dark figure emerged from the woods, sprinting towards Darren with terrifying speed.

"Darren—look out!" Emily's shriek cut through the storm, her voice merging with a deafening roll of thunder.

Darren turned just in time to see the figure barreling toward him, but it was too late. In the faint glow of the phone's screen, they saw the glimmer of a blade arching through the air. Darren instinctively raised his arms to block, but the knife plunged into his side, slipping just below his left rib cage. His eyes bulged with shock and pain as the blow sent him staggering backward.

"Nooo!" Emily's scream was filled with horror as she watched Darren collapse to his knees.

Jen was already sprinting, but she knew it was too late. The figure—quick, efficient—yanked the knife from Darren's body and disappeared back into the cover of the trees, vanishing into the shadows as if swallowed by the night itself. The darkness seemed to close in tighter around them, the rain intensifying as if the sky itself was mourning what had just happened.

"Darren!" Emily reached him just as he fell to the ground, crumpled in pain. "Darren, talk to me!"

The pale light from Darren's phone cast an eerie glow over his face, just enough for Jen to see the raw agony etched into his features. Darren's breaths were shallow, labored, each one a struggle. She glanced toward the forest, where the figure had disappeared. Was he still watching? Still lurking, waiting to strike again?

Emily knelt in front of Darren, tears streaming down her cheeks as she pressed her forehead to his, their breaths mingling as his grew more ragged. His eyes fluttered, struggling to stay open, his vision blurring. He tried to speak but only managed a weak, choked gasp.

"It's okay, baby," Emily whispered, her voice cracking as she tried to hold it together. "I'm right here. You're gonna be fine."

Jen's chest tightened, the weight of helplessness crushing her. She ripped off her jacket and sweatshirt, shoving the sweatshirt into Emily's hands. "Here—hold this to it. Put pressure on it." She swallowed hard, forcing herself to stay calm. "This is gonna hurt, Darren, but we gotta keep the pressure on, okay?"

Darren nodded weakly, his face contorted in pain. He hadn't said a word since the attack, only letting out a deep, guttural groan as Emily pressed the sweatshirt to his wound, applying pressure. His body trembled with every breath, the pain overwhelming.

Jen grabbed Darren's phone off the ground, her hands slick with rain and mud. "Hello," she barked into the phone, hearing the faint voice of the dispatcher on the other end. "Is everything alright?"

"Just get the fuck out here! My friend was just stabbed!" she yelled before hanging up, shoving the phone into her jacket pocket and zipping it closed. She crouched next to Darren, her heart racing. "Can you walk?" she asked, her voice tense with urgency.

Darren groaned again, nodding slightly, though his body was shaking from the effort of staying upright.

"Okay, let's go." Jen positioned herself behind Darren, carefully lifting him to his feet. Darren swayed, his legs barely able to support his weight, leaning heavily on both girls.

"Where are we going to go?" Emily asked, her voice trembling as she glanced at Jen, fear and uncertainty in her eyes.

"Back to the road," Jen replied, nodding toward the forest path. Her heart pounded in her chest. The forest loomed before them, dark and menacing, the shadows between the trees seeming to shift and crawl.

"No way, Jen!" Emily shook her head, her voice rising in panic. "We can't go back in there!"

"We don't have a choice!" Jen snapped, trying to hold Darren upright as he groaned in pain.

"The police are on their way. We just have to make it back to the Jeep."

"How do you plan on doing that?" Emily's voice wavered, her eyes darting between the shadowy path and Jen.

"We have to try. He needs help," Jen said firmly, her gaze shifting to Darren, who was pale and struggling for breath. "We go slow, and you keep an eye out. One in front, one in back. It's not that far."

Jen knew it was going to be a slow, painful journey. Darren was barely holding on, and the path ahead was treacherous. Every step would be a gamble. But what other choice did they have? Darren was bleeding out, and time was running out. Jen's gut twisted with dread. Could they even make it back to the Jeep alive?

Emily hesitated but finally nodded, understanding the gravity of the situation. "Okay," she whispered, though fear still gripped her.

Jen took a deep breath, her heart heavy with the weight of the situation. She slowly started toward the forest, Darren leaning heavily on her. Each step was careful, deliberate, the forest ahead seeming darker and more foreboding with every inch they covered. The rain continued to fall, soaking them to the bone, every drop a reminder of the danger that still lurked in the shadows.

But they had to keep moving. They had no choice.

Chapter 13

The rain had slowed to a steady drizzle by the time Jen and Emily had to switch places for the first time. The once relentless storm had turned into a soft but constant tap on the canopy above, yet the weight of the situation pressed harder than ever. Darren was weak, barely able to bear his own weight. Jen had tried to carry him as far as she could, but the strain had become too much. Each step had felt like dragging dead weight through quicksand.

"Just leave me," Darren managed to choke out, his voice hoarse, barely audible over the hiss of the rain. His vision was blurring, the edges of the world around him growing dark.

"There's no way we're leaving you!" Emily said, her own voice shaking with exhaustion, though she tried to sound firm. She took Darren's arm, slinging it over her shoulders, motioning to Jen. "I've got him for a while. You look out ahead."

"You sure?" Jen protested. Her eyes scanned Emily's face, noting the strain there, but she knew her own body was faltering, and this was their only option.

"Go!" Darren gurgled, the wet, rattling sound from his throat sent a chill down Jen's spine. It was the sound of someone on the edge, someone barely clinging on. She didn't know how much longer he had.

"We have to hurry!" Emily urged, her voice quivering with fear and urgency. She started down the path again, struggling to keep Darren upright. His weight seemed to drag her down with each step, his body growing heavier, like dead weight, sinking deeper into the mud.

Jen took the lead, her movements cautious, her senses on high alert. Every step felt calculated, her eyes darting from side to side, checking every shadow, every shape that seemed to twist in the periphery of her vision. The forest was dense here, the trees looming overhead like ancient sentinels, their gnarled branches tangled together, blocking out what little light the storm allowed. The world felt claustrophobic, as if the very air around them had thickened, making it harder to breathe.

The damp, earthy smell of wet leaves and mud filled her nostrils, and the constant patter of rain against the canopy created a low, steady hum. It was almost hypnotic—dangerously so. Jen shook her head, forcing herself to stay alert. She knew they were out there—whoever it was. Watching. Waiting. The shadows seemed alive with their presence, shifting, growing, shrinking with every flicker of her flashlight.

She glanced over her shoulder at Emily and Darren. His breathing was ragged now, every inhale a struggle, his body slumping more with each passing minute. Emily's face was pale, her lips pressed into a thin line as she gritted her teeth, pushing forward despite her own exhaustion. They didn't have much time. Jen just hoped the police would get there before whoever was hunting them made their next move.

The forest around them felt endless, a maze of twisting branches and dark, muddy paths that all seemed to blend together. The rain dripped from the leaves in steady streams, soaking through their clothes, making them colder, heavier with each passing moment. Jen's boots sank into the mud with every step, the sucking sound of it pulling at her feet, threatening to drag her down.

"We're almost there," Jen whispered, though it was more for herself than anyone else. The Jeep was close. If they could just reach it, maybe—just maybe—they could find help.

But then, through the thinning trees, the shape of the vehicles slowly came into view. Her heart leapt, only to sink again as her eyes scanned the clearing. The SUV was gone.

Jen's pulse quickened, a cold sweat forming at the back of her neck despite the rain. How? It had been there moments ago, hadn't it? Her eyes darted around the clearing, scanning the dark shapes of the forest for any sign of movement. The air was thick with tension, as if the world itself was holding its breath.

"We've gotta move faster," Jen urged, her voice barely above a whisper as she glanced back at Emily. Darren's weight was dragging them down. His breaths came in shallow, wheezing gasps, his body swaying with every step.

"We're almost there, just a little further," Emily coaxed, though her voice trembled with fear.

Jen's eyes were fixed on the Jeep now. The vehicle stood out like a beacon in the dark, but something felt wrong. The silence was oppressive, and the absence of the SUV gnawed at her, like a piece of the puzzle that refused to fit.

Jay came to again as he was making his way along the path. His steps were becoming more labored, each one slower, as if he were fighting a fatigue that came in waves. The rain, now a steady drizzle, felt colder against his skin, sending a chill through his already weary body. His muscles ached with every movement, and the outer edges of his vision blurred, like he was looking through fogged glass.

He blinked, confused. Lost.

Why was he on the path? What had he been looking for? His mind felt hazy, like he was slipping in and out of consciousness. The forest around him seemed to press in closer with every step, the thick canopy above muffling the world into eerie quiet, save for the steady drip of rain.

Jen!

The name hit him like a shock. His heart raced as the memory of her running flooded his thoughts. But... running from what? From him?

No. That didn't make sense. He shook his head, trying to clear the fog. A sharp throb pulsed behind his eyes, sending a wave of dizziness through him. Where was she?

He remembered them running. His breath catching, his legs pushing through the thick underbrush—but then... nothing. A blank space in his mind. Why was he so confused?

Get it together, Jay. He forced the words through his mind like a mantra, trying to focus, trying to hold on to something solid. He was here for a reason. There was something he had to do. Jen was in danger. They were all in danger.

Will.

His best friend.

Where was Will?

He stumbled forward, his feet sinking into the mud with every step. Flashbacks started to hit him, random and disjointed, like flickers of broken memories spliced together out of order.

He saw himself as a child—Christmas morning, unwrapping his PlayStation at ten years old, the joy lighting up his face as vividly as if it were happening now. His mother's smile, warm and full of pride, stayed with him for a moment longer before the memory shifted.

Another flash. He and Will on their first day of school, sitting together at their lunch table. A first shared meal that cemented their friendship—a tradition that lasted through the years, right up to today. But then, that memory, too, warped into something darker.

Suddenly, Jay was seeing their lunch table at school, just like the other day. Darren was there, laughing loudly, making some crude joke that sent George into a fit of laughter, mashed potatoes nearly falling out of his mouth. Jay had been laughing too, pointing at George, mocking him in good fun.

But something was off. Will's seat was empty.

Jay stared at it, confused. Where was Will?

Then, in the blink of an eye, Will appeared. He was wearing that same hoodie, the one he always wore. His face just stared at Jay. Almost as if he were looking at Jay as he watched the
scene unfold.. But... something was wrong. Jay blinked again, staring at Will as his image flickered like a bad TV signal. There, then gone. Then back.

Like a ghost.

The cafeteria scene around them seemed frozen, stuck in a pause, while Will flickered in and out of existence. Jay felt his heart racing, his skin prickling. The last flicker felt wrong—it wasn't Will anymore. It was something darker, something that sent a cold shiver running down Jay's spine, making him snap back to the present.

He gasped, blinking hard, trying to ground himself. The forest came back into focus around him, but his pulse wouldn't slow. His head still throbbed with confusion, his memories blurring into something he didn't understand.

Where was Jen?

Jen forced them to trudge on through the last few agonizing steps. The rain had eased to a steady drizzle, but the forest still felt suffocating, the air heavy with dampness. The ground was slick beneath their feet, mud sucking at their shoes with every step, as though the earth itself was trying to pull them down. Darren's breathing had become a labored rasp, each inhale sounding like it was scraping against his lungs. He was sagging more with every second, his weight deadened by exhaustion.

"Hang on," Jen murmured, her voice barely cutting through the thick, wet air. She leaned on her knees, taking in a deep breath, the moisture clinging to her face like mist. She scanned the edge of the forest, her flashlight's beam cutting across the dark, twisted trees.

The forest was eerily still now, save for the soft patter of rain hitting leaves, the quiet dripping as water collected and fell in tiny streams.

She raised her flashlight, moving it slowly along the tree line, inspecting every inch, her eyes straining in the half-light. Each gnarled branch and cluster of foliage seemed to shift and move under her scrutiny, shadows playing tricks in the dim glow. Was that a figure? No, just the wind teasing the branches. They were alone. But for how long?

"How much longer till the cops get here?" Emily's voice was thick with emotion, her face puffy from crying. Her words came out in quick bursts, her breath visible in the cold, wet air. She felt a wave of relief that they'd finally made it to the vehicles, but that relief quickly drained away when the harsh reality set in—they were still stranded. They still had to wait.

"I don't know," Jen admitted, her voice hollow as she continued to scan the surrounding trees. The silence pressed against her ears, unnerving her more than the storm ever had. Every sound seemed amplified in this strange lull, the creaking of branches, the soft rustle of leaves, all of it setting her on edge.

Darren lay on his side, slumped against the deflated rear tire of the Jeep, his face pale and slick with rain. His breathing came in shallow, wheezing gasps, his chest rising and falling with painful effort. He looked small against the towering trees, vulnerable and broken, the life draining from him as the minutes ticked by. He shivered, his body shaking uncontrollably, though his eyes were half-lidded, barely aware of his surroundings.

Jen's gaze shifted from the dark forest to Darren, her heart aching at the sight of him. He wasn't going to make it—she knew it, felt it in the pit of her stomach. The grim realization tightened her throat as she looked down at Emily, who sat beside him, cradling his head in her lap. Emily's hand stroked his wet hair, her fingers trembling, as she whispered something to him—soft, soothing words that Jen couldn't quite hear, words that sounded like goodbye.

Jen's chest tightened as her thoughts shifted to Jay. The pain hit her like a punch to the gut, sudden and sharp, catching her off guard. In all the chaos, in the terror and adrenaline, she hadn't had a moment to process what had happened to him. She couldn't believe it. Jay... gone.

Just like that.

Tears blurred her vision as the heartache overwhelmed her, wrenching her stomach in knots. She tried to blink them away, tried to focus, but it was all too much. This entire week had been a nightmare, a never-ending hell of death and fear, and through it all, Jay had been the one thing that kept her grounded. The one person she could always count on, the person who made it all bearable.

How could he be gone?

For a fleeting moment, she stopped caring. She didn't care about the forest around them, didn't care about the creeping danger or the slashed tires or the suffocating darkness pressing in on them. None of it mattered. Jay was gone. The thought crushed her. Her world had shattered, and she felt like she was standing on the jagged pieces.

But then the moment passed. She could almost hear Jay's voice, scolding her for giving up, telling her to snap out of it. He'd hate to see her like this. He'd want her to fight—he always pushed her to be stronger, to never back down. He was her rock, the foundation of her world, and she needed to hold onto that now more than ever.

She swiped at her tears with the back of her hand, forcing herself to focus through the haze of grief. They still had to survive. For Darren. For Emily. For Jay. The thought of him pushed her forward, igniting something inside her.

The light from her flashlight was just completing another slow rotation around the perimeter when she saw it—a movement. Her heart skipped a beat. She froze, the beam of light catching something in the trees, something that shifted just out of reach.

Was it an animal? A bird disturbed by the rain?

Another rustle. More deliberate this time.

Jen's pulse quickened, her body going rigid. Her flashlight's beam trembled slightly as she tried to steady her hand, the light flickering over the undergrowth. Someone—or something—was out there. Watching. Waiting.

They had caught up to them. Whoever it was, they had found them.

Jay stumbled forward, his feet dragging through the wet mud, each step more difficult than the last. The forest around him blurred, the edges of his vision smudging like an old photograph, the rain seeping into his clothes, chilling him to the bone. His body ached, but his mind was worse—fractured, confused, lost in a sea of memories that didn't fit together.

He knew he was on the path. Knew he was supposed to be finding Jen.

But Will. He had seen Will on the path too, right? He had been following him, hadn't he? There—there he was again! A fleeting shadow, a figure in the distance.

"Will," Jay tried to call out, but his voice cracked, the effort sending a wave of pain through his skull. His head throbbed, a dull ache that pulsed with every heartbeat, every memory that flashed before his eyes.

More images. More flashbacks.

He saw them all again—the group at the Warehouse, planning this ill-fated trip. Darren, grumbling about something Emily had done. George, stuffing his face with a breadstick while Amy rolled her eyes. Jen laughing at Darren's whining, her voice bright and full of life.

And there was Will, in his usual spot, hoodie pulled up, his eyes locked on Jay. But something was wrong. Will wasn't part of the conversation. He wasn't laughing with the group. He was just... watching. Staring at Jay, flickering like a faulty lightbulb. There, then gone. There, then gone again.

Jay blinked, trying to clear his vision, but the image persisted—Will, fading in and out, a ghost at the edge of his mind.

Jay stumbled forward, his feet slipping in the mud. He looked up, squinting through the rain. Ahead, a figure stood in the clearing—someone familiar.

It was Will.

Jay's heart lurched. He took another step, but as he approached, Will's form flickered one last time and disappeared into the mist.

Jay staggered out of the clearing, his breath coming in ragged gasps. His vision was swimming, but through the blur, he saw them—Jen and Emily, huddled over Darren.

Jen stood, her body tense, her flashlight aimed at the darkness. She was guarding them, protecting them from whatever was lurking in the shadows.

Was it Will? Had he come back?

Either way, Jay was relieved to see her. But something was wrong. His head throbbed harder, his legs wobbled beneath him as he tried to make sense of the scene.

"Jen?" he croaked, his voice barely above a whisper as he blinked through the haze, trying to focus.

Jen's head snapped toward him, her heart leaping into her throat. The flashlight beam wobbled as her hands began to shake. She could hardly believe what she was seeing. It had to be a trick, her mind playing cruel games on her. But no—there he was, standing at the edge of the path.

It was Jay.

For a fleeting second, relief flooded through her. She had thought he was gone—dead, like the others. But then, that relief twisted into something darker. There was something wrong with the way he stood, something off about the way he looked at her.

She straightened up slowly, her mind racing to make sense of the situation, but a creeping sense of dread coiled in her gut.

Why was he looking at her like that?

"Jen, it's me," Jay called softly, his voice cracking with exhaustion. He took a step toward her, his movements slow and unsteady, like he was barely holding himself upright. "He can't hurt you anymore. I'm here."

He reached out for her, his hand trembling as it extended, but Jen didn't move. She couldn't. Her body had gone rigid, locked in place by a growing, suffocating fear.

Her breath caught in her throat as she looked down.

Jay's legs wobbled beneath him, unsteady, as if they might give out at any second. His clothes were soaked through with rain, sticking to his skin, and his hand—his hand was reaching out to her, but... but why did it look so heavy?

Her eyes drifted down further, following the line of his arm, her breath hitching in her chest.

Jay's hand wasn't empty.

He was holding a knife. A long blade, its edge glinting faintly in the dull light of her flashlight, dripping with blood. The blood dripped in slow, steady drops, pooling at his feet, staining the mud beneath him in dark, crimson streaks.

Jen's heart raced, her pulse pounding in her ears so loud that she couldn't hear anything else. She couldn't even speak. Her mind screamed at her to run, to grab Emily and Darren and get as far away as possible, but her feet wouldn't move.

She looked back up at Jay, her eyes wide with horror.

Jay looked down at the knife in his hand, his face slackening with confusion as if he hadn't realized it was there until that very moment. His brow furrowed, his mouth opening in a silent question.

Why?

His gaze shifted back to Jen, his eyes filled with bewilderment, with anger, with... terror.

"I... I don't understand..." he stammered, taking another shaky step forward. "Jen, it's not what you think..."

But the words were lost on her. Jen felt her entire world tilt as she backed away, stumbling slightly over the uneven ground. The rain, the mud, the suffocating darkness around them—it all seemed to close in tighter, like a vice squeezing the breath from her lungs.

"Stay the fuck away from me!" Jen's voice cracked with a mixture of fear and fury, her hands trembling as she raised them in a desperate gesture to ward him off. Her pulse was racing, her body screaming with adrenaline as she backed away further, trying to shield Emily and Darren from whatever this was—whoever this was.

Jay's face twisted with confusion. Why was she doing this? Why was she afraid of him?

"Jen..." his voice broke, but she wasn't listening.

"Stay the FUCK BACK!!!" Jen screamed, her voice raw with terror.

Jay's hands shot up in surrender, but as they did, he felt the weight of the knife in his left hand. He looked down again, and for the first time, he truly saw it—the blood, the slick, wet handle of the knife. The crimson droplets splattering onto the muddy ground below.

His heart dropped.

His mind went blank.

What... what had he done?

He looked up at Jen, his eyes wide with panic. "I... I don't know..."

Jen's breath hitched. Her body was trembling uncontrollably now, her back pressed up against the Jeep as she tried to shield Emily and Darren from the man standing before them. She couldn't believe what she was seeing. Couldn't believe the words coming out of his mouth.

"Jen, I figured it out," Jay said, his voice rising with a desperate, manic edge. He took another step forward, the knife still clutched in his trembling hand. "It's Will... it's been Will this whole time. He's lost it, babe. He's the one who's been doing this!"

Jen's heart ached as she listened to the broken, frantic words tumbling from Jay's mouth. She couldn't understand how she had missed this—how she hadn't seen the signs. It was all unraveling before her, and she had no idea how to stop it.

"Will?" she sobbed, the word barely escaping her lips as she watched her boyfriend—no, the person she thought was her boyfriend—struggle to make sense of his own actions.

"Yeah, babe. Will," Jay insisted, his face brightening as though he had solved everything. "It's been him this whole time. I saw him, Jen. I saw him... just now... on the path."

Jen's tears fell harder, her chest heaving as the reality of the situation crashed down around her like a tidal wave. She wanted to believe him. God, she wanted to believe him. But the truth—what she had known for so long, but hadn't wanted to admit—was staring her in the face.

"Will is dead, Jason," she whispered, her voice breaking as the words left her mouth.

Jay stopped, the smile faltering on his face. He blinked, confusion clouding his eyes as he shook his head.

"No... no, I just saw him. I just saw him..." His voice trailed off as the knife in his hand grew heavier, the blood on it seeming to pulse in time with his heartbeat. His mind raced, memories flashing before his eyes, disjointed and jumbled, flickering like old film reels.

"Will is dead, Jay," Jen repeated, her voice stronger this time. "He's been dead for six months.

He's gone."

Jay staggered backward, his knees buckling as the memories started to hit him harder. Images of Will. Of their friendship. Of that night. The night everything changed. His breath came in ragged gasps as his mind tried to reconcile what he knew with what Jen was telling him.

"No..." he whispered, his voice hoarse. "No, I don't believe you..."

But the truth was there. It had always been there, lurking at the edges of his consciousness, waiting to strike. His body trembled as the weight of the knife grew unbearable, his grip tightening involuntarily around the handle.

"He's gone, Jason," Jen said, her voice softening now, but her words were firm, final.

"I don't believe you..." Jay sobbed, but the images wouldn't stop. His mind was unraveling, every flicker of memory blurring into the next. Every conversation with Will, every shared moment—they all began to fracture, pieces of the puzzle that no longer fit together.

Jay's breathing grew erratic, his chest rising and falling in rapid, shallow bursts as his mind spun in chaos. He could feel it now—the creeping tendrils of doubt, of reality unraveling in his hands like loose threads. The more he tried to hold on to what he thought was true, the more it slipped away, disintegrating into nothing but fragments of memory, distorted and warped.

His grip on the knife tightened.

"No...no, I saw him. He was here, Jen. He was with me... He was always with me," Jay stammered, his voice cracking under the weight of his own disbelief. His legs wobbled beneath him, his body unsteady as if the very ground beneath him had turned into quicksand.

Jen's eyes were wide, her heart shattering with every word that came out of his mouth. She wanted to scream, to tell him to stop, to wake him up from whatever nightmare he was trapped in. But there was no waking him. He was slipping further and further away, lost in the dark labyrinth of his own mind.

"Jay, please..." she whispered, her voice thick with emotion. "Will is gone. You have to believe me. He's not here anymore."

But Jay wasn't listening. His mind was a storm, swirling with half-formed memories and flickering images that didn't make sense. He could see Will—standing next to him, laughing, running with him through the woods, sitting beside him at the lunch table. And then—gone. Flickering like a dying light, there one second, gone the next. It didn't make sense. None of it made sense.

"He told me..." Jay's voice wavered as his eyes darted around wildly, searching the dark forest as if Will might materialize from the shadows. "He told me it was his idea... He told me he had to do it. It wasn't my fault..."

Jen swallowed hard, tears streaming down her face as she took a cautious step forward, her hands trembling. "Jay... Will didn't tell you that. He couldn't have. He wasn't there. Don't you see?"

Jay's heart pounded in his chest, his pulse deafening in his ears. The rain had picked up again, the drops falling heavier now, pounding the earth beneath them, the rhythmic patter merging with the frantic beating of his heart. His mind throbbed with every passing second, the flashes of memory becoming more erratic, more violent.

Will's voice echoed in his mind, distorted now, as if coming from a great distance.

"You ever look back and wish you could have done things differently, Jay?"

Jay's vision blurred, the forest spinning around him in a dizzying whirl of dark greens and shadowy browns. He swayed on his feet, barely able to keep himself upright as the weight of everything pressed down on him, crushing his chest, squeezing the breath from his lungs.

"I remember... I remember it all," Jay muttered, his voice barely above a whisper. His gaze dropped to the knife in his hand, the blade slick with blood, glinting faintly in the dim light. His grip tightened even further, the edges of the handle biting into his palm, but he couldn't let go. He couldn't stop.

Jen watched him with wide, tear-filled eyes, her heart pounding with fear and sorrow. She took another step forward, her voice soft but urgent, trying to pull him back from the edge. "Jay, please... put the knife down."

But he didn't hear her.

His mind had already spiraled back to that night, six months ago—the night everything changed. The night Will's family was killed.

"Darren and George were over... Will was there... We had a few drinks... After they passed out..."

The memories were coming faster now, barreling toward him like a runaway train, unstoppable and relentless. He could see it—the flash of Will's face in the dim light, the sound of his voice, low and cold, the way he had leaned in, whispered something that had changed everything.

"I promised him I wouldn't tell anyone..."

But Jen's voice cut through the fog like a knife. "Jay, Will's dead. He's been dead for months.

You have to remember."

Her words hit him like a hammer, shattering the last remnants of the illusion that had held him together. The memories he had clung to, the truth he had convinced himself of—they were nothing but lies. Lies he had told himself to survive. To cope with the guilt, the horror of what had really happened.

"I... I didn't..." Jay's voice cracked, his knees buckling as he sank to the ground, the weight of the truth finally crushing him. His hands shook, the knife slipping from his grasp and landing in the mud with a dull *thud*. He stared down at his hands, his breath coming in ragged gasps as the full realization hit him.

Will wasn't there.

He never was.

Jen took a hesitant step closer, her heart breaking as she watched him crumble before her. "Jay..."

Jay's head snapped up, his eyes wide with terror as the truth crashed over him, suffocating him.

His body shook violently, the memories flooding his mind in a chaotic storm of images, sounds, and emotions. He could see it now—the moments with Will, the conversations, the laughter. None of it was real. None of it ever happened. It had all been in his mind.

And the blood... the blood on his hands...

It was his.

The sickening truth clawed its way up from the depths of his mind, choking him, suffocating him. He had been the one. He had killed them. Not Will. Not anyone else.

Him.

Jay's breath hitched, his vision swimming as the world tilted on its axis. His hands trembled violently, his body convulsing as the weight of what he had done crushed him. He had killed them—his friends, his family. All of them. He had become the monster he had feared all along.

"No..." Jay whispered, his voice barely audible. "No..."

Jen's heart shattered as she watched the man she loved unravel completely, consumed by the darkness that had been festering inside him for months. She took a step back, her hands trembling, tears streaming down her face as she realized there was nothing left to save.

Jay was gone.

The man standing before her was someone else entirely—someone she didn't recognize.

And just as the realization settled over her, a blinding flash of light filled the clearing.

The roar of an engine cut through the rain, and Jen barely had time to react before the SUV came barreling toward them, its headlights slicing through the darkness like a knife.

She dove to the ground, her heart pounding in her chest as she heard the sickening *crack* of metal slamming into flesh. The impact reverberated through the clearing, the sound so loud it seemed to split the night in two.

The SUV plowed through the forest, crashing into a massive tree with a deafening *thud*. The rain poured harder now, drumming against the roof of the wrecked vehicle as the world seemed to freeze in place, the silence deafening in the aftermath of the chaos.

Jen slowly lifted her head, her heart in her throat as she looked toward the wreckage.

Jay was gone.

Pinned between the SUV and the tree, his body lifeless, crumpled like a ragdoll.

The rain continued to fall, washing away the blood as the flashing lights of distant sirens illuminated the darkness.

They were finally going to be okay.

The silence that followed was deafening. The rain fell harder, pounding against the earth and trees, washing away the blood that had soaked into the mud. For a moment, Jen couldn't move. Her body was frozen, her mind unable to process what had just happened. She lay there, her heart pounding in her chest, the cold rain mixing with her tears as they slid down her face.

Her eyes were locked on the crumpled figure pinned against the tree—the body that had once been Jay. The man she had loved, the man who had protected her, who had been her rock through everything, was gone. The realization hit her like a tidal wave, knocking the breath from her lungs.

Jay was dead.

And yet, a part of her had known. She had felt it in her gut, in the pit of her stomach, even before he revealed the truth. The man standing before her in those last moments hadn't been Jay. It had been something else—something darker, something twisted.

But now... now it was over. The nightmare was over.

Jen slowly pushed herself up from the ground, her limbs shaking from the cold and the adrenaline coursing through her veins. The rain soaked through her clothes, chilling her to the bone, but she didn't care. All she could think about was Emily and Darren, huddled behind her. Were they safe?

Her body ached as she stumbled toward them, her legs weak, trembling with every step. The forest around them was eerily quiet now, the sounds of the storm and the distant sirens the only thing breaking the suffocating silence. The trees loomed above them like dark sentinels, their branches swaying in the wind as the storm continued its relentless assault on the world below.

She found Emily still cradling Darren's head in her lap, her face streaked with tears, her body shaking with sobs. Darren's breaths were shallow, each one a painful, rasping struggle. His skin had turned an unhealthy shade of pale, and Jen could see the life slowly slipping from him with every passing second.

But they were alive.

Jen dropped to her knees beside them, her hand resting on Emily's shoulder, squeezing it gently. Emily looked up at her, her eyes red and swollen from crying, her lips trembling as she tried to speak, but no words came out. She didn't need to say anything. Jen knew.

They had survived.

But at what cost?

Jen swallowed hard, her throat tight as she looked down at Darren. His eyes fluttered open, just barely, and he managed a weak smile. It was a broken smile, one filled with pain and exhaustion, but it was a smile nonetheless.

"You're okay," Jen whispered, her voice shaking. "You're going to be okay."

Darren didn't respond. He didn't have the strength. But his eyes spoke volumes—the gratitude, the relief, the sadness. Everything he had been through, everything they had all been through, was written there in his gaze.

The sound of the sirens grew louder, the flashing red and blue lights cutting through the trees, casting long, eerie shadows across the forest floor. Help was finally here.

Jen closed her eyes for a brief moment, letting out a shaky breath as the weight of everything settled over her. She wasn't sure how much more she could take. The past few hours had felt like a lifetime, and yet they had passed in a blur of terror, confusion, and heartbreak.

The paramedics arrived in a flurry of motion, their voices quick and efficient as they assessed Darren's condition, loading him onto a stretcher and whisking him away toward the waiting ambulance. Emily clung to him, refusing to leave his side as she climbed into the back of the vehicle, her face a mask of fear and desperation.

Jen stood there, watching them go, feeling as if the world was spinning out of control around her. Everything she had known— everything she had believed—had been shattered. She had lost so much. George. Amy. Jay.

Jay.

Her breath caught in her throat, and for a moment, she thought she might collapse under the weight of it all. The grief, the guilt, the pain. It was too much. Too overwhelming. How could she have missed it? How could she have been so blind to what Jay had become?

But it wasn't her fault. She knew that. Deep down, she knew that. And yet the guilt still gnawed at her, clawing at her insides, refusing to let go.

She had loved him.

And in the end, it hadn't been enough.

The officer that had lent her his jacket approached, his footsteps heavy in the mud as he came to stand beside her. Jen felt his presence before she saw him, the weight of his hand on her shoulder grounding her, pulling her back to the present.

"You did good, kid," he said softly, his voice gruff but kind. "You did everything you could."

Jen nodded, her throat too tight to respond. She wasn't sure she believed him, but it was comforting to hear nonetheless.

The officer sighed, glancing toward the wrecked SUV, its front end crumpled against the tree, the steam from the engine hissing in the rain. "Damn shame," he muttered, shaking his head.

Jen's heart skipped a beat, her mind snapping back to the present. The SUV. The driver.

Liz.

"What happened to the driver?" she asked, her voice barely above a whisper, afraid of the answer.

The officer hesitated, his gaze shifting toward the wreckage. He rubbed the back of his neck, as if considering how much to tell her, before he finally spoke.

"Dead on impact, I'm afraid."

Jen's heart sank, her stomach twisting in knots. Liz. She must have known. She must have realized what Jay had become—what he was planning. But why? Why had she thrown herself into the middle of this? Why had she risked her life to stop him?

Jen stared at the wreckage, the twisted metal and shattered glass, and felt a deep, aching sadness settle over her. Liz had been part of this too—part of the nightmare that had consumed them all.

And now she was gone.

Jen turned away from the scene, her hands trembling as she hugged the officer's jacket tighter around her shoulders. She felt the weight of his hand on her back, offering silent comfort as the reality of it all began to sink in.

They had survived.

But nothing would ever be the same again.

The officer gave her shoulder a gentle squeeze before walking away, leaving her alone in the clearing, the rain still falling softly around her. The flashing lights of the ambulances and police cars reflected off the wet ground, casting long, eerie shadows across the forest floor.

Jen stood there for a moment longer, her eyes fixed on the wreckage, the memories of the night replaying in her mind like a broken record. She knew that this would stay with her forever. The pain, the loss, the guilt. It would haunt her for the rest of her life.

But she was still here.

She was still alive.

And somehow, she would have to find a way to keep going.

The sound of the sirens faded into the distance, and the world around her fell silent once more.

About the Author

CJ Tuttle is an award-winning writer whose passion for storytelling started with songwriting and grew into a love for writing novels. "Killer Secrets: Buried Truth" is CJ's first novel, which began as a personal challenge to see if he could write a book. What started as a casual project quickly turned into a gripping story that CJ couldn't put down, drawing inspiration from the thrill of creating a world from scratch.

For CJ, writing is more than just words on a page—it's an escape from reality, a way to channel creativity and embrace the madness of life. Having won multiple awards for his songwriting, CJ is no stranger to crafting narratives that captivate and engage.

When he's not writing, CJ enjoys spending time with his family, playing guitar, gaming, and whipping up delicious meals in the kitchen. He hopes readers love the twists and turns of "Killer Secrets: Buried Truth" as much as he loved writing it.

Read more at https://cjtuttle.com.